Fated Salvation
The Sendaxa Chronicles, Book 3

By

REBECCA HEFNER

Contents

For everyone who supported this steamy dystopian trilogy. Thank you from the bottom of my heart. I love writing these books and am honored you spend your time and money to read them. I hope Dani, Arianna, Grace and their team save the world! Happy reading.

PART I

THE PAST

Chapter 1

Over ten years before the events of
Scorched Redemption...

Grace Albright never forgot the day she met Tristan Holder. Everything about that day—from the scent of the burning birthday candles to the sound of popping champagne corks—was embedded deep in her soul.

Her father had organized an elaborate twenty-fifth birthday party for her, and it was endearingly over-the-top, as were most things Robert Albright did for his daughter.

"What's the point in being rich if we don't spend it, dear?" her father would ask, love shining in his eyes as he patted Grace's shoulder. "And Mom would want me to take care of you. She'd be thrilled that I make you smile."

"You *spoil* me, Dad," Grace said, her smile kind since she loved him more than anyone in the world. "Mom would probably say you're making me soft."

"Soft," he said with a *pfft*. "Never. My daughter has balls of steel."

"I don't have balls at all, and don't talk like that at the party tonight. Your rich friends might faint from shock."

"Screw 'em." Robert winked. "I say what I want, and I'll spoil my daughter whenever I want. Lawrence will be here at seven, so make sure you're ready," he said, referencing their driver.

"Ten-four," Grace responded with a salute.

As she dressed for the party, Grace took a moment to reflect on turning a year older. Sometimes, she felt old. After all, most of her friends were already married to their country club husbands, and several had children.

Other times, she felt young, reminding herself she had her entire life ahead of her. Determined to seize the moment, she dressed in a gorgeous green gown that hugged her breasts and the curve of her hips like a glove. After applying a coat of makeup that accentuated her almond-shaped blue eyes, she regarded herself in the long mirror of the bedroom she still inhabited in her father's Great Falls, Virginia, mansion.

"Not bad," she murmured, running her palms over the satin of the dress. "You don't look a day over twenty-four." Snickering at the sentiment, she grabbed her clutch and headed downstairs to meet the driver.

She made uneventful small talk with her father in the limo and felt her pulse quicken as they approached the restaurant.

"Dad! The parking lot is full. How many people did you invite?"

"All your friends, and all of mine. Why waste a perfectly good party?"

"Is Luthor coming?"

"Of course," Robert said with a nod. "He's my most important client and thinks of you as a daughter, Grace."

Grace pursed her lips, biting her retort so she didn't upset him. In truth, she found Luthor to be skeevy and disingenuous, and something about him always made her feel uneasy. But his business relationship with her father was responsible for their lavish lifestyle, so she remained silent as they pulled into the parking lot.

"I also hired extra security at Luthor's request. He's paranoid now that he's the tenth richest man in the world, and thinks everyone is out to get him." Robert arched a sardonic eyebrow. "So, if you see any men with guns holstered to their belts lurking in dark corners, that's why."

"I'll try not to get shot," Grace murmured drolly as she exited the limo.

Her father smiled as he walked to her side, offering his arm. "You look beautiful, dear. Your mother would be proud."

"Thanks, Dad." Grace lifted her chin in the regal way she'd been taught from countless hours of etiquette lessons. Her mom had insisted on them, reminding Grace that acceptance into the upper echelons of society was never guaranteed. One must act refined and proper to exist in their lavish world.

Grace always thought the lessons a bit ridiculous, but she also enjoyed the spoils of her father's wealth, so she bit her tongue and did her duty. Her mother had passed away several years ago from a brain aneurism, leaving Grace as the matriarch of the family. While other women her age spent their nights dancing in dark, pulsing nightclubs, Grace spent most of her time accompanying her father to charity galas and fundraisers. Others might have found it boring, but Grace hadn't yet found her purpose in life, and going to fancy parties was familiar, so she figured she'd continue the status quo until something in her life changed.

Little did she know, it would be that evening.

She entered the party on her father's arm, noting the lavish decorations and balloons. Robert had tasked his assistant with hiring a decorator, and the room sparkled in her favorite colors—gold and green.

A band played in the far corner of the room, the music filling the room with a soft beat that was drowned out by the cheers at their entrance.

"Grace, you look stunning!" her friend Margaret said, rushing toward her and encircling her wrists. "You might just find a husband tonight."

"I'm more concerned with finding the bar," Grace replied, glancing toward the far wall. "Come on, let's get some champagne."

Margaret nodded and beckoned to her husband, Charles, who followed her like a puppy. Grace thought him incredibly boring—as were most men who ran in their circles—and she had no desire to tie herself to one of them any time soon.

After securing a glass of chilled champagne, Grace began her rounds. She understood her duty—smile, nod, and be cordial. Appearances were meaningful in her father's world, and she aspired to please him. Although she didn't necessarily crave his approval, she did crave his love. He was the only person she'd ever truly been close to, besides her dear mother, and she had an inherent desire to see him happy. Traveling in their societal circles brought him joy, so she'd continue to play her role.

Sure, it was lonely sometimes. Grace had no idea why she had trouble connecting with people. She considered herself smart and polite, and perfectly capable of interesting conversation. A casual observer would probably think she had several close friends.

But Grace was also aloof, sometimes feeling adrift in a world that seemed so big but somehow small at the same time. She often found herself wondering why people in her wealthy circles didn't want *more*. Despite all the charity galas and fundraisers, most people she knew didn't actually do anything else to change the world. Giving money was one thing, but action was another. Perhaps when she got a bit older, she could set the example by implementing positive change in the world.

For now, she pushed away the thoughts in order to mingle with the partygoers.

After two hours, Grace felt restless, yearning for a break from talking about yachts and trips to Greece. Craving fresh air, she ordered a refill on her champagne and slipped outside onto the restaurant's second-floor terrace.

The stars twinkled above as she rested her forearms on the cool stone of the terrace wall. Sighing, she closed her eyes and listened to the faint humming that leaked from the restaurant's main room. Something shuffled behind her and she whirled around, narrowing her eyes to scan the darkened corner behind her.

"Is someone there? I thought I was alone."

A man stepped forward, hazel-green eyes flashing in the moonlight as he lifted his chin. His shoulders were broad and a black holster rested at his belt. He was dressed in a black suit, his hands crossed above his belt buckle as he regarded her.

"I'm one of the security personnel your father hired tonight," he said, his deep voice possessing a gravel-laden tone that made her shiver. "I saw you slip outside and wanted to make sure you weren't alone."

Her eyes darted between his as her pulse pounded, although she wasn't sure if it was from surprise or...something else. His gaze was piercing as he regarded her, and it made her slightly uncomfortable. Heat crept up her neck as she stared back, wondering if he would break first.

The stubborn bastard stood firm, drilling her with those limitless eyes, before he smirked.

"Well, this might be the most enthralling staring contest I've ever had," he drawled, arching an eyebrow. The gesture made him appear incredibly sexy in the dim light, and Grace cleared her throat.

"It's rude to stare," she said, thrusting up her chin.

He just shrugged a dismissive shoulder.

"You can go inside," she continued. "I assure you, I'm perfectly safe. This restaurant is one of the nicest in Virginia and the only threats to my life are the dreadfully boring conversations I'm forced to have with the area's elite."

His eyes widened with surprise. "Aren't you one of the elites?"

"Yes." Her lips fluttered as she expelled a slightly exasperated breath. "Maybe the worst kind of all. I'm an elite who thinks I'm still down to earth."

A low chuckle left his throat, surrounding Grace in a blanket of warmth that caused bumps to rise along the sensitive skin of her nape. She slowly lifted her hand to rub the tiny pricks, aware that the mysterious man's eyes traveled to where her fingers caressed her skin. A sizzling energy vibrated between them, his nostrils flaring as he observed her.

Something raw and animalistic curled in her belly, and she realized it was lust. For the first time in her quarter-century on Earth, Grace felt the unassuageable tug of pure, unchecked desire.

"I don't think—"

"You're not supposed to think on your birthday," he interrupted, shifting his weight from one foot to the other. Grace's eyes roved over his tall frame, and she licked her suddenly parched lips.

"I don't have the luxury of making impulsive decisions. I think about everything."

He glanced over his shoulder to the main room where the Great Falls aristocrats laughed and mingled. Turning back, he tilted his head. "Seems to me like you have all the luxury in the world."

"The prettiest illusions are always the easiest to believe," she said, lowering her arm from her neck to wipe away the chill upon her forearm.

He took a step forward, causing Grace's spine to straighten.

"Don't bristle, little empress," he said, assessing her. "I'm just taking another look at you. If you're an illusion, I want the whole mirage."

"Empress?" she scoffed, unable to control her smile.

"Well, aren't you? All these people are here to celebrate you tonight."

Grace bit her lip as she contemplated. "I think they're all here to celebrate my father. My birthday is just the occasion."

"And is there a 'Mr. Empress?'" he asked, his tone filled with mirth and curiosity.

"No."

His eyebrows lifted slightly. "No one with a fancy boat or a portfolio full of condos waiting in the wings."

Grace's lips thinned. "Most of the eligible men I meet are about as exciting as watching eggs boil."

"Maybe you should slum with the rest of us sometimes. We're not so bad."

Breathing a laugh, she nodded. "Maybe I should."

Her breath caught when he took another step closer, the warmth from his body tangible against hers as he gazed into her eyes. He was several inches taller, and Grace tilted her head, forcing herself to meet his gaze. In other situations, she might have backed down, but for some reason, she felt a need to respond to the slight challenge in his eyes as he loomed over her.

"Damn..." he whispered, placing the backs of his fingers against her jawline. Slowly, he traced the skin there, and Grace felt her knees buckle.

"You're not what I expected, empress," he said, the tender movements of his fingers against her jaw mesmerizing. "If you know what's good for you, you'll head back inside before I show you how fun it can be to join the peasants." Leaning closer, his breath washed over her cheeks. "Or maybe that's what you secretly want."

Grace couldn't deny that she desperately wanted him to kiss her. Never had she felt the pull of consuming desire like this. Hell, she'd only had two boyfriends—one in high school and one in college—and both had been terrible in bed. She was sure neither one even knew a woman possessed the ability to orgasm.

But this man? Somehow, Grace knew that he would know *exactly* what to do with her trembling body. He would know how to find the sensitive little pearl that was now throbbing between her legs. His lips would understand how to travel over every inch of her body. And those long fingers... God, they would probably set her on fire.

"I see the dirty thoughts swirling in those pretty eyes, Grace," he whispered, sliding his fingers under her chin. Tilting her head back, he brushed his lips over hers. The touch was feather-soft, but it elicited a lusty purr from deep in her throat.

"Tell me to stop," he murmured.

Grace remained silent, her body thrumming as she contemplated whether to kiss him back or ask him to release her.

Resting his forehead against hers, he sighed. "I'm on duty, so I have to let you go." His teeth gently nipped her lip before he drew back and released her.

Grace felt the loss of his warmth in every cell of her skin.

"As much as I want to kiss you, I need this job and can't chance your dad finding us in a precarious position."

"I'm an adult and can kiss a man without my father's permission," she said, her tone regal since she was slightly offended.

His slight smirk indicated he believed otherwise, and she straightened her shoulders, embarrassed at her reaction toward him. Aiming to dismiss him, she pivoted and headed back toward the terrace doors.

"It's Tristan Holder," he called, a knowing lilt in his voice as she halted and looked back over her shoulder. "For when you come looking for me—if you're brave enough to leave Daddy's mansion."

Shooting him a glare, she planted a hand on her hip. "Screw you. I could have you fired."

His resulting smile turned his face into something so sexy Grace could feel the heat intensify deep in her core.

"See you around, empress."

Giving him her best look of disgust, she whirled around and reentered the party.

An hour later, Tristan Holder was still on her mind.

When she arrived home after midnight, he'd somehow overtaken every thought in her addled brain as she brushed her teeth and washed her face.

As the early morning light streamed through her bedroom window, Grace awoke, sweaty and groggy from a restless night full of dreams of her sexy, and undeniably rude, hazel-eyed stranger.

"Why were his lips so soft anyway?" she muttered, punching her pillow. "Guys aren't supposed to have soft lips."

But Tristan had. They were somehow soft *and* firm, and as the week wore on, she couldn't stop thinking about having them on every inch of her body.

By Friday, Grace resigned herself to the fact she would never get Tristan Holder out of her mind unless she saw him again. He'd twisted something inside her, and she needed to set it right. While her father was at work, she tiptoed into his office, not wanting the housekeeper to see her.

Shuffling through the documents, she scrolled the wheel on the mouse. In the folder labeled "Grace's 25 Birthday Party," she found a spreadsheet of all the vendors.

"Trident Security Services," she whispered, accessing the company's phone number and dialing. It rang twice before a polite woman answered.

"Uh, hi. I'm looking for one of your security personnel, Tristan Holder. He performed private security for a birthday party organized by Robert Albright last week. I think he left his...er...wallet on the terrace and I wanted to return it to him."

"Oh, that's nice of you," the receptionist chimed. "Let me give you our address and you can mail it to us."

"I was hoping I could speak to him first. Just to, um, you know, verify it's his. His license isn't inside, but there are some other identifying pieces of information."

The receptionist paused. "We can't give out our employees' information, but if you want to email me the info, I'll be happy to ask him."

Sighing, Grace rubbed her forehead. "It's fine. Sorry to bother you."

Feeling like an idiot, Grace hung up the phone.

"He left his wallet? A week ago? For god's sake, Grace. That's ridiculous." Rising from her father's desk, she stuffed her phone in her pocket and wrung her hands. "Let it go. You're two people from completely different worlds, and you'll eventually stop thinking about him. He was just...*hot*," she continued, talking to herself as she exited her father's office and trailed down the marble-floored hallway. "There are plenty of other men to obsess over. Get a grip."

Determined to move on, she plopped on the couch and turned on the latest episode of *Real Housewives*, hoping the diversion would rid the enigmatic man from her mind.

Twenty minutes later, her phone buzzed. Drawing it from her pocket, she gasped at the text message.

Unknown Number: I told you you'd come looking for me.

Furious, Grace gritted her teeth.

Grace: I don't know who this is or what you're talking about.

Sweat beaded at her temple as the text bubble appeared.

Unknown Number: Liar.

"That arrogant son of a bitch..." She quickly saved his number before her thumbs moved furiously over the keyboard as she typed.

Grace: Don't text me again or I'll call the police.

Tristan responded with an eyeroll emoji.

Tristan: Are you always this dramatic?

A surprised laugh left Grace's lips.

Grace: I'm not dramatic. And leave me alone.

He didn't respond for several minutes, causing Grace to frown at the thought that he might actually obey her order. Then another text appeared.

Tristan: If you want to see me again, all you have to do is ask.

Grace: How did you get my number? I'm pretty sure that's illegal.

Tristan: I'm in security, and we have a log of everyone who calls the firm. It wasn't hard.

Grace: I could get you fired for stalking me.

Tristan: Says the woman who needs to return my "wallet."

Grace emitted a frustrated groan.

Grace: Forget it. I never want to see you again. I had a momentary lapse in judgment. Goodbye.

Several more minutes passed before another text appeared.

Tristan: 345 Dogwood Lane, Apartment 7, Sterling, VA. If you're brave enough. I'm off on Sunday. If not, I'll lose your number. The ball's in your court, empress.

Grace pulled up the address on her phone, noting it was in the next town over. She'd planned to spend Sunday at the club playing tennis with the kids. She'd played in high school and liked to help the instructors when they held their Sunday lessons. She didn't get paid, but she didn't need the money and it allowed her to give back, if only a little.

Or...she could tell the club's pro that something had come up.

"You can't go to his house alone!" she squeaked to herself. "He could be a serial killer!"

Telling herself she'd become delusional since meeting the sexy stranger, she dismissed the idea of visiting him at all.

And promised herself she'd stick to that decision.

Which definitely made her the liar Tristan had called her when she pulled up the rideshare app on Sunday morning and hailed a car to his apartment.

Her heart pounded furiously in her chest the entire ride, and she told herself a hundred times she was crazy for visiting a stranger's home without telling her father where she'd gone. He was on a fishing trip for the weekend, so as far as he knew, she was at the club.

After the driver dropped her off, Grace rubbed her wet palms on her pristine slacks and walked down the slightly cracked concrete walkway that led to Tristan's building entrance. She located his unit number and rang the bell with shaking fingers.

"Yes?" his deep baritone chimed over the speaker.

Grace stood frozen, unable to speak as she struggled to breathe.

His sultry chuckle echoed through the speaker, both infuriating her and sending little shivers of desire over her rapidly heating skin.

"It's on the second floor, empress."

The buzzer on the front door sounded, jolting Grace as she faced the entrance. Swallowing thickly, she pushed the heavy door open and headed toward the stairs.

Wondering if she was making the worst decision of her life...

And reminding herself she didn't kiss men she didn't know...

Even if the man who awaited her inside was the sexiest man she'd ever met in her affluent but sheltered life.

Chapter 2

G race walked up the stairs, telling herself not to be a snob. The rickety steps desperately needed cleaning, and a dead bug greeted her as she crested the second floor, but not everyone had a live-in housekeeper. Although the building was a bit dingy, it wasn't squalid. And after all, was she really here for the décor?

"What in the hell *are* you doing here?" she muttered, rapping on the door as her heart threatened to burst from her chest.

Tristan slowly opened the door, the hinges creaking as he loomed in the doorway.

"I wasn't expecting company," he drawled, cocking a brow as Grace's eyes traveled over his bare chest and down to gray sweatpants above his bare feet.

"Well, you could've thrown on a shirt since you knew I was here," she said, annoyance in her tone.

"Where's the fun in that?" Opening the door wider, he gestured her inside. "I promise I won't bite—unless you ask."

Grace shot him a glare before breezing past him. The interior was small but clean, and she rubbed her wet palms on her jeans as she approached the plaid-covered couch. "Should I sit here?"

"Sure. Want a drink? I've got light beer, shitty wine, bottled water or whiskey."

"Water is fine. Thank you."

He disappeared through a doorway that must've led to his bedroom, because he reemerged a few moments later wearing a t-shirt. Grace frowned, silently admitting she enjoyed the view without the shirt much better.

Tristan padded over and handed her a water before sitting beside her and popping open his beer. Lifting it, he made a toast. "To slumming it."

Breathing a laugh, Grace tapped her bottle against his. "It's not so bad. And your apartment is very clean. Maybe they can hire you to remove the bugs from the stairway."

His sultry gaze lingered on her as he took a slow sip of his beer. "Yeah. We're not quite up to white-glove standards here."

Smiling, Grace forced herself to relax into the soft cushions. "Some standards are overrated."

Silence lingered as he contemplated her, and Grace was surprised at how...*easy* it was. For some reason, although her body was a frayed mass of nerves, she felt comfortable with Tristan.

"I'll be honest," he said, crossing an ankle over his knee, "I'm not sure what to do here. I don't know what your expectations were when you came here today, but I'll make polite conversation until you're ready to tell me." Tilting his head, he flashed a brilliant smile that made her stomach flutter. "So, Grace Albright, tell me about yourself."

Sighing, she ran a hand through her thick golden tresses, reveling in the desire that flashed in his eyes. "Sadly, there's not much to tell. As you know, I just turned twenty-five, but nothing much has happened to me yet. Maybe I'm here to change that."

His eyebrow lifted slightly.

"Anyway," she continued after taking a huge gulp of water. "I've probably got the same ol' boring rich girl story as every debutante in Great Falls. Wealthy father. Tragically departed mother. Trying my best to figure out life in a world I have no business complaining about but still find incredibly dull."

"I'm sorry to hear about your mom," he said softly.

"Thanks. She died of a brain aneurysm. One day she was vibrant and alive, and the next day, she was gone." Grace snapped her fingers. "It reinforced the importance of seizing each day. That's for damn sure."

Tristan nodded as his foot tapped above his knee.

"And you? Tell me about your family."

"My parents live in a retirement home in Texas. They love the community there and are thrilled to participate in the daily rounds of bridge." His lips twitched. "And I have a sister, Jessica. She's two years younger than me."

"Does she live close by?"

"She's in Florida and engaged to a douchebag who's going to ruin her life. I've given up on trying to stop the wedding. I'll just be here to pick up the pieces when she inevitably gets divorced."

"Well, that's cynical. Maybe it will work out."

Tristan scoffed. "Happy ever after only happens for people like you, empress. The rest of us just do our best while we wait for the other shoe to drop."

The sentiment made her sad, and she shook her head. "Maybe someone will prove you wrong one day. I hope they do."

"We'll see," he murmured, his expression doubtful. Shifting, his gaze grew curious. "So, what's it like to run in Luthor Cromwell's circle? He's up there with Jeff Bezos and Richard Branson. That fancy mansion he lives in must have warm bidet sprays for all his guests."

Tossing back her head, Grace broke into laughter. "He does have bidets, although I can't say if they're warm." She shrugged. "What can I say? He and my dad are close."

"They work together?"

Grace nodded. "My father is the CEO of the largest CDMO in the country—"

"CDMO?" Tristan asked.

"Contract Development and Manufacturing Organization. Companies like my father's help pharmaceutical companies like Sendaxa get drugs to market faster."

"And getting drugs to market faster makes them more money."

"Exactly. There's so much that goes into drug production, from the equipment needed for storage, to the raw chemicals, to setting up distribution channels. My dad helps Sendaxa release drugs quicker and satisfy all the FDA regulations."

"Sendaxa isn't known for adhering to FDA regulations," Tristan said. "That painkiller they released a few years ago was taken off the market."

"Yeah, that was definitely a blunder." Grace rubbed her forehead as she recalled the shitshow that ensued after the drug was recalled. "My dad lost millions in fines, and Sendaxa was fined over a billion dollars."

"All in a day's work for Luthor Cromwell, huh?"

"Sadly, yes. Sendaxa paid the fine and that was it."

"You don't seem particularly...satisfied at the outcome."

Sighing, she bit her lip as she pondered. "I mean, I'm happy Dad was able to just pay a fine and move on. He's a good man and didn't mean any harm."

"And Luthor?"

Grace's teeth fidgeted with her lower lip. "I'm not sure he's as good of a man. The experience seemed to reinforce that he can continue the bad behavior and only get a slap on the wrist."

"To living a life where a billion-dollar fine is considered a slap on the wrist," Tristan joked, lifting his beer.

Chuckling, Grace tapped her water bottle against his. "For real. Anyway, Sendaxa is Dad's most important client, which means Luthor is here to stay. Although he's not my favorite person, I understand his importance to my father's legacy."

"If he's not a good person, couldn't that be detrimental to your father's legacy?"

Shivering, Grace rubbed the bumps that rose on her arm. "Maybe. I hope that doesn't happen."

"There's that unfailing belief in happy endings again. It's in direct contrast to my ever-present pessimism."

Grace smiled, inwardly wondering if she could somehow change his mind one day. After all, being optimistic was a more positive way to life, right? What was wrong with having hope?

Tristan drank the last of his beer and shook it. "I can open another one, or I can pour us both a glass of whiskey. Your call."

Clearing her throat, she contemplated whether it was a good idea to have whiskey at ten a.m. on a Sunday with a stranger in his home.

Moving closer, he leaned toward her and whispered, "I'm not going to roofie it, Grace. Believe me, if we ever get to the point where I touch you, I want you to be perfectly aware of what's going on."

She whipped her head to face him, her nose almost grazing his. "I didn't come here to have sex with you."

A knowing glint flashed in his eyes. "Then have some whiskey with me. You're wound up and it will help you relax."

Her eyes darted between his before she nodded. "Okay."

His lips curved before he rose, striding into the kitchen and returning with two tumblers full of brown liquid.

"Sheesh," Grace said, taking the glass he extended. "What happened to two fingers?"

His eyes turned molten at the double entendre. "Why, Grace, I thought you weren't interested in having sex." The teasing lilt of his voice washed over her, drawing her further into his seductive web.

Grace didn't know much about uncontrollable desire, but this man had a magnetic stronghold over her. The energy that pulsed between them was tangible, and she leaned closer, craving it as warmth emanated from his skin.

"I'm not sure what I'm interested in," she droned, lifting the glass. "Maybe the whiskey will help me decide." Tristan clinked his glass with hers, and she took a hefty gulp.

Grace coughed and sputtered as the whiskey burned her throat. Tristan scooted closer, the side of his body pressing against hers as he patted her back.

"Jesus, woman. You're supposed to sip it." His hand caressed her back in a soothing gesture as tears stung her eyes.

"Fuck it," she whispered before tossing back another swig. "Seize the moment, right?"

Tristan grinned as he shook his head. They drank in comfortable silence until Grace felt the warm liquid coursing through her veins. After a few more gulps, she finished the glass and set it on the table. Emitting a high-pitched hiccup, she rubbed her mouth with her arm.

"That's good. I like whiskey."

"You don't say," he teased, playfully pressing his shoulder into hers. "Do I need to worry about you puking on my cheap couch?"

"Nope." Mesmerized by his strong arms as they rested on his muscular thighs, she slowly reached over and touched one of the tattoos. Emboldened by the alcohol, she gently traced the black ink that formed the shapes of a skull, a snake and an anchor.

"Did they hurt?" she asked, her voice raspy.

"Not really. I'm guessing you don't have any."

"I've always been too afraid of the pain. But with all the whiskey I just drank, maybe it wouldn't be so bad."

Gliding his fingers under her chin, he forced her to meet his gaze. "Since we've decided you didn't come here for sex, maybe you came here so I could convince you to get a tattoo. I can take you to my guy in town. He's got years of experience and will take care of you."

"I can't get a tattoo!" she exclaimed before hiccupping again. "And I'm wasted. That's a terrible time to make decisions."

Tristan arched a sexy brow. "Or maybe it's the *best* time."

Grace stared into his eyes as curiosity welled. What if she actually did something unexpected for once?

"Oh, yeah," he said, tucking a strand of hair behind her hear. "You're going to get your first tattoo today. Let me get dressed and we'll call an Uber." He tossed back the last of his whiskey and disappeared into his room before she could argue.

He emerged two minutes later, looking sexy as hell in jeans, a black t-shirt, and black sneakers. Trailing toward her, he extended his hand as he loomed above her. "Ready?"

Grace resisted the urge to shrink away. Was she actually considering this? It was completely against her nature.

"Come on, empress. Live a little."

Inhaling a deep breath, Grace clutched onto every ounce of courage she possessed and pressed her hand to his.

Chapter 3

Tristan stood beside the tattoo chair, arms crossed against his chest as he pursed his lips. He struggled not to laugh at the gorgeous creature who reclined beneath him, her face a mask of fear and anticipation as she gazed at him with those limitless blue eyes.

"Stop laughing at me!" she demanded, causing his lips to twitch. Damn, she was tougher than she appeared, and he was quickly realizing that the multiple layers of her spitfire personality ignited all sorts of feelings deep within his stoic soul.

When he'd met her on the terrace in the moonlight, his heart had stopped for one soulful moment. His eyes had traveled over her wistful expression, those plump, kissable lips, and farther down to the green dress that hugged every curve. Lust had roared in his brain, and his palms ached to caress those flared hips...

And then she'd turned, and he'd gazed into those azure eyes, and something clicked into place. One solemn, possessive word echoed in his mind as they spoke under the stars.

Mine.

Tristan had given her his name on a whim. Something about her feisty nature caught him off guard, and he thought there might be a chance she would attempt to track him down.

Albeit, a *small* chance—but he'd been overcome with the need to see her again. To feel the strange, pulsing energy that sizzled between them. He'd never felt anything like it in his life.

When she'd shown up on his doorstep, he'd been surprised and...elated, if he was being honest. Tristan took it as an indication that she was just as curious about the sparks that had flown between them. For someone who was rather unemotional, Tristan found the indisputable connection between them intriguing.

"I'm not laughing at you, empress," he lied. "Take some deep breaths and relax. It will feel better. I thought you were drunk?"

"It's quickly wearing off," she grumbled as the tattoo artist leaned over her, the sound of the buzzing gun causing her to flinch.

"Micah will take good care of you," Tristan said, sliding his palm over hers and squeezing. "Right, man?"

"You bet." Micah gave a nod and got to work, pressing the tattoo gun to the drawing he'd made next to Grace's hip bone.

"That's a painful place to get a tattoo," Tristan said, his eyes darting over the pale skin of her hip. Jealousy flared that Micah had a front row seat to the intimate patch of skin.

"I had to choose a place my father wouldn't see," she said, squeezing her eyes shut against the pain. "He'd kill me if he knew I was doing this."

The tattoo gun buzzed and hummed as her breath grew labored. Threading her fingers through his, she squeezed so tightly Tristan thought he might lose circulation. And still, even through the threat of involuntary amputation, he held tight, wanting to comfort her. There was something about her that inspired a deep-seated need to protect, and Tristan realized he'd have a hard time letting her go when she eventually tired of hanging with the riffraff on the other side of the tracks.

Tristan was a realist, and he knew that rich women like Grace never slummed with his kind for long. Once the excitement wore off, she'd run back to her fancy country club and marry someone named Dennis who teed off at four o'clock every afternoon and then hurried home for two minutes of vanilla missionary-style sex.

But for now, Tristan clutched the hand of the regal beauty he'd met the night of her twenty-fifth birthday. She was his, if only for the moment, and he wouldn't squander his good fortune.

Hell, if he was lucky, he might just kiss those pretty lips.

He wasn't boorish enough to push her into sex. Tristan was too proud to be anyone's mistake or dirty little secret. But he wasn't above tasting that hot, regal mouth while she purred beneath him. He was perfectly fine with taking her home, giving her one last glass of whiskey, and sucking every drop from her sexy lips. Then he'd send her on her way, armed with a tattoo that would ensure she'd never forget their time together.

And maybe, just maybe, she'd come back for another taste before she married ol' Dennis.

Tristan felt his lips curve at the slightly optimistic thought. Perhaps she was already rubbing off on him; his majestic little optimist.

Tristan focused on the ink Micah injected into her skin. He thought she might pick something dainty, like a flower or a fairy, but she'd surprised him and picked a dragon. It was a simple design, with a dragon's head and a long body that ended in a curled tail.

"Why the dragon?" he asked, hoping to distract her from the pain with conversation.

"Because they're misunderstood. They have these built-in defense mechanisms like breathing fire and bony scales, but underneath, they're probably just a little lost like we all are."

The words were lonely, and he wondered how someone as wealthy and pampered as Grace could feel lost.

"I told you," she said, her lips forming a poignant smile. "Pretty illusions."

Tristan smiled back, holding her hand as Micah focused on finishing the job.

An hour later, Grace sat up and chugged the shot Micah handed her. "On the house for surviving your first tattoo. I'm impressed. Thought you were going to puke for a second there, but you proved me wrong."

"It looks so cool," she said, setting down the glass and examining her tattoo before Micah covered it with a bandage. "How long will it take to heal?"

"Use the ointment I recommended a few times a day," Micah said, shaking the tube she'd purchased to take home with her. "You want to clean with sterile, lukewarm water and fragrance-free soap at least twice a day."

"Okay," she said as he patted the bandage to make sure it was secure.

Micah helped her into a sitting position, and she swayed atop the chair. Grasping her shoulders, Tristan steadied her. "You okay?"

"Yeah." She quickly shook her head. "Just gotta get used to the discomfort."

"It will heal in two to three weeks if you follow the regimen," Micah said. "And Tristan can help you. He's gotten a few of these."

Grace pulled her American Express black card from her designer purse. "You take AmEx?"

Micah shot Tristan a droll look. "Where'd you find her, man?"

Laughing, Tristan shook his head. "Don't ask."

"Excuse me," Grace said, shaking the card. "Or would you rather I didn't pay?"

"We take cash here, princess. Nobody in this neighborhood has one of those."

Tristan pulled two hundred dollars from his pocket. "Here you go. Thanks, Micah. Keep the change."

"Always a pleasure," Micah said, standing and stuffing the cash into his back pocket. "I'll be in the back smoking a bowl. Let me know if you need anything before you leave."

"I'll pay you back," Grace said, gazing up at Tristan as she frowned. "I don't usually carry cash."

"Don't worry about it." Grasping her hand, he helped her stand, making sure she was steady on her feet before they called the rideshare back to his place.

As they sat in the back seat of the rideshare, he eyed the hip where she'd gotten the tattoo. "You feeling okay? I probably shouldn't have dared you to do this."

"Honestly?" she asked with a cheeky grin. "I feel amazing! I never do anything like this." Covering his hand atop her thigh, she squeezed. "Thank you. I feel...*free*."

As the warmth from her hand seeped into his, Tristan marveled at the joy on her stunning face. Lost in her brilliant eyes and breathtaking smile, he had the insane thought that nothing else in the world mattered other than making this woman happy.

Recreating the incandescent glow in her expression and the shine of reverent admiration in her eyes was all he cared about.

And that's when Tristan realized that even though he'd only known this woman for a matter of hours in the scheme of things, time was irrelevant when it came to matters of the heart.

Whether he was ready or not, he was falling for a rich debutante he could most likely never have.

And still, although it seemed impossible, his heart thrummed with the uncharacteristically optimistic thought that, perhaps, in some small way, Grace felt the undeniable chemistry between them too.

As they approached his building, she dug her perfectly manicured pink nails into his skin, sending pricks of pleasure-pain through his body as he gazed into her eyes.

In that moment, Tristan was overcome with the agony of ever letting her go.

So, he led her inside and promised himself he'd do everything in his power to make her want to stay.

Chapter 4

G race followed Tristan inside his apartment, cognizant of the stinging of her freshly minted tattoo. Glancing at her watch, she noted there were hours left before her father would be home around nine p.m. She'd have to make sure she was back when he arrived—otherwise, it would lead to questions she wasn't ready to answer.

For some reason, she wanted to keep her visit with Tristan to herself, if only for the time being. Not because she was ashamed or embarrassed. Instead, it felt nice to have something that only belonged to *her*. Since her mother died, her life had been inexorably tied to her father's and his lavish world, and it was freeing to have something of her own.

Striding to the window, she glanced out toward the courtyard behind Tristan's building. She'd been truthful about not visiting him to sleep with him. That was something she wasn't ready for—yet. But the man occupied several corners of her mind, and she wanted to understand why.

The object of her musings approached, gently pressing his body to hers as he slid an arm around her waist. Grace's eyes fluttered before closing as he tenderly nuzzled her neck.

"I'm guessing we're still on the 'no sex' policy," he murmured, grazing his lips over her nape.

"I don't want to ruin this," she whispered, shaking her head. "I don't even understand it." Lifting her lids, she gazed into his eyes. "Do you?"

His palm flattened over her belly as he drew her tighter against him, the curve of her bottom fitting into the juncture of his thighs as if she were made to fit there.

"No," he rasped, his eyes sweeping her face as he studied her. "It's...intense."

She breathed a laugh. "Yeah. I'm slightly terrified, but that could just be the pain and the booze talking. But I have a couple of hours before I need to go and...I just don't want to leave yet."

"Okay." He glanced out the window. "There's a garden down the street that's pretty if you want to walk there. We could grab some food at the deli along the way. It won't be fancy, but I don't think you were expecting fancy when you searched me out."

"You've really got a chip on your shoulder about me being rich. It's annoying. I can't help what I was born into and I do a lot of charity work." She lifted her chin to emphasize her words. "And I don't look down on people who don't have the same means I do. I was just born lucky where others weren't."

"I have a chip on my shoulder because you're the most beautiful woman I've ever seen and I hate that you're going to leave eventually." Grace's heart slammed at his words. "And once you go, I'm afraid you'll never come back."

Her hand glided over his jaw, his prickly stubble so stark against her softness. "I'll come back."

"That's a lofty promise, empress."

Nodding, she ran her thumb over his bottom lip. "I know. Lock it away because I don't make promises I won't keep."

Tristan nipped her thumb and grinned. "I'll hold you to it. Come on. Let's get you some food. You must be starving."

After stopping at the deli to grab some sandwiches, they strolled to the garden. A flower-covered arch covered the entrance, and Grace found it quite pretty and serene. They walked along the gravel path until they found a bench.

Once they were seated and enjoying the sandwiches, Grace surveyed the tiny park.

"Lots of butterflies here," she said in between bites. "I love butterflies."

"I definitely thought you'd go for the butterfly tattoo. You surprised me with the dragon."

"I think I was feeling bold." She flashed a grin. "Maybe I'll get a butterfly on my other hip when I get my next tattoo."

"Told you," Tristan said in that arrogant way that should've pissed her off but she found endearingly sexy. "Once you get one, you become addicted."

Grace grinned as she wiped her hands, thinking of how livid her father would be if he ever discovered the tattoo.

"I guess you're not going to tell your dad about our day together since you're hiding the tattoo."

"I don't plan to tell him…yet," she said, lifting a shoulder. "I love him very much, but he has this idea of who I'm supposed to be. I play the part and it works for us."

"Don't you get tired of pretending?"

Lifting her eyebrows, she pondered. "Yes. I think that's why I came looking for you."

Tristan nodded as he gathered their trash and walked toward the nearby receptacle to toss it in. Returning, he extended his hand. "I'm honored to be someone you don't have to pretend with."

Grace slid her hand in his, allowing him to tug her to her feet before they wandered around the garden. It was a few hundred feet in diameter, and they walked in comfortable silence as she threaded her fingers through his.

"Oh, it's an Olympia Marble butterfly!" she exclaimed, pointing to the white butterfly that perched on a nearby bush. "See the dark marbling on the white wings? They're endangered. One of the charities I volunteer for protects endangered butterflies and moths."

"It's pretty," Tristan said, squeezing her fingers. "Inspiration for your next tattoo."

Grace chuckled, wondering if she'd truly ever have the courage to get another tattoo. She'd settle into her dragon first and see how it healed. "Maybe."

Eventually, Tristan led her back to his apartment and offered her more whiskey. She declined and checked her phone.

"My dad will be back in a few hours. I should probably head back."

Tristan's gaze bored into her, filled with a yearning that shook her to her core. Closing the distance between them, he placed his broad hands on her waist and rested his forehead against hers.

"I don't want you to leave," he whispered. "And I sound like a fucking pansy for saying that, but it's the truth—"

Grace lifted to her toes, pressing her mouth to his and inhaling his words. His hands slid to her backside, cupping her and lifting her into his arms. Her legs wrapped around his waist, her arms encircling his neck as she thrust her tongue into his warm mouth.

Tristan groaned, a low hum that shot down her throat and straight to the core of raw energy buzzing deep within her rapidly heating body. He carried her into his bedroom, placing her on the bed as he devoured her mouth.

"I won't fuck you," he rasped, thrusting his fingers in her hair and twining the tresses around them as he tugged. "But I need this. I need to taste you, empress. Please let me taste you."

"Yes..." she cried, tossing her head back on the soft com-forter as he nibbled her lips...and the skin that covered her collarbone...before moving lower and dragging her shirt and bra from her trembling body.

Those full, skillful lips tasted every inch of her straining frame. He tasted her tight nipples, budded into sensitive points when they hit the cool air...and then relieved when his silken tongue lapped and sucked...

And then he moved lower, dipping his tongue into her navel before he deftly unzipped her jeans and tossed them aside. He pressed tender kisses to the sensitive skin beside the bandage that covered her new tattoo. Groaning, he almost tore the scrap of lace that covered her core as he yanked it from her legs before burying his face in her dripping center.

Her sexy lover worked his tongue and fingers over the straining little bud between her legs as Grace begged for more. Spearing her fingers in his thick hair, she pulled him closer, pushing into his wanton mouth as he growled with lust.

There in a nondescript apartment with a man she barely knew but somehow trusted implicitly, Grace experienced her first earth-shattering orgasm from a lover.

After exploding beneath him, she struggled to contain the convulsions that rocked her ravaged frame. Tristan blew on her wet, ravaged core before placing soft kisses along the flesh. Slithering over her, he removed his shirt and pants and threw his thick leg over her still-trembling thighs.

"You took off your clothes," she droned, wondering how she was still able to speak.

"Left my underwear on," he said, nuzzling her neck as he held her. "Otherwise, I'll definitely fuck you, and I don't want to betray your trust. But I need to feel you against me, empress. Just a few minutes before you leave, okay?"

"Mmm kay..." she agreed, her tone sleepy as she yawned. "Just a few minutes and then I'll go..."

His satisfied hum vibrated against her skin as his limbs tightened around her. Grace reminded herself she could only sleep for a few moments and then she would leave.

Yes, just a few moments before she had to return to a reality that now paled in comparison to lying in Tristan's warm embrace on a lazy Sunday afternoon...

Chapter 5

G race awoke to the sound of metal and wood being pulverized outside Tristan's bedroom. Rising with a gasp, she covered her breasts with her arms, shielding herself as two men stormed into the room.

"What the fuck?" Tristan yelled, moving in front of Grace to shield her.

Grace observed her father enter the room, rage lining his expression. "This is where I find you, Grace? Naked in a stranger's dingy apartment in Sterling?"

"What the hell, Dad?" she asked, peering over Tristan's shoulder as she hid behind him to cover her nakedness. "You weren't supposed to be home until nine o'clock."

"I got home a few hours early and was terrified when you weren't there." His eyes narrowed to angry slits. "I traced your location on your phone and we rushed over. I thought you were in danger!"

Grace's gaze roved over her father's two security guards as anger welled in her chest. "I'm a grown woman and can visit whomever I want—"

"Not as long as you live in my house!" He jabbed his finger as he spoke. "Do you hear me? I won't have you getting pregnant with some vagrant's child so he can steal my inheritance!"

"Your daughter searched me out, sir," Tristan said, nostrils flaring as his hands curled into fists. "And I make my own money."

"Not anymore you don't," Robert said, lifting his chin. "I'll have you blacklisted from every security job in the state if you don't stay away from my daughter. Do you hear me?"

"Dad!" Grace said, confused by the angry man in front of her. Sure, her father had always been a bit pretentious, but she'd never thought he was classist. "Tristan is right. I came here on my own free will."

"Well, we're going home now. Get dressed. And you're not to see each other again. Do you hear me? I'll be outside." He ushered the men out the door and closed it behind him.

"I've never seen him this way," Grace said, rubbing her forehead as the shock of his reaction set in. "I'm so sorry—"

"It's how the world works," Tristan said, his face impassive as he rose and gathered her clothing. Thrusting it at her, he shrugged. "I knew you'd leave eventually. At least you'll have the tattoo to remember me by."

Grace scowled as they dressed, annoyed that he would give in to her father's ridiculous behavior so easily. "This isn't over. I *will* see you again."

Tristan glanced toward the door as he contemplated. Sighing, he lifted her hand and kissed the palm. "I doubt it. Go live the life you were meant to live, Grace. I'm grateful for the day we had."

Yanking her hand away, she straightened her spine. "I just need time to figure this out. I'll be in touch."

Trying to appear composed even though she was a shaking mass of frayed nerves, she opened the door and joined her father and his security team on the other side. Robert led her down to the limo and ushered her inside before sitting across from her. As they began the drive home, he stared out the tinted window, fury evident in his expression and in the hunch of his shoulders.

"That was unacceptable behavior, Dad. I don't know what's gotten into you. Tristan was nothing but a gentleman with me."

Releasing an exasperated breath, Robert faced her and spoke in a low, solemn tone. "I've tried my best to shelter you from the evil in the world, Grace, but I fear I might have inadvertently forgotten to teach you what evil actually is.

Men like *that*"—he pointed back toward Tristan's apartment building—"never go after women like you for reasons other than money or power."

Scoffing, she ran a hand through her hair. "I've never thought you were elitist, but I'm ashamed of you. It breaks my heart—"

"I'd rather you be heartbroken than broke and pregnant," Robert said, slicing his hand through the air. "And if you see him again, I'll cut off your inheritance and donate your trust fund to the local pet rescue. I mean it, Grace."

Tears welled as she struggled not to cry. "He's a good man, Dad."

"You're not to speak to him again and this subject is closed."

Overcome with emotion, Grace turned away, blindly staring out the window as she contemplated how things had gone so horribly wrong.

One thing she knew for certain was that she would see Tristan Holder again. In fact, her father's reaction had the unintended consequence of making her want to see him even more. To make things right and apologize at Robert's terrible behavior.

Little did Grace know that this night would be her first lesson in irreversible pain and heartache.

In the future, she would have many more nights where she sobbed uncontrollably and railed at the world.

But this would always be the first night her innocence was shattered.

Chapter 6

Three months later

Tristan sat on his couch studying his phone, frustrated because he knew it wasn't going to ring. His thumb trailed over the screen in a slow, sad motion, representative of the despondency that had crept into his soul when he'd blocked Grace's number.

They'd been sneaking around for several months, and the lying and deception had worn on Tristan until he couldn't take it anymore.

He'd done his best to try to win Robert to his side. Tristan had shown up at his office, and when the secretary refused to let him inside, he'd waited on the sidewalk outside the corporate building. When Robert exited, dressed in his pristine designer suit with briefcase in hand, Tristan stepped in his path, blocking him from the limo where his driver was waiting.

"Sir, if I could just have a few minutes—"

"How dare you approach me?" Robert interrupted, his cheeks growing ruddy with anger. "I have nothing to say to you."

"I'm in love with your daughter, sir, and want to earn your trust," Tristan said, encircling his forearm.

Robert yanked his arm away. "My daughter will inherit this one day." He gestured to the building. "She's all I have left since her mother died, and I won't watch her waste her life on an interloper who has no chance of giving her the life she deserves."

"You don't know me, but I'm resilient, Mr. Albright. All I want is to build something with Grace and make her happy—"

"Grace needs a man who can give her stability. Someone who came from *her* world and understands the life she's meant to have. Not someone who will build a life on her back with her money."

"I don't want her money," Tristan said, angry at the accusation. "I make my own money, sir."

"Not if I ensure you can't," Robert threatened, his nostrils flaring. "And if you don't stop seeing her, that's exactly what I'll do. Do you think I don't know she's been sneaking around with you? You have no honor, son, and your actions prove that."

"You forbade her to see me!" Tristan exclaimed. "Without even giving me a chance. And it's laughable that you would accuse me of having no honor when you're obviously having her tracked. Or are you exempt from the misdeeds of the rest of us commoners?" He crossed his arms and lifted his eyebrows.

"I had to have her followed to ensure she was safe. For all I know, you're trying to entrap her to steal her fortune."

Sighing, Tristan shook his head. "Is it so unfathomable to you that someone could love your daughter for who she is? I don't give a damn about her money. If you took any time to get to know me, you'd realize that, and you do a grave disservice to her to assume otherwise."

Robert's gaze fell to the ground as he contemplated. Returning his gaze to Tristan's, he gave a dismissive shrug. "I've been around too long and know how the world works, son. Go and find someone who fits you. Grace isn't meant for you."

"I could *make* us fit," Tristan said, a slight pleading in his voice. "In so many ways, we already do. I apologize for sneaking around, but *she's* the one visiting me. We both want this to work. Let me earn her."

A resigned expression overtook Robert's features. "You'll never be able to earn her, Tristan. The fact that you don't understand that shows me how naïve you are. It's not personal. It's just the way it is. Stay away from her before I blacklist you with every security firm from Miami to Maine." Lifting his finger, he said sternly, "I mean it. Leave. Her. Alone."

Backing away, he slid into the limo before the driver shut the door and drove away.

Leaning back on the worn cushions of his couch, Tristan expelled a defeated breath as he remembered the disastrous conversation. That night, he'd returned to his apartment with a sense of finality. Moments later, he'd blocked Grace's number. Although he wanted to make it work, he had too much pride to sneak around with a woman whose father would never accept him.

That had been two nights ago. Rubbing his hand over his heart, Tristan acknowledged it felt like two years. In the scant time he'd ceased communication with Grace, the heartache had set in. He considered himself a tough soul, but there were some connections that transcended normal feelings. His feelings for Grace exceeded anything he'd ever imagined, and he wondered how long it would take for them to abate. Would he feel them for a month? A year? Forever?

Deciding he needed to drown his sorrows, he tossed on some jeans and haphazardly combed his hair before heading downstairs, ready for a drink at the local bar on the corner. When he approached the front door of his building, he noticed Grace standing outside, her blond hair plastered to her cheeks and neck as rain drenched her.

Pulling open the door, he asked, "What the hell—?"

Her palm slapped across his cheek, the sound echoing in the vacant atrium of his building.

"You fucking blocked me?"

Tristan clenched his teeth, simultaneously admiring her gumption and wanting to wring her neck. "If you're here to win me back, knocking out several of my teeth isn't the way."

She sputtered as the rain continued to sluice over her skin and hair. "A gentleman would invite me in so I can get out of the rain."

Tristan arched a brow. "A lady wouldn't hit someone in the face."

Emitting a frustrated groan, she lifted her eyes to the darkened sky. "Lord, give me strength. I'm going to kill him before we make it down the aisle."

"What?" Tristan asked as shock ran through his veins.

Lowering her gaze to his, her eyes were filled with fire and determination. "No one makes decisions about my future but me. That includes my father. As much as I want to murder you right now, you also happen to be the one person I've ever felt free with in the entire world." Stepping closer, she jabbed her finger in his face. "You're the only man who's ever come close to making me scream—and I'm not just talking about the sex, although it's pretty fucking great."

Pride swelled as he stood silent, digesting her tirade.

"Every second I'm not with you, I feel *numb*. I feel like an imposter in a world where everyone else is human." Dropping her hand, her expression softened slightly. "But with you, I feel...*everything*." Grasping his wrist, she splayed his palm over her heart before covering his hand with hers. "And I won't give that up. So, you're going to marry me. And that's the end of this discussion."

Tristan absorbed each beat of her heart beneath his palm as he gazed into her eyes. They shone back at him filled with deep emotion and a slight fear that nearly shattered him. "You're scared I'll say no," he whispered.

"A part of me is," she said, nodding. "Because it means I'll have to fight harder until you say yes. And you *will* say yes. I think it's best if you just save us both some time and get me to a damn courthouse. *After* I dry off."

He breathed a laugh. "Your father will never let it happen—"

"It's not his choice."

"Grace," he murmured, cupping her cheek. "If I marry you, he's going to ensure I never get a security job again. My options to support us will be extremely limited."

"I have plenty of money."

"No," he said, drawing her inside and running his thumb over her lip. "I won't live on your fortune. I have to do things my way if we do this."

"A marriage involves two people, Tristan. I know we can figure this out. How about, instead of your way, we do it *our* way? Together."

Tristan mulled the sentiment. He was a lone wolf in many ways, and wasn't sure he understood the first thing about compromising in a relationship. "I'm not sure we'd be able to figure it out. And what happens then? When your father has disowned you and we're living in the real world? Have you really thought about this, Grace?"

Placing her hands on his face, she softly asked, "Do you love me?"

He released a slow breath. "Yes."

Her brilliant smile eroded every ounce of loneliness he'd felt in the past two days.

"Then marry me."

Elation at the prospect of marrying her warred with the fear they were doomed to fail.

"Tristan?"

In that moment, although it went against his better judgment, all he could focus on was her. Those stunning eyes, full of hope and love. The earnestness in her expression as she waited for him to answer.

God help him, even though he knew the odds were against them, he couldn't deny the woman he loved more than he'd ever thought possible. Sliding his fingers into the hair at the base of her neck, he tilted her face to his.

"It won't be easy, empress."

"I don't care."

Pressing his lips to hers, he sealed their fate with a poignant, solemn kiss.

"I'm going to do my best," he whispered, resting his forehead against hers. "Nothing has ever meant more to me than you. I promise to cherish you and make you happy, sweetheart. Or die trying."

"No one's dying," she said, grinning. "But we need to make it official before my father banishes me from his life forever. Once we're married, he'll have to give you a chance. I know he's going to change his mind."

Tristan's lips thinned. "I appreciate the optimism, but I doubt it."

"Well, there's only one way to find out. I think the court-house opens at nine in the morning."

He laughed at the challenge in her voice. "Don't you want to wait and get a pretty dress or whatever women want when they get married?"

"Nope. I just want to get on with our lives."

"Okay. I'll call out of work tomorrow so we can seal the deal." He pecked her lips. "This is crazy. You know that, right?"

"Honestly? It feels like the smartest thing I've ever done," she said, shrugging. "And now, your future wife would like a towel please. I'm freezing."

Tristan took her hand, threading their fingers as he led her to his apartment. Once she was dry, he drew her into his arms, thankful she had the courage to seize their future when he'd seen no viable path to forge ahead.

And as he held her on the last night before they promised to love and cherish each other for eternity, he acknowledged it would be the easiest vow he ever made.

The next morning, Grace stood before Tristan, full of hope as they repeated their vows in front of a judge. She knew their future was uncertain and they had nearly insurmountable obstacles ahead, especially with her father's insistence they weren't meant to be.

But she'd never felt anything more in her soul than the knowledge she was meant to be with Tristan. He'd unlocked something inside her—something bold and fierce—and she'd come to crave it in the short months they'd been together.

She was certainly no expert on love, but in her mind, a connection like hers and Tristan's was extremely rare and almost impossible to find.

There, in one of the most important moments of her life, she gripped his hands and spoke her truth: Tristan was the only man who would ever inhabit her heart.

The young woman she was at that moment could never have foreseen the disastrous future ahead. Could never have imagined so much heartache and pain could follow such a happy, auspicious day.

In many ways, the last rays of innocence that had been shattered the night her father first discovered her with Tristan would soon begin to erode until only heartache and grief remained. The coming weeks and years would teach her harsh lessons about loss and disaster, and humankind's penchant for grave evil.

Eventually, she would exact retribution against those who hurt her and craft careful, meticulous plans to dismantle a malevolence that rendered the world broken and bereft.

But in that moment, as she held Tristan's hands and stared into his gorgeous hazel eyes, she was still just a woman vowing to love the man who owned her heart.

In the quiet courthouse under the soft glow of the fluorescent lights, she cemented her union and became Mrs. Tristan Holder...

Till death do they part.

PART II

THE PRESENT

Chapter 7

Three weeks after the events of
Scorched Redemption

"Darling, I'm the one leading the rebellion."

Tristan worked his jaw beneath Grace's warm palms as she held his face. After several attempts to speak, he finally found the words, although they were less than eloquent. "Holy fucking shit."

Her pink lips curved in that sexy way that set his body on fire, and he fought the urge to grab her shoulders and shake her. *She* was the rebellion leader? Since when? And how? And why in the hell hadn't she let him help her?

"Because you were too close," Grace said, reading his thoughts as she'd often done when they were together all those years ago. Lowering her hands, she shrugged. "You're too invested in Luthor's death, and I need things to play out a certain way."

Scratching his head, Tristan regarded her. "The night Zayne kidnapped you..." He trailed off and scowled at Zayne, who was standing beside the desk in the small cabin where Tristan found them in the Pennsylvania woods. "That was a ruse?"

Arching a silken eyebrow, Grace grinned. "Pretty stealthy, right? Maybe I should've been the one that special forces recruited."

A shocked laugh escaped his lips. "Maybe so." Glancing over her porcelain skin, the swell of her breasts beneath her brown sweater, and the flare of her hips, Tristan accepted she was unharmed. "I thought you were in danger. I wanted to save you."

"Sweet but unnecessary." She batted her eyelashes, making him feel like an absolute dolt for assuming. "But we definitely need to talk. Walk outside with me? My cabin's behind this one. We have a few in this cluster, but Zayne and the men let me have my own."

"She's the boss," Zayne said, his voice filled with respect. "We're all aligned for the cause and believe in Grace's plan."

Tristan surveyed the others in the room, noting there were six additional men besides Zayne. "This is John and Caleb," he said, pointing at the soldiers who'd accompanied him. "They helped me search for you and hate Luthor as much as I do."

"You're probably hungry," she said with a nod in their direction. "Zayne, see that they get some food while Tristan and I chat outside."

"Yes, ma'am."

Gesturing for Tristan to follow her, she headed toward the cabin door and down the wooden stairs.

Tristan followed her, the act symbolic of how easily she could command him. Of how willingly he would always follow her, even when she'd left him and shattered his heart by marrying the man he loathed more than anyone on the planet.

His eyes darted to the swell of her backside in her worn jeans, so different from the fancy clothes he was used to seeing her in. He'd memorized the curves of her body long ago, although he was man enough to admit he was more entranced by her body now than when they were young. Something about the way she carried herself, and the confidence with which she swayed as she walked...

"This should do," she said, pivoting as they approached another cabin, which he assumed were her private quarters. "There are enough trees to dampen the noise if we start yelling."

Shifting his weight, he rested a hand on his hip. "I'm not planning on yelling. I just don't understand how you became the leader of the rebellion. What the hell, Grace?"

"Pity" was her soft reply as her eyes roved over his face. "I miss you yelling at me sometimes. At least when you screamed at me, I knew you cared. When you stopped yelling, I knew I'd truly lost you."

"I've always cared, even when you married that fucking bastard." Stepping forward, he pounded his chest. "Even when you ripped my goddamned heart out, Grace—"

"Okay, I take it back," she said, showing her palm. "Don't yell. I'm not ready to fight yet. I need to explain some things to you."

"You think?"

Her gaze lowered to the ground, surveying the fallen leaves as she gathered her thoughts. "There's so much and I don't know where to begin." Her blue orbs lifted to his, swimming with deep emotion. "But I guess I should tell you that I never loved Luthor."

"Your husband?" Tristan asked sarcastically.

"*You* were my husband," she said, swallowing thickly. "Luthor was a plan. A well-executed plan that I've been slowly implementing for years."

"Well, I kind of missed that when you were divorcing me in favor of marrying him," he said, angrily rubbing the back of his neck. "I thought you couldn't forgive me because I wasn't here when our daughter..." Clearing his throat, he continued. "I thought you wanted someone rich who could replace what you'd lost when your father died—"

"I know. I counted on you believing I chose him over you. It was an integral part of my plan."

Floored, Tristan's mouth fell open. "You're saying you divorced me as part of a fucking scheme? Did you fuck him for the rebellion too?"

Wrinkling her nose, she bristled. "Don't be crass. I understand you're upset—"

"He's an old man, Grace!" Tristan yelled, stepping forward and gripping her shoulders. "How could you let him touch you?"

"Who I let touch me is no longer your concern." She swatted his arms away as anger reddened her cheeks. "And we have more important things to discuss."

He scoffed. "Who touches you will *always* be my concern."

Her nostrils flared as she pinched the bridge of her nose in frustration. "I approached Luthor with the idea of marriage shortly after my father died. I had just lost the baby and was understandably distraught. You weren't here, and I had to do the best I could with the circumstances I had."

Tristan studied her, noting the secrets that lurked in her stunning eyes. "You're not telling me the whole story. I want to know *everything*, Grace."

"I'm telling you the basics," she said, her tone firm. "You can believe me or not, but Luthor and I didn't have a passionate marriage. That's why he always had women around. I wanted him to, although I'm sorry Jessica got caught up in his sick obsession. I wish I could've prevented that."

"Me too," Tristan said, sighing. "My hope is that Danica can cure the world of this fucking drug and my sister will never have to suck that bastard off again."

Stepping forward, she placed her palms on his chest. "We want the same things, Tristan. It's time to align. We need to end this once and for all."

Cognizant of the rampant throbbing of the organ beneath her palm, Tristan covered the backs of her hands. His thumbs caressed her soft skin as he gazed into her eyes. "Why didn't you tell me? I would've helped you."

"Because you get in your own way too often," she whispered, her fingers tightening on his chest in a possessive gesture that nearly caused his knees to buckle. "I couldn't have your hatred of Luthor or your doubt in me derailing my plans."

"I've never doubted you," he rasped, leaning closer so his breath mingled with hers.

"Darling, you've always believed the worst about me." Emotion shone in her eyes as she spoke. "You could never shake the belief that I shared my father's notion that you weren't right for me. Your lack of faith in my feelings for you was the one thing I knew I could count on. After all, you told me on the day I got my dragon tattoo that I'd eventually leave and never come back." Her chin wobbled. "It broke my heart that day as much as every other day you continued to believe it."

"But you *did* leave and never come back," he said, frustrated at her insistence on blaming him.

"*You* left *me*. To prove something that never needed to be proven—to me at least."

"Your father—"

"Was an old man who wanted to protect me. His views weren't personally about you. He was just a product of his environment and the forces that eventually led to his death. It was never about you, Tristan."

Needing space from her scent and her touch, Tristan backed away and studied her. "What forces that led to his death? I thought he died of a heart attack."

Grace's lips fluttered as she released a breath. Gnawing her lip, she hesitated. Finally, she straightened her shoulders and spoke with gravity. "Luthor murdered my father. I saw it and wasn't able to stop it. Shortly thereafter, I went into early labor with our baby." She covered her abdomen, a look of sharp pain covering her features. "And after I almost bled out and lost *everything*, I declared in that moment that I would bring Luthor Cromwell down."

Closing the distance between them, she straightened her spine. "And that, my dear ex-husband, is when I began plotting my revenge...and ultimately, the rebellion."

Chapter 8

G race observed the shock that covered Tristan's face, still overcome with how gorgeous he was after all this time. Although he was almost forty, he'd somehow managed to become more attractive as he aged. The hair at his temples was a sexy shade of gray, and the wrinkles beside his eyes only highlighted the glints of green and honey that swirled in his hazel orbs.

Allowing herself a small moment of reprieve, she lost herself in those mesmerizing eyes as he gaped at her. Tilting her head, she remembered the small moments when they were happy...when she'd drowned in that heated gaze as he worked his body deeply into hers...

"Grace?" he called, causing her to flinch and clear her throat.

"Hmm?"

"Are you seriously going to stand there and not acknowledge that you just told me Luthor murdered your father? And you witnessed it? What the hell?"

Sadness swamped her as she covered her throat, a protective gesture against the terrible memories. "It was the worst day of my life, and you weren't here..." The words drifted off as she reminded herself now wasn't the time to get lost in memories. As much as she wanted a soulful reunion with her ex-husband, she had more pressing issues at hand.

"But we don't have time to discuss that now," she said, glancing back toward the cabin where the men she commanded waited. "How did you find me? If you tracked me down, Luthor's men can't be far behind."

"I'm not going to let you sideswipe this conversation. I need to know everything so I can help you—"

"And I'll tell you," she said, holding up a hand. "Once I figure out our next steps. We can't stay here now that I know it's vulnerable."

Sighing, Tristan placed his hands on his hips. "I'm an expert tracker, Grace. One of your men drove directly to the Scranton black-market compound to pick up supplies. Once I had his trail, you were easy to track down."

"Andy," she said, rolling her eyes. "I told him to park at least ten miles from the compound in a wooded area and carry the supplies back."

"It was sloppy, although it was pouring rain so he might've thought no one would be around to track him." Tristan's eyes narrowed. "Did Solomon Grange help you?" he asked, referencing the leader of the Scranton compound. "I've heard he's not friendly to outsiders."

"He's harboring George Luddington," Grace said. "George has promised him a position in the new government once we defeat Luthor, so Solomon has been...somewhat agreeable."

"Does George have the right to make that promise? If Arthur Reyes has his way, he'll be the leader of the new government after Luthor falls."

"George has been stockpiling weapons in a bunker near Scranton for years. Arthur will need them to take back the DC Sen City. Therefore, George can promise whatever he wants. Weapons are worth more than gold in this hellhole we find ourselves in."

Tristan arched a curious eyebrow, as if he was trying to juxtapose the savvy woman in front of him with the young woman he'd loved all those years ago.

"You won't find her here," Grace said, splaying her arms and allowing him to look his fill. "The girl you loved is dead. She died when her father was murdered by an evil narcissist and her child was ripped from her womb while you were halfway around the world. I'm the commander of the rebellion, Tristan, and I refuse to fail."

The corner of his mouth curved, jolting her heart in the way it always had. With a resigned nod, he asked, "What do you need from me? I have a direct line to Arthur Reyes through a shortwave radio channel. Do you want to contact him?"

Grace's lips formed a slow, satisfied smile. "Darling, *now* we're getting somewhere."

CHAPTER 9

A rianna Lawson placed two fingers in her mouth and whistled. The ninety soldiers who stood in formation before her froze, planting their feet as they awaited instruction. Pacing in front of the first line, she perused each soldier she passed.

"I'm impressed with your skills, men," she called before stopping in front of the three female soldiers on the right flank. "And women," she added with a nod.

They saluted, each showing respect before Arianna said softly, "At ease."

The female soldiers dropped their hands to their sides, and Arianna took her place in the center of the formation.

"We have ninety members in this militia. When I fought with you all the night Luthor sent his army, I was impressed with your fortitude." She lifted a finger. "But fortitude will only get you so far. Trained soldiers who fight as a team are needed to beat the Sen Force soldiers, especially if Luthor blasts them full of the super-serum."

"Yes, ma'am!" they chimed in unison.

"We've had three weeks to train, and I see improvement every day. I'm honored to serve with you all, and appreciate the time you've taken to condition your bodies and learn the skills Dominic and I have taught you."

Dominic stood behind her, feet planted far enough apart to anchor his weight as his hands crossed behind his back.

"We're working with Arthur to form a plan to take back DC once and for all. Know that your hard work will be worth it. My sister has perfected the antidote, and as soon as we wrest control of the manufacturing plants inside the DC walls, we'll begin producing and distributing the cure. This nightmare will be over, and we can go back to doing whatever the hell we did before the world fell apart."

Arching an eyebrow at one of the nearby soldiers, she grinned. "You can go back to blogging about insects on Instagram, Jones. I'm sure your fanbase misses you."

"Insects are the most interesting species on Earth, ma'am," Jones replied, deadly serious as several of the men laughed at Arianna's teasing.

"I'm sure they are, cadet. Proud of you for having the fastest ten-mile finish yesterday." Lifting her chin, she projected her voice. "Let's all aim to finish today's ten-mile run in less than seventy minutes. Our bodies won't condition themselves." She circled her finger above her head. "Get to it!"

The soldiers gave one last "Yes, ma'am!" before darting toward the far-off wall to begin the laps. Glancing to her right, Arianna leaned down and placed her hands on her knees. "You'll make sure they have water at the finish, Chris?"

The boy nodded, his face glowing with excitement at being Arianna's chosen helper for the troops.

"Good man." She patted him on the shoulder. "I'm going to have to get you something extra special for your eleventh birthday."

"Jenny and I can celebrate with our mom since Dani fixed her," he said, beaming. "We're going to have a party. Maybe you can come?"

"Tell me the time and place. And I'll bring this one too, although he's not as much fun as I am." She pointed at Dominic.

"I'm fun," Dominic said, crossing his arms as he scowled.

"Okay," Chris said before turning to jog toward the grassy knoll where the soldiers would finish their run. "Gotta make sure the water's ready. Bye, Arianna!"

Arianna watched him scamper off as Dominic sidled up beside her.

"He's obsessed with you. It's cute."

"He's got good taste," she said, grinning.

Facing her, Dominic slid his hands over her hips. "But he's not *nearly* as obsessed with you as I am." Leaning forward, he stole a kiss. "You gonna marry me today or not, Lawson?"

Squinting one eye, Arianna studied him. "Are you seriously going to ask me that every day? It's annoying. I told you, we'll get married once we defeat Luthor."

His pout was adorable, causing Arianna's heartbeat to pulse in her ears as he leaned closer. "Why wait? I want you to be my wife when we beat that bastard."

"I never knew you were so traditional," she said, unable to control her smile at his insistence on tying the knot. "Isn't it enough that you were literally inside every part of my body last night?"

Growling, he snaked his arm around her waist and pulled her against him. "I love claiming your body, but I want to claim your soul, sweetheart."

Taken by his sweet words, she tenderly cupped his cheek. "You have it." Allowing one more poignant moment before returning to reality, she brushed her lips against his and whispered, "I love you."

His resulting shiver was the perfect response to her endearment.

"Okay, enough PDA." Playfully pushing him away, she placed her palm over her forehead to shield the sun and looked off into the distance. "The troops look good. I think we have enough of a foundation to plan an attack."

"Thanks to you," Dominic said, admiration crossing his features beneath the jagged scar that ran from the corner of his eye, over his nose and to the opposite corner of his lips. Arianna found it incredibly sexy, and combined with his pride in her, it damn near made her year.

"I miss running my own squadron, so returning to the role is second nature. You're a good second-in-command. I wondered if you'd be able to let me lead, but you step up in the moments I need you, and defer during the others I don't. It's seamless."

"Because I get you, Ari, and I'm man enough to know when to follow a powerful woman into battle. With you leading us, we're poised to succeed."

Embarrassed at the tears that stung her eyes, she sighed. "Stop saying nice shit. I'm supposed to appear tough."

Chuckling, he ran his fingers over her arm. "I don't think you'll have any trouble there."

"Screw you."

"My point exactly."

She swatted his arm away before pointing toward the high steel wall that surrounded the compound. "I'm going to go help Chris prepare the water rations. You coming?"

"I told Mav I'd look over the old architectural archives of DC with him again. He's determined to find ways to infiltrate the city that aren't on modern maps. He thinks we can find several old tunnels and underground highways to gain access during the offensive. Once he memorizes them all, we'll strategize the attack with Arthur."

"Good plan. Whenever you all are ready to bring me in, I'm here. In the meantime, I'm committed to getting the soldiers ready. See you at dinner?"

"See you then."

She turned to walk away and Dominic gripped her wrist. Tugging her back, he planted a firm kiss on her lips. "Bye."

Clutching his chin, she reveled in the desire that flared in his eyes. "Don't manhandle me, Cavalleri." Drawing him toward her, she swiped her tongue over his lips. "Bye."

Groaning, he wiped his mouth as she slowly backed away, a wide grin spread across her face.

"You're going to pay for that tonight, Ari."

Lifting her hands in invitation, a challenge laced her expression. "Promise?"

Dominic just stood firm, slowly rubbing his lips as she retreated.

Flicking a dismissive wave, she turned and strode toward the wall. "God, he's so fucking sexy. Down girl. Training *then* sex. Get a grip."

Breaking into a joyful whistle, she headed to join her soldiers.

Dr. Danica Lawson-Ward stood beside the bed in the infirmary, nodding as she scribbled notes on her clipboard.

"And you're not experiencing any lingering pain at the injection site, Mr. Clarke?" she asked.

"No, ma'am," the man with kind brown eyes said, rubbing the russet skin of his arm where she'd given the injection over two weeks ago. "Everything feels fine. I believe you've cured me, Dr. Lawson-Ward. I haven't had a craving in days and I'm steady. No shaking or tremors either."

Breathing a sigh of relief, Dani smiled. "Excellent. You're our last patient, Sam, on this compound at least. Can I call you Sam? You can call me Dani."

He smiled and nodded.

"Well, Sam, I'm thrilled to say that you conclude my real-life clinical trial on this compound. Everyone is cured of EverLife addiction, and I feel comfortable producing the serum I've tested here for the masses."

"You've done a wonderful thing here, Dani," Sam said, his eyes clouding with tears. "I feel something I haven't in so long..." His voice drifted off as he cleared his throat. "Hope," he rasped. "I feel hope, ma'am."

Dani allowed the conflicting emotions to war within. Anger and doubt collided with the small sparks of longing in her gut as well. "I'm glad to hear it, Sam." She softly squeezed his arm. "I did a lot of damage, and I won't be able to live with myself until I fix what I can. Even if it will never be enough."

"It's enough," he said firmly. "You didn't have to help anyone, but you did. It's admirable. All we can hope for when we make terrible mistakes is the chance to make it right."

"From your lips to God's ears," she said, flashing a cheeky grin. "And I'm an atheist, but I still like that saying."

"Well, I'll believe for both of us." He patted her hand. "Thank you, Dani. I wish you luck on your endeavor to cure the world. I'm too old to fight in the rebellion, but I'll offer my services where I can. I want to help defeat Luthor and live in peace again."

"I'll let Arthur know of your willingness to help. There are always positions that need to be filled. Rikina will continue to monitor you during your follow-ups, but otherwise, you're free to resume a normal life. Whatever that looks like nowadays."

Sam rose and gave her one last nod, affection in his gaze, before he strode out of the room. Taking a moment to appreciate the gravity of the achievement, Dani rested her palms on the bed and closed her eyes.

"One compound down, countless more to go," she whispered. "You can do this, Dani. You *have* to do this."

Inhaling a fortified breath, she straightened her spine and trailed from the room to find her husband.

She found Maverick and Dominic in the old home economics room, studying various maps of DC. Dani approached them and cupped her husband's shoulder as she placed a kiss on his head.

"Have you identified some tunnels that will allow us entry?" she asked.

"We've found a few," Maverick said, leaning back and tapping his cheek. "But I need another kiss first, please."

Laughing, she leaned down and nipped his lips before kissing him. "How's that?"

"It'll do...for now." He winked before turning back to the maps and tracing the outline of the city in one of them. "Washington, DC, has several underground catacombs, train tunnels and old prohibition tunnels. Many of them are sealed, but we can blast through them during an attack if we need to."

Arthur Reyes walked into the room, the air of confidence and purpose surrounding his broad shoulders. Dani found him an extremely capable leader, and felt he was the perfect person to take over the new government if they defeated Luthor Cromwell.

Scratch that. *When* they defeated Luthor Cromwell.

"What have you got for me, Maverick?"

"Dom and I think these two dormant tunnels will work the best," Maverick said as Arthur sat beside him. "There's one on the northwest side and one on the southwest side. Both will probably need to be blown open at certain spots, but Dom and Arianna are excellent at creating improvised explosive devices."

Leaning back, Arthur crossed his arms over his chest. "That's good to know, but what if we didn't need to create IEDs? What if someone could supply them to us, along with all of the ammunition we need to attack Luthor?"

Maverick's eyebrows lifted. "Well...that would be great. How do you propose we accomplish that?"

"I've just been contacted by Tristan Holder," Arthur said, making eye contact with everyone as he spoke to indicate the seriousness of the moment. "He's found the rebellion leader, and we're going to chat over shortwave radio in thirty minutes. I'd like you all to join, as well as Arianna."

"Tristan found Zayne Danvers?" Dominic asked.

"He found Zayne, but he's not the leader of the rebellion," Arthur said, excitement lacing his features. "In a rather shocking twist, it turns out that Grace Cromwell is the leader."

"What?" Dani asked, lowering her stunned gaze to Maverick's.

"I'll know more when we discuss further. But it seems she has stockpiles of weapons, and she's ready to align with us."

"Wow," Dominic said, rising and rubbing the back of his neck as he digested the information. "Tristan was under the impression she was quite helpless the night she was abducted."

"Which must've been part of her plan," Dani said, eyes widening as she realized the woman's brilliance. "Good for her and very impressive."

"I'm not sure we can trust her yet," Arthur said, "but it's certainly an interesting development. We're at the point where we're going to have to take some risks, and if Grace comes through, we could be very close to ending Luthor's reign."

"I'll go find Arianna and make sure she's in the meeting with us," Dominic said. "If the rebellion truly has a stockpile of weapons they're ready to share, we should plan an attack soon. Luthor is close to perfecting his super-soldier drug, and Anthony and his men are vulnerable inside the walls."

"Agreed," Arthur said, standing and tapping the map. "Can you have a preliminary multipoint attack plan prepared by this afternoon?"

"You bet your ass I can," Maverick responded confidently.

"Excellent. And the cure is ready, Dani?"

"Everyone on the compound is cured, and the serum is also preventative from my observations. As a scientist, I'd love several more rounds of trials, but as a realist, I've seen the results and they're better than I could've hoped for. I'm prepared to distribute the cure to the masses."

"The first thing we'll do once we defeat Luthor is revamp the pharma production plants so we can produce the cure in mass quantities. Then we'll need to safely distribute it across the country and the world."

"Society will take some time to recover, but I'll walk from compound to compound if I have to," Dani said, lifting her chin. "I won't rest until everyone is free from the ravages of EverLife."

"As discussed, I'll still have to put you on trial, Dani. You'll plead your case in front of a jury of your peers, but I can't guarantee the outcome." Sympathy clouded his expression.

"I'll accept whatever outcome a jury decides. If they want to execute me, it's certainly justified—"

"Like hell it is," Maverick muttered.

Dani held up a hand. "It is, Mav. I hurt so many..." Shaking her head so she wouldn't dwell on the destruction, she continued. "But I would be honored to live out my days working for the new government to help eradicate EverLife and create more cures for deadly diseases like cancer. I hope the people will allow me the chance."

"As do I," Arthur said. "I'm proud of your efforts and honored to align with you."

Sentiment clogged her throat at the genuineness in his gaze. "Thank you, Arthur. Let's take back the world. I'm ready."

Arthur's chest rose with pride as he smiled. "See you all in an hour," he said before marching from the room.

"No way in hell are you getting executed," Maverick said, snaking an arm around her waist and resting his forehead against hers. "I won't let that happen."

"Let's hope it doesn't come to that," she said, palming his cheek. "I was really getting used to the idea of having a baby or two with you. But we're not naming them Goose."

Maverick playfully nipped her finger. "We can name them anything you want, babe. My grandma's name was Gertrude. Little Gertie would be cute, right?"

Dani grimaced. "I'm definitely going to have to let that one grow on me."

Dominic chuckled behind them. "While you all ponder baby names, I'm going to go find Arianna. I'll see you in a bit."

When they were alone, Maverick pulled her closer and pressed his lips to her ear. "My grandpa's name was Lester."

Tossing back her head, Dani laughed. "We are *not* naming our child Lester. I do want them to have *some* friends."

"They'll have my good looks, so they'll be fine," Maverick said, drawing back to point at his face. "You can't argue with genetics, babe."

Overcome with love for her gorgeous husband, she bit her lip. "I think I'll continue to be the genetics expert in this conversation, thank you very much. But you are cute."

"Oh, I'll show you cute later tonight," he said, his voice sultry. "Now that your body remembers me each morning without watching the videos, you've become very randy, my little geneticist."

"I'm remembering so much more every day, and I do recognize you when I wake up. I write about it in my journal a lot. It's this warm, musky scent that surrounds me and makes me feel safe, even when I'm scrambling to remember where the hell I am."

Empathy clouded his gunmetal-gray eyes. "One day, you'll remember everything, sweetheart. I know it." He ran a soothing hand over her chestnut locks.

Lacing her fingers through his, she tugged him toward the door. "Want to say hi to Sam Clarke before your meeting? He's my last patient on the compound, thank goodness, and he's so sweet, Mav."

"Sure, I can always squeeze in time to see my wife's brilliant work. Lead the way."

Clutching her husband's hand, Dani clung to the hope their fortune would soon change for the better.

Chapter 10

Zayne offered to accompany Grace to the clearing where Tristan's truck was parked, but she declined.

"I need you to stay here and make sure everything is packed and loaded. Then ensure the vehicles are functional and the tires are full of air. I don't feel comfortable staying here now that we've been located." She shot a pointed glare at Tristan.

"Hey, my intentions were good, and it's better I found you before Luthor."

"You've already communicated the basics to Arthur through Morse code, correct?" she asked, pointing at the telegraph machine atop the desk.

"Yes," Tristan said. "My radio and the microphone are in a backpack under the passenger seat of the truck I drove here."

"We'll be back within the hour. Make sure we're ready to move quickly," Grace said to Zayne before beckoning Tristan outside.

"Zayne is protective of you," Tristan said, slight annoyance in his voice as he led her through the woods to the faded red truck in the distance.

"It took me a while to confirm I could trust him, but he's been invaluable to my plan." She patted the frame of the truck bed as she approached. "This reminds me of the one you had when we got married."

"Shitty vehicles were all I could afford when we were married."

"We had some good times in your shitty truck," she said, running her hand over the smooth metal. "Especially in the woods where we used to hike near your apartment."

"We never had trouble making good use of a flat surface," he droned. "Until everything fell apart."

Sadness crept into the dark corners of her heart that remembered times when they were young and believed it was them against the world.

"And Zayne?" Tristan continued. "Are you and he..."

Laughing, Grace shook her head. "Not that it's any of your business, but no. I don't have time for romance, Tristan. In case you've forgotten, I'm trying to bring down my evil husband. Let me defeat him first, and then I can focus on trivial things like sex and love."

Closing the distance between them, he covered her hand atop the truck. "I still can't believe you're the rebellion leader." He slowly traced a finger down her arm, causing her to shiver in the shadows of the trees.

"Then I did a good job," she said, slowly recoiling. His proximity conjured too many memories, making her yearn for the times he'd pressed those firm lips to her ear and whispered her name... "Where's the radio?"

Tristan's eyes narrowed as he contemplated her, and Grace had a nagging suspicion he was mired in memories too. He eventually tore his gaze from hers and opened the door of the truck. Reaching beneath the seat, he drew out a backpack.

Walking toward the back of the truck, he pulled down the bed door and opened the pack. After pulling out a short-wave radio, he located the small microphone and inserted it into the transmission port. He lifted the antenna, extending it the full length, before turning the knob. A green light glowed on the radio as Tristan adjusted the dial to 4930 kHz.

Lifting the microphone, he spoke into the receiver. "This is Dragon Rider to Bird Catcher. Do you copy?"

"Interesting names," Grace said, grinning.

"It's what we came up with in a pinch," he said, with a shrug. After a few moments, he repeated the call.

"Bird Catcher here. Are you with Olympia Marble?"

Olympia Marble? Grace mouthed, pointing to her chest.

"I'm with her. Is your team there?"

"Yes, everyone is assembled and listening."

Grace took the mic from him. "Bird Catcher, this is Olympia Marble. Do you think this channel is secure enough to use our real names?"

"I believe it is," Arthur confirmed.

"Excellent. As Tristan told you, I have a supporter who has stockpiled weapons in a bunker outside the Scranton black-market compound."

"Are you willing to allow us to use them and to transport them to us?"

"Yes. My team is capable, and I assume Tristan and his men will help me."

Tristan nodded.

"How many days do you need?" Arthur asked.

Squinting, she pondered. "We have a sedan, two SUVs, and Tristan's truck now. We should be able to gather the weapons in a few days and convene with you at your compound. Once we're there and we've evaluated our stockpile, we can plan the attack."

"And we're supposed to trust this isn't a Trojan Horse plan?" a gruff woman's voice called over the radio. "That Luthor Cromwell's wife just wants to help us out of the goodness of her heart?"

"Hello, Arianna," Grace said, unable to control her smile. "It's a pleasure to finally speak to you. I don't blame you for being wary, but I assure you, my goal is the ultimate destruction of Luthor Cromwell."

"Not to be a dick, but that's exactly what a double agent would say."

Grace couldn't argue with her there. "I know trust isn't easily given in our world. All I can say is that Luthor took everything from me, and I won't rest until he's paid for every ounce of pain he caused me and everyone else. If you can't trust me, I'll forge ahead on my own, but we'll be stronger united."

Grace listened to the muffled voices on the other end as they discussed. Finally, Arthur said, "We're ready to align. We'll await you and your men. We'll need to search every vehicle, team member and weapon before you're allowed entry to our compound."

"I accept your terms. We should all arrive within the week. We'll do our best to stay off of Luthor's radar. If we're caught, I urge you to contact George Luddington at Scranton and ask for his help. He has powerful connections even though he's in exile."

"I will, although I have faith in you, Grace. I look forward to getting to know you and your team. Do you think Luthor knows you're leading the rebellion?"

"He might not know yet, but it's only a matter of time. Once he figures it out, he'll publicly execute me if we fail, so I'm counting on you, Arthur. I'm not ready to be tortured for public entertainment."

"The only person who's going to be tortured is Luthor," Tristan interjected. "I'm going to kill that fucking bastard, and he's going to choke on his own blood."

"We wish you well on your mission," Arthur said. "Tristan, please contact me with updates."

"Will do."

The static settled and Grace realized Arthur had turned off his radio. Tristan packed up the supplies before stuffing the bag inside the truck. "Should I drive the truck closer to the cabins?"

"Yes," Grace said, trailing around to the passenger side and hopping in. "We'll stuff every inch of every vehicle with as many weapons as we can before heading to Arthur's compound in Maryland."

Tristan slid behind the wheel and hot-wired the truck before putting it into gear. He drove over the high grass until they reached the cabins. Putting the truck in park, he turned to face her.

"What do you mean when you say Luthor cost you every-thing? Are you talking about Raquel?"

Grace's nostrils flared at the question. She could've pretended he was referring to Danica's sister, who had recently died at the hands of Luthor. But they both knew he was referring to their daughter, who'd they'd also planned to name Raquel before Grace went into premature labor at five months and lost the baby.

"Yes," she said, holding up a hand when he opened his mouth to question her further. "Not now. Let's make it to Scranton and our quarters there. They'll allow us privacy to have this conversation."

"I want some fucking answers, Grace—"

"Don't curse at me," she said, grabbing the handle and swinging open the truck door. "I'm not the same little rich girl who looked at you with stars in her eyes and hung on your every word. I was forced to become something much stronger—and much colder—when you left me behind with a baby on the way and zero support system."

"Grace—"

"Not now," she gritted, exiting the truck and slamming the door. Striding around, she waited until he got out. "When we get to Scranton, we'll have a safehouse where we'll have privacy. I want you to drop it until then."

Tristan scowled. "I will, but once we're alone, you're going to tell me everything. I won't operate in the dark."

"Fine," she said before turning to stalk to the cabin. "And don't speak to me that way in front of my men," she called over her shoulder. "I'm the commander here, and you'd damn well better remember that."

Cognizant of the emotion swirling through her body, she reminded herself to remain calm. Tristan had always stirred up more emotion in her than anyone on the planet. He'd always been the one person able to infiltrate her ice queen façade.

But she owed it to her men to show strength, and had learned long ago that emotion only led to heartache. Leaving her ex-husband behind, she marched up the stairs, ready to prepare her team for the next phase of their plan.

Chapter 11

Luthor Cromwell paced in front of the expansive conference room table in his penthouse office in downtown Washington, DC. His side ached from where that little bitch Raquel Lawson had stabbed him the night everything went to shit. At least her death brought him a small sense of satisfaction. No *one* stabbed Luthor Cromwell and got away with it.

"Are you all right, sir?" Dr. Ziegler asked from his seat at the table. "If your side is hurting, I can give you a painkiller."

"I'm fine," Luthor said with an absent flick of his hand. The constant stream of EverLife in his system should've led to faster healing, but Dr. Ziegler had informed him that Raquel had nicked a major vessel near his kidney. Although he'd eventually heal, the incapacitation was frustrating—especially for someone who needed to exhibit strength and confidence.

Striding to the long windows, Luthor glanced across the city. The buildings no longer seemed to sparkle in the midday sun. Instead, there was a gloomy pallor over his once-promising metropolis. Smoke rose in the distance, causing him to scowl.

"I thought I told you to arrest anyone who started a bonfire," Luthor snapped. "They're signs of the rebellion that need to be eradicated."

"My men have been advised to arrest anyone who makes sympathetic gestures toward the rebellion," Colonel Mc-

Grath said, rising and walking to stand beside Luthor. His eyes narrowed as he observed the smoke, and he lifted the walkie talkie from his belt. "Major Martinez, please send some soldiers to address the bonfire near Pennsylvania Avenue and E Street."

"Yes, sir," a voice crackled over the radio.

"Major Martinez failed in the attack on Arthur's compound, and yet, he's still in a leadership position." Luthor rubbed his chin. "How odd. Do we accept failure in our ranks, Colonel McGrath?"

"We lost Lieutenant Colonel Jackson in that battle, sir," McGrath said, a slight twinge of anger and regret in his tone. "Tony has earned the respect of his battalion, and removing him would cause strife amongst the soldiers."

"What's the point in having the strongest army in the world if we lose?" Luthor shot him a glare before heading back to the table. "Sit down, Colonel McGrath. We have lots to discuss."

Once McGrath was seated, Luthor rubbed his forehead and sighed. "I'm not sure how I've lost my grip on peace. All I've ever wanted was for humanity to live together in harmony. Long, unanimous harmony where everyone benefits from the spoils of my labor—and where I don't get arrested for the crime of being rich."

Gripping the high-backed leather chair, he slid onto the seat and rested his forearms on the table. "We must make everyone remember that I am a generous, peaceful ruler. But I am also practical, and I realize the only way we can maintain peace is to destroy the rebellion."

"Our spies have been reporting back to me consistently," Colonel McGrath said. "There's been some movement near the Scranton compound, and we'll continue to monitor that, as well as Arthur's compound in Maryland."

"I would be worried that shady bastard Solomon Grange is harboring George Luddington since he disappeared after Grace was kidnapped, but George is too much of a pretentious snob to hide on such a disparate compound. My guess is that he's hiding somewhere in the Philly Sen City. The mayor I've installed there complies with my wishes, and I've let them continue to use power and some basic technology for now."

"We haven't located your wife, sir, but it is our highest priority."

"Yes, she must be found. I can't be the most powerful leader in the world if I can't rescue my own wife."

Colonel McGrath cleared his throat. "Plus, I'm sure you want to make sure she's unharmed."

"Yes, yes," Luthor said dismissively, waving his hand. "Of course, I hope she's okay."

Luthor observed the uncomfortable looks his men gave each other and pounded his fist on the table. "Three weeks is too long! I want Zayne and Grace located immediately. Am I understood?"

"Yes, sir."

"Dr. Ziegler, are we ready to inject the first two hundred soldiers with the enhancement serum?"

"I completed the two-week observation of the first ten men I injected, sir," Dr. Ziegler said, his voice racked with nerves. "As we discussed, two are incapacitated. Their bodies went into shock and they are now in stroke-induced comas. The other eight soldiers are tolerating the drug well enough. They've all shown bouts of increased anger and irritability, but each man can now lift twice what they were able to before."

"And their healing properties?" Luthor asked.

"The strength enhancement serum combined with the EverLife in their system seems to have a positive healing effect. I cut a small gash on each of the eight men's forearms, and they all healed without a scar within seconds. A cut like that would normally take a week to heal."

"So, they could effectively sustain injuries during a battle and be able to bounce back quickly."

"In theory, yes," Dr. Ziegler said with a nod.

"We'll inject the two hundred soldiers we discussed, Colonel McGrath. They were all recruited from poor families, most of whom were ravaged when they decided to succumb to addiction rather than take the watered-down antidote I generously provided."

"Yes, sir," Colonel McGrath said. "They have all consented to receiving the super-soldier drug and have been advised of the possible side effects."

"I want to be there as they're injected. Let's plan on two o'clock today in the barracks building on Eighth Street."

"Sir, some might go into cardiac arrest or experience a stroke when injected," Dr. Ziegler said. "I'll need a full medical triage station set up in the barracks."

"Fine. Get him whatever he needs," Luthor said to Dr. Johnson, a white-haired man who he'd nominated as head of what remained of the hospital system in the city.

As Dr. Johnson nodded, Luthor addressed Colonel Mc-Grath. "And I want the exact locations of Zayne Danvers, Grace and George Luddington ASAP. Don't make me ask again, Colonel."

"I'll have a report when we meet at fourteen hundred hours to inject the soldiers, sir."

Rising, Luthor placed his palms on the cool wood, leaning forward to emphasize his words. "I haven't done a public execution yet, but controlling the entire power structure and television streaming channels allows me to communicate directly with my constituents. I believe Zayne Danvers is an excellent choice for the first public execution. Find him so I can remind the good people of our city what happens to dissenters."

The men rose and filtered out of the room, many of them appearing slightly dejected as their shoulders hunched.

Squeezing his hand into a fist, Luthor clutched so tightly his knuckles turned white. If only power was as easy to grasp...

"You'll win them back," he murmured to himself, slowly approaching the window again. "They just need to be shown the consequences of dissension."

Placing his palm on the glass, he pressed his nose to the cool surface. "I'll remind you *all* who gave you renewed life. And once you remember, we'll all prosper together."

Silence surrounded him as he clung to the pristine glass, his loose grasp a metaphor for how quickly things could slip away if he didn't retain control.

Luthor refused to return to a world that saw him as a criminal monster. He was meant to be a leader, and the people just needed to remember his benevolence.

Failure was not an option.

Pushing away from the window, he walked to the adjoining bathroom to check his wound. Small sparks of doubt flared that Grace could somehow be involved in the rebellion, but he quickly dismissed the thoughts.

His wife was a gorgeous trophy. Someone whom he'd allowed to live because of the very lucrative business deal she'd proposed when she suggested they marry. And since her heir had died, she was the last of the Albrights, allowing Luthor to assume Robert's wealth and company.

Yes, in a cruel twist of fate, the death of Grace's daughter had secured Grace's life.

Another advantage to his marriage with Grace had been George Luddington's support. Luthor hated the fat bastard, but he'd been powerful before the world fell and had many connections. The fact that George and Grace had disappeared was certainly suspect.

"For god's sake, Luthor," he said to his reflection in the mirror as he examined the injury to his side. "What could Grace possibly gain from helping the rebellion? And even if it benefited her, she's a doormat who would never abandon her wealthy life."

Lowering his shirt over the bandage, he shook his head. "She's being held by Zayne for leverage. That's all."

Confident he understood the situation fully, he headed to inject a round of EverLife before continuing his day.

Chapter 12

The cars were ready by three o'clock, and as clouds darkened the sky, Grace realized a storm was about to roll in.

"It seems luck is on our side," she said to her team as they stood outside the main cabin. "The rain will make us much harder to track. As discussed, we'll all follow separate paths. Zayne, you and I will take the direct route, following old Highway 81. Tristan, you and your men will take the old Route 11."

Tristan nodded, his face impassive.

"Charles and Kent will drive the SUVs, taking the long northern routes so we don't draw attention. If you pass Ardor Creek, you've gone too far north. I think we all should arrive by dusk."

Grace splayed her hands to emphasize her next words. "Solomon Grange is skeptical of visitors, even though he knows we're friendly. He'll have his men search us, and we need to remember not to be antagonistic."

Tristan shot her a glare, as if he knew she was talking to him.

Flattening her lips at his angry look, she continued. "If you notice someone following you, make sure you lose the tail before you approach Scranton. Are there any questions?"

Silence followed as they shook their heads.

Steeling herself for the fact that all her planning was finally coming to fruition, Grace lowered into the vehicle beside Zayne and set off for Scranton.

Tristan approached the imposing steel walls of the Scranton black-market compound as thick clouds loomed above. The rain had let up slightly, but the ominous clouds in the distance warned more was on the way.

The perimeter compound wall was caked with mud in several places, and Tristan wondered how often it was cleaned, if ever. Narrowing his eyes, he noticed several spray-painted warnings, including *Stay Out* and *Do Not Enter.*

"It's possible we'll be separated inside, so make sure you stay alert. Keep a mental log of everything and let's make sure we compare notes. Something innocuous could end up being important."

"You got it, boss," Caleb said.

When they reached the front gates, they were met by two armed guards, rifles in hand. Stepping out of the truck, Tristan showed his palms.

"I have a gun holstered on my belt and a knife in my boot," he said. "I'm assuming you're going to frisk us. Caleb is in the passenger seat, and John is in the truck bed. They also have handguns and knives."

"Stand here," one of the guards said, pointing to an open area beside the truck. The three men complied and were frisked.

Annoyed at the loss of his armaments, Tristan reminded himself to be cordial. "When will we get our weapons back?"

"When you leave the compound," the guard said. "Grace has already arrived. She's waiting for you inside. We'll confiscate the truck and park it inside the walls until we're ready to load it with weapons."

Tristan nodded before the guards pulled open the thick steel front doors. "Walk three hundred yards down the road and you'll arrive at the old Scranton post office. It's Solomon's home base now, and they're waiting for you."

Tristan started down the damp dirt road, John and Caleb walking silently beside him as they took in the surroundings. What used to be minor Scranton roads and buildings were mostly burned out, melted to crisps and meager frames. Discarded vials and needles lined the ditches on either side of the road, and Tristan noted it had once been paved. Cracked asphalt still lined small patches along the edges, but otherwise, the road had returned to dust.

As he walked, Tristan searched for signs of life. One glaring difference between the DC Sen City and the Scranton compound was the lack of homeless people.

"I thought we'd see more people living in tents like in DC," John said.

"I heard Solomon allowed shitty, contaminated EverLife on his compound and all the addicts died," Caleb said. "He's not as altruistic as Arthur Reyes, who has a reputation for at least *trying* to only allow clean EverLife and antidote on his compound."

"And allowing shitty EverLife leads to big payoffs from dealers," John said. "Killing people has probably made Solomon rich."

"Which means he's not much higher on the sliding scale of asshole than Luthor," Tristan warned. "Stay sharp and don't trust anyone you meet here. Blind trust will get you killed."

"You trusted Grace pretty fast even though she's Luthor's wife," Caleb said. "It all seems a bit strange to me. She'd be a perfect double agent."

"She's not a double agent," Tristan said as they neared the former post office. The lettering at the top of the building had been torn away and replaced with black spray paint that read *Scranton Compound Headquarters*.

"How do you know?"

Halting, he turned to face them. "Because before she was his wife, she was mine. And I trust her implicitly, which means you both do too. Are we clear?"

They glanced at each other, each urging the other to ask the question both wanted answered.

"How in the hell did your wife end up married to Luthor Cromwell?" Caleb asked.

"Because I made a lot of mistakes I'll pay for forever." Tristan harshly rubbed his forehead. "Any other questions? Or can we get on with our fucking mission?"

They both shook their heads as Tristan struggled to contain his annoyance. Facing the headquarters, he climbed up the stairs, ready to meet the infamous Solomon Grange.

Grace observed Tristan enter the building, his two counterparts close on his heels. Solomon sat in a makeshift throne of sorts at the top of the marble stairs, and he hooked his fingers, beckoning them forward as the large doors closed behind them.

"Ah, the infamous Tristan Holder," Solomon said, gaps in his smile where several teeth had eroded. "The man who has his hands in everything, but still knows nothing."

Tristan halted at the bottom of the stairs and planted his hands on his hips. "I'm just trying my best to survive in this shithole world and take care of those I love." His eyes darted to Grace, and her heart skipped a beat at his intonation. Although he was referring to Jessica, his searing gaze left no doubt he was also referring to *her*.

Grace remained impassive, refusing to allow emotion into her expression. Love had never been the problem between her and her enigmatic ex-husband. *Believing* in their love for each other had always been the issue. Somewhere along the way, she'd lost faith in his feelings for her. Although she knew a part of him still loved the girl she'd been, he didn't know the woman behind her cultivated shell.

Tristan loved someone she would never be again. A part of her mourned that idealistic version of herself, but she'd become the person she needed to be to protect those she hadn't yet lost.

"We're all doing our part," Solomon said, gesturing toward Grace. "And your ex-wife is doing a fine job. Thanks to her efforts, our compound has remained off the radar, but I fear that luxury is now over."

"We knew this day would come eventually," Grace said, refusing to allow men to speak on her behalf any longer. "We need to mount an offensive and take back DC from Luthor once and for all. Now that Arthur's compound has been attacked, there's no reason to wait."

"The weapons George has been funneling here over the past few years are all safe in the bunker by the northern stretch of the wall. I might have confiscated a few for my own use, but most are there, along with the ammunition and other supplies."

George Luddington, who'd been lurking in the shadows behind Grace, stepped forward, balancing on a cane as he advanced. "I had a feeling you'd swipe a few," he muttered, arching an eyebrow. "But I appreciate your alliance, so I won't grumble about it."

Solomon elicited a hefty chuckle. "Good. I'll allow you to remain in your luxurious suite in the old hotel by the Lackawanna River. That's how alliances work, George. You take a little, I take a little...and everyone's happy."

Grace lifted her hand to retake control of the conversation. "Now that we're all happy, let's get on with the mission. My men and I need to get a good night's sleep so we can inspect the bunker first thing in the morning and catalog the weapons. We'll load all of the vehicles by tomorrow afternoon and leave for Arthur's compound around midnight. The darkness should provide some good cover."

"My dear," Solomon said, his voice dripping with fake affection. "You can stay longer. You've only just arrived."

"We've set things in motion that can't be undone," she said firmly. "I'll return once we've defeated Luthor, and we can discuss your future."

Solomon lifted an eyebrow, a warning in his gaze. "My future is up to me, Grace. You'll do well to remember that."

"Of course." She gave an affirming nod, acknowledging now wasn't the time to anger the man sheltering her and a shitload of weapons. "I look forward to that day. Do you have a place where we can stay the night?"

"There are several vacant rooms in George's hotel, although none as nice as the one he claimed. You're welcome to stay there. It's a ten-minute walk from here, but you'll need to drive to the bunker with the weapons."

"Thank you. Our vehicles were confiscated when we arrived—"

"I needed to check them for drugs, Grace. I can't have you smuggling in the shiny new antidote I've heard about on Arthur's compound. We have trade alliances with antidote dealers, and they wouldn't be pleased if I diluted their stash with cleaner serums."

Gritting her teeth, Grace took a second to tamp down her anger. One of her goals after defeating Luthor was to eradicate *all* of the black-market drugs with nefarious components. But she had to accomplish one thing at a time, and focusing on shady drug dealers wasn't on her agenda yet.

"Well, I'm sure you found the vehicles clean, and I'd like them back so we can load the weapons."

"My men will be outside the hotel at first light ready to drive you to the bunker. Any other questions?"

"That's it for now. Will you be accompanying us to the bunker?"

Solomon wrinkled his nose. "I wish you well, but I have no desire to dirty my hands in a war. If you win, I'll be here to enjoy the spoils. If you lose, I can claim that I never truly joined the cause."

"A man with strong conviction," she muttered. "How noble."

"Just a man who's learned to survive." His eyes narrowed. "As I know you have, Grace."

Fear darted up her spine at his tone. Did he know something? She glanced at George, and he slightly shook his head, indicating Solomon was just blustering.

"We'll head out to the hotel before it starts to rain again," she said, looking toward the high windows. "I'll report back tomorrow once we've loaded the vehicles. Thank you for your help, Solomon."

Extending her hand, she waited for George to take it. "You going to walk with us?"

"I've got no choice since the golf cart I was using ran out of gas." Gripping her hand, he sighed. "I don't move as fast as I used to before I stopped taking EverLife. Thankfully, I was able to bribe Luthor's maid to steal a stash of his clean antidote before I fled the city."

"I'm glad you're free of that garbage," she said, squeezing his fingers. "And Marcia would be too," she said, referencing George's wife, who'd passed away in her sleep a few weeks before Grace's "kidnapping." "Once we defeat Luthor, I'm happy to exercise with you to rebuild those muscles. I want you with me for a long time, George. Dad would be proud of your dedication to our cause."

"I hope so, dear. Lead the way."

She slowly led him out of the post office and down the dirt road, cognizant of Tristan, Zayne and their men following close behind.

"Once you're settled in the hotel, come to my suite," George said softly so only she could hear. "I think it's best if we talk privately."

Grace jerked her head to gaze into his eyes. "Should I be worried?"

"I overheard Solomon discussing towns along the Susquehanna River, including Dundore. I found it strange. It's a small town that's been mostly deserted since the fall of society."

"That is strange," she whispered, acknowledging the nagging worry in her gut. "I'll stop by your room around seven to discuss. Thank you, George."

When they arrived at the abandoned hotel, George gave them a quick tour of the four-story building. "The second floor is mostly vacant, except for the families that stay in rooms 201 and 202. The doors are unlocked and you can have your pick."

Grace chose room 208 since it was located in the middle of the floor near the defunct elevator bank. A stairwell ran parallel to the elevators, so she had a quick escape in the event something went wrong. The rest of the men filtered into the vacant rooms, and she noticed that Tristan claimed room 210 beside hers.

"There are some jugs of bottled water in the lobby I paid some kids to bring from the well," George said as he headed toward the stairwell to climb the last fight to his third-floor suite. "There's no power, so it's barebones, but if you search the hotel, you might find a toothbrush and some other toiletries. Use the water sparingly. Good night."

Lifting his cane, he tipped it before disappearing into the stairwell. Grace entered her room, taking note of the dust that covered every surface. Scrunching her nose, she took a fleeting moment to remember times in her life where everything had been clean and pristine.

Acknowledging those days were over, she searched through the closet, hoping to find some sheets that hadn't been infested with moths or rat droppings.

Chapter 13

Tristan heard Grace's room door close, followed shortly by the stairwell door. Pulling the stethoscope from his bag, he placed the ends in his ears and stood on the bed. Pressing the receiving end to the ceiling, he waited.

He'd overheard Grace and George speaking in hushed tones and didn't like the secrecy. Were they hiding something from him? If it was detrimental to their cause, he needed to know.

He'd learned surveillance during his time in special ops and would put the skills to good use. Did he feel guilty for spying on Grace's conversation? Absolutely not. She'd kept her role in the rebellion secret, so he considered his efforts fair play.

When she finally told him everything, there would be no need to spy.

Straining, Tristan struggled to hear the muffled words through the ceiling.

"...*can't guarantee Arthur will accept the package or handle it with care...*" Grace said.

Footsteps shifted above, as if she were pacing, before George answered.

"...*safer with Arthur than Solomon...*"

Tristan's eyes narrowed as he wondered what this "package" could be. Realizing they were going to continue to speak in code, he lowered to the bed and ran his hand through his hair.

One thing he'd learned over the years was patience. Leaning back on his hands, he crossed an ankle over his knee and waited. Minutes ticked by as he absently shook his foot, waiting for Grace's return.

Eventually, the stairwell door closing echoed in the hallway, and Grace's room door creaked shut moments later. Ready for some answers, Tristan strode to her room and firmly knocked on the door.

Grace scowled at the pounding on her hotel door. She was in the middle of brushing her teeth, thanks to the toothbrush she'd stowed in her bag. As part of her preparation, she'd armed Zayne with a toiletry bag for her before he'd "kidnapped" her. Having small luxuries like a toothbrush, nail clippers, and Q-tips were more invaluable than gold.

It was amazing what you learned to appreciate when your husband destroyed the world.

Speaking of husbands, her former one was banging down the door as if the room was on fire. After rinsing, she gripped the sink with both hands and sighed.

"You did promise him answers, Grace. Just be careful."

Striding to the door, she yanked it open and frowned. "Are you trying to wake everyone up? Our men need sleep."

"And I need answers. *Now*," he said tersely.

She arched an annoyed brow. "I'm exhausted. Can we do this in the morning—?"

He splayed his palm on the door and pushed it open another inch. "What package are you and George referring to?"

Gripping his wrist, she dragged him into the room and closed the door.

"That's confidential," she gritted, aware of the muscle ticking in her jaw.

"No more secrets." Leaning forward until their noses almost grazed, his eyes burned with anger and frustration. "I mean it, Grace."

"Fine." Walking to the bed, she sat down and removed her sneakers. Her feet were killing her, so she massaged her swollen toes as she contemplated where to start.

"Feet hurting?" he asked, his expression softening.

Nodding, she continued her ministrations. "I worked out often in DC, but nothing prepares you for hiking along dirt roads on a shitty compound. To say my circumstances have changed is an understatement." She circled her hand, indicating the sparse, faded decoration.

"Slide back to the headboard," he softly commanded.

Grace's eyebrows drew together, but she complied. Perhaps due to muscle memory from all the times in the past he'd commanded her with that deep voice.

Tristan trailed over and sat on the edge of the bed. Lifting her feet onto his lap, he began to massage them.

"*Oh, god...*" she moaned, eyes closing with pleasure as she leaned her head against the headboard. "It feels *way* better when you do that."

His warm chuckle surrounded her, making her feel like the gooey center of a hot brownie. God, she'd always loved his voice...and his laugh...and those golden-flecked irises that gazed into her soul...

"I'll keep going while you talk. Hell, maybe it will soften you up."

Squinting one eye, she grinned. "Good plan."

They sat in silence for a few moments, each easing back into the comfortability they felt when they'd been the most important people to each other on the planet.

"This is nice, empress," he said, his thumb moving gently over her arch. "I missed touching you."

Sighing, she shook her head. "I missed it too."

His gaze was hooded as it bore into hers. "What did you mean when you said you and Luthor didn't have a passionate marriage?"

She played with a nonexistent thread on her pants. "It was a stipulation of my marriage proposal to him—that he never touch me sexually. And he never did."

Questions swirled in Tristan's eyes. "That seems impossible."

"It's easy to tell a man you're not interested in sex when you've just had…"

"A miscarriage?" he asked softly.

Emotion welled in her throat. "Yes," she whispered. "Among other things."

"Tell me," he said, running his thumb over the pads of her toes in a soothing gesture. "My promise not to yell still stands."

Needing space, she drew her legs from his lap and stood. "Remember that last time we really yelled at each other? Our last terrible fight before you deployed?"

Regret marred his features as he slowly ticked his head in acknowledgment. "I relived it every day for years. It was the biggest mistake of my life."

"Fighting with me or deploying when I was four months pregnant?"

"All of the above. I never should've left." Rising, he closed the distance between them and cupped her face. "I'm so sorry, Grace. I thought I was doing the best thing for us. Your father blacklisted me, and I couldn't get a security job to save my life. It was the only path I saw to supporting our family."

"I know you thought it was best," she said, overcome by the sentiment in his eyes. "But I could've supported us—"

"No. There's no honor in that. I had to earn you and support you and our daughter."

"Darling," she warbled, overwhelmed with grief as she stroked the stubble that lined his jaw, "you had me from the second you met me on that balcony. I never needed anything else."

"It didn't make sense to me then," he murmured, running his thumb in a slow, tender stroke over her chin. "That I could be enough. I was a young fool deeply in love. Age has given me more perspective. Now, I realize that only an idiot would leave his pregnant wife and ask her to stay behind in close proximity to her father who hates him until he returns from deployment." He slowly shook his head. "I just couldn't see it then."

"I know you thought you were doing the right thing, but it broke me. I chose you, Tristan, and you chose some misplaced sense of...*obligation* to prove that you deserved me. Hell, I showed up on your doorstep three months after we started dating and demanded you elope with me."

He breathed a laugh. "You were always excellent at showing up on my doorstep and bending me to your will. You're a fantastic manipulator. I should've realized it ages ago. It makes sense you've scaled up to plan an entire rebellion."

Pride swelled at the glow of admiration on his handsome face. "I'm used to people underestimating me. It's how I survived this long."

"I need you to know that our time together was the happiest of my life, Grace." He cleared his throat as emotion laced his words. "Such a short time, but it meant everything to me."

"Before it all fell apart," she said softly, encircling his wrists and drawing his hands away from her face.

"I'm sorry I wasn't there when you lost the baby." His eyes were glassy as he flexed his fingers at his side, as if he could still feel her skin upon them. "It's unforgivable. When I returned home and you asked for a divorce, I knew it was futile to fight it. I promised to be there for you and I broke my vow. You deserved more."

"Like I said, I knew I'd truly lost you when you stopped fighting with me." She tilted her head. "I'd take arguing with you over a boring conversation with anyone else any day."

"You gave up too," he said, lowering to the bed and leaning back on straight arms. "You buried our daughter without me."

"Things moved quickly after Dad died, and I had no idea when you'd return. I had to make hard choices."

"Walk me through the choices. I need to know what happened. We never had any closure, and I can't help you defeat Luthor if I don't know everything."

"Okay, but stay there while I tell you." She pointed at the bed. "I can't think straight when you touch me. It brings back too many memories."

Crossing his outstretched legs at the ankles, he nodded, his face lined with understanding and empathy. "What did you mean when you said Luthor murdered your father?"

Grace rubbed her forehead, allowing the painful memories to surface.

"I'm going to tell you how everything unfolded, but please don't interrupt me. You can ask questions when I'm finished."

"All right."

Wanting to rid her shaking frame of its nervous energy, she began to pace as she recounted the tragic events of the past...

Grace wandered aimlessly around her father's large home, restless as she stroked her slightly distended abdomen. Ever since Tristan had deployed for his special ops mission in the Middle East, she'd been despondent. She'd begged him not to leave, but her husband was stubborn and immobile.

"Your father has blacklisted me for every security job on the East Coast, Grace," Tristan said as he furiously threw clothes into his backpack. "This special ops assignment will set me up for our future. I was lucky to get a four-month deployment and will be back before you have the baby."

"You might be back," she said, dread filling her heart. "You said they could extend the operation if circumstances change on the ground."

"I'm going to fight like hell so that doesn't happen. There are certain terrorist leaders we need to take down, and I'm going to ensure they're eradicated. Once I prove myself to the special ops commanders, I can parlay that into a job at the Pentagon. Your father has a wide reach, but it doesn't extend that far. I'm determined to support our family, and I won't depend on your father's money to raise my child."

"It's my money," she said, stomping her foot. "My mother left her family's trust to me when she died. Dad has no control over that."

"He's assured me he does, and I won't raise our child with inherited money. I'm going to build my own path and show those high society assholes that I deserve you and the family we've created."

"I don't need you to prove anything," she pleaded, grabbing his arm and halting his furious movements. Placing his palm over her belly, she pressed. "We both just need you here. Please don't go."

That had been one of many moments Grace had begged him not to deploy, but it had been no use. He'd been adamant that his way was the only way he would earn her.

Ultimately, it was the reason everything fell apart.

Before Tristan deployed, he added her to his lease and set everything up so she could maintain the apartment. But Grace quickly grew lonely and missed her father, even though their relationship was strained and she sensed Robert's disapproval of the child she'd conceived with her husband. Of course, he hadn't been on board with their elopement either, so she really shouldn't have been surprised.

Hell, couldn't a girl just fall in love and live happily ever after?

She found herself returning home often—to the place that represented happier times, when her mother was still alive and she was on good terms with her father. Although she tried her best to bury the hatchet with Robert, he'd become increasingly angry and unreasonable as he entered his sixties and grew closer to retiring and leaving the company in Grace's hands. Although she would become majority owner, she had no desire to run the day-to-day business. Still, she respected her father's legacy, and would inherit her rightful place as owner and president of the board while delegating duties to those who were better suited for Corporate America. Perhaps, then, he would forgive her for the misdeed of falling in love with someone he deemed unworthy.

To make matters worse, her father's business had become inexorably tied to Luthor Cromwell's Sendaxa Corporation. The pharmaceutical company was under all sorts of investigations and violations, and the relationship between Robert and Luthor was rapidly deteriorating.

Grace didn't understand all the details, but she knew Luthor was trying to get her father to push through approvals on certain drugs whose outcomes had been falsified. Although Grace and her dad weren't on the best terms, she believed Robert was an honest businessman and would never approve commercial production of drugs he believed would harm the public.

As Grace wandered the mansion, she heard Luthor arrive. He kindly greeted the butler and was escorted to Robert's home office. Curious, Grace crept down the hallway, noting the staff had mostly gone home since it was late. Their butler, Jerry, offered the men a drink, and Robert declined.

"Luthor's only staying a moment, and we won't need anything else, Jerry," Robert said. "You can head home. See you in the morning."

"Yes, sir." With a nod, Jerry retreated down the hallway, unaware that Grace stood in the shadows a few feet away. Minutes later, he exited the house, and she was left alone with her father and Luthor.

"I told you you're not welcome in my home, Luthor," Robert said, his tone acerbic as he sat behind his desk. Grace watched them through the slit in the cracked door as Luthor sat on the edge of her father's mahogany desk. His leg kicked back and forth in a gentle rhythm, as if he were comfortable and had no reservations that he was an unwanted guest.

"Your lack of respect is becoming dangerous, Robert," Luthor said, tracing the wood as he spoke. "With the last release of the weight loss drug to market, I'm now the richest man in the world. Some would say that makes me a very undesirable enemy."

"That weight loss drug is the last drug I'll ever push to market for you, Luthor," Robert said, leaning back in his leather chair. "I'm convinced you falsified the data about the outcome to the pancreas. In ten years, if we see a wave of pancreatic cancer, I'm going to blame you."

"People want a miracle weight loss drug," Luthor said with a shrug. "They'll do anything for it. The side effects are written on the product insert."

"Which no one reads," Robert gritted. "Regardless, you need to find a new CDMO. My company won't do your dirty work anymore."

"Pity since I'm under all these pesky investigations." Rising with the elegance of a panther, Luthor slowly paced around the desk, reminding Grace of a shark circling its prey in bloody waters.

"That's your own fault," Robert muttered.

"Perhaps. It's a shame I get punished for giving the people what they want." Halting, he gazed out the nearby window. "I have plans for a new drug. One that channels the fountain of youth and doubles a person's lifespan. I want to call it EverLife." He splayed his hand in a circle as he dramatically spoke the word. "What do you think?"

"I think developing a drug like that is expensive and requires the best minds in the world. It also would require cellular reconstruction, which, in turn, would require painkillers. Sendaxa doesn't have the best track record with safe painkillers."

"What's a little addiction when you can live two centuries?" Luthor asked, his tone sinister.

"Who in the hell wants to live two centuries? I'm barely surviving in this one."

"Ah, yes. I heard Grace's pregnancy is coming along nicely even if you hate her husband. You'll have an heir soon, Robert. Congrats."

"I told Grace I'd deny her my inheritance if she married him, but I can't bring myself to do it." He scrubbed his hand over his face. "Even though she defied me, she's my daughter and my only living relative."

"And if she were gone before she has the baby, that would leave you without an heir. In that instance, your company would automatically be absorbed by Sendaxa."

"What?" Robert asked, straightening in his chair. "No, the board would vote on what to do with Albright Industries—"

"Yes, and I, as CEO of Albright's largest pharmaceutical partner, would make a compelling case to fold your company under my wing. Don't worry, Robert. I assure you, I would take good care of it."

Something sinister trickled up Grace's spine as she listened, and she realized it was the cold rush of fear. Leaning closer, she watched through the crack as the next events unfolded.

"Well, Grace is young and has a child on the way, so I think Albright Industries is in good hands. She knows that I want George Luddington to take over as CEO if something happens to me. He's head of the board and will guide the company into the future."

"That fat bastard," Luthor said with a pfft. "He can't even guide himself away from a cheeseburger."

"We all have our vices," Robert said, glancing at his watch. "Regardless, it's time for you to go, Luthor. I don't begrudge you finding another CDMO. But our time as partners has come to an end, and my business goals don't align with yours. We've had a profitable arrangement for years, and although I no longer consider us friends, I wish you the best." Rising, he extended his hand. "I'll be polite to you in our social circles, but I think it's best for us to part ways."

Luthor slid his hands into his pockets, his lips curling into a malevolent grin. "You think you can dismiss me so easily? I'm the most powerful man in Corporate America, Robert. In time, I'll most likely become president. And you think you can just shoo me away?" He made a flicking motion with his hand. "I don't think so."

Drawing his other hand from his pocket, he appeared to clutch something in his fist. Slowly rounding the desk, he pressed his hand to Robert's shoulder and pushed him back into the chair.

"What the hell, Luthor—"

Luthor jabbed a needle into Robert's neck, pushing the stopper on the syringe forward. Cloudy liquid exited the syringe as Robert sank back in the chair, his muscles going lax.

"This is a hefty dose of that painkiller you disparaged, Robert," Luthor murmured, leaning closer as Grace covered her mouth to stifle a scream. "You see, I'm kind in my destruction. The opium inside will ensure you have a painless death. You're welcome, you bastard."

"Fuck...you!" Robert rasped, struggling to breathe as the drug coursed through his body.

Grace stood frozen, her mind screaming for her to intervene, but terror causing her to remain immobile. Petrified into a powerless statue, all she could do was watch as Luthor murdered her father.

"There, there," Luthor soothed, patting Robert's chest as he removed the empty vial and stuck it back in his pocket. "Don't worry, I've got another one in here for Grace. I'll make sure she and her unborn brat die quickly too."

Robert kicked and sputtered, fighting for his last breaths as the drug stole the life from his body.

"Once they're gone, I'll kill George Luddington and then I'll convince the board to sell Albright Industries to Sendaxa. I've always wanted an in-house CDMO. Too much red tape working with idealists like you, old friend. Now, I can approve everything to market much quicker."

"Grace... will... stop... you." Robert gasped. "She's smart."

Tossing back his head, Luthor broke into an ominous laugh. "Your daughter is a mindless twit who can't tie her own shoes without asking you first. I'll be doing her a favor by murdering her. One less vapid debutante in our elite circle, hmm?"

The words sent a jolt of anger through Grace, and she slowly regained the ability to move her fingers. Testing, she flexed them, wondering why in the hell her body was furiously shaking but she couldn't move.

"The drug is manufactured to mimic the effects of a heart attack. The Great Falls medical examiner has been paid an exorbitant sum to document that as your cause of death. Grace's death will be ruled the same."

Robert's eyes drifted closed as his head lolled on his shoulder. "Bastard... You'll burn in hell..."

"Perhaps. But I have plans, and I can't have you standing in my way, Robert. I'm sorry it's come to this, old friend." Robert exhaled his last breath as his body slumped in the chair. "Rest in peace."

No! The word shot through Grace's mind, and she willed her body to move. If she could just run to her father, perhaps she could do CPR and resuscitate him…

At that moment, a sharp pain ripped through her abdomen. Covering her belly, she screamed in pain and collapsed on the floor. Luthor's head snapped toward the door and he ran over, crouching beside her as she writhed in pain.

"Grace? I was meeting with your father. Did you overhear—?"

"Grace?" Jerry called, rushing down the hallway before kneeling beside her. "I forgot my phone and came back to get it. Are you all right?"

"Robert clutched his chest and fainted as we were meeting," Luthor said, pointing to her father's lifeless body behind the desk. "We need to get an ambulance here for both of them now!"

"Yes, sir," Jerry said, dialing 911 and lifting the phone to his ear. "I'm calling from 735 Crestwood Drive. We have a sixty-two-year-old man who's suffered a heart attack and a woman who's just over five months pregnant in distress…"

As Jerry spoke to the dispatcher, Luthor slid his hand behind Grace's neck. Having his skin against hers made her want to retch, but she knew she couldn't indicate she'd overheard his interaction with her father.

"Did you hear us speaking, dear?" Luthor asked, his dark eyes assessing her.

"No," Grace said through clenched teeth as another wave of pain shot through her trembling body. "Was just walking to the kitchen…"

"The ambulance is on its way, Grace," Jerry said, rubbing her shoulder in a soothing gesture. Closing her eyes, Grace thanked every god above that he'd forgotten his phone. Otherwise, she'd also be dead at the hands of the evil man who loomed above her.

Another wave of pain crested in her abdomen, and she realized she was having contractions.

"It's too early," she cried, tears streaming down her cheeks. "Call Tristan. Please…"

"We'll try, dear," Jerry said as sirens wailed in the distance. "The ambulance is almost here..."

Delirious from the agony of her father's death and the excruciating pain, Grace closed her eyes and allowed the darkness to overtake her...

Chapter 14

Tristan observed Grace crumple to the floor, burying her face in her hands as her body racked with sobs. Unable to comply with her request to stay away any longer, he rushed toward her and enveloped her in his arms.

"Shhh," he soothed, sitting on the floor and drawing her between his legs. She pressed her face to his neck, her tears wetting his skin as she curled into his body. "I'm here, sweetheart, and I'm so sorry."

"They couldn't reach you on your deployment. I asked the nurse to call you so many times..."

Tristan squeezed his eyes shut as shame and regret rolled through him. "I should've been there," he said, stroking her soft hair. "I can't imagine how painful losing the baby was. And you were all alone without your father. Fuck..." He tightened his arms around her. "I hate myself for leaving you."

Her tears eventually abated and she drew back, swiping her arm under her nose. Although her face was red and swollen, she was still the most gorgeous creature he'd ever seen. Cupping her cheek, he swiped the tears with his thumb. "I wish I could go back and change it."

"I know," she whispered, her throat bobbing as she swallowed thickly.

"Why didn't you tell me Luthor murdered your father?"

She pursed her lips as she contemplated. "Because by the time you came back, I'd already made my deal with Luthor...and accepted that we were over."

"Tell me why you made the deal, Grace. I'm just not getting it."

Sighing, she ran a hand through her hair. "I was the heir of Albright Industries. Luthor murdered my father in order to overtake the company. It was only a matter of time before he killed me too. So, I offered him a partnership that would give him what he wanted so I could live."

"You promised him control of Albright Industries."

"Yes. I made an offer that granted him everything he wanted but also ensured my future. I didn't want him to know that I'd seen him murder Dad. I needed to bide my time and earn his trust. I was understandably distraught after so much loss, so I needed time to mentally recover before I could plan revenge. Unfortunately, things took a bit longer than I expected. I didn't see the EverLife crisis occurring. Chalk that up to bad foresight, I guess."

"No one could've anticipated that," Tristan muttered. "And of course you needed time to mentally recover. Losing your father and the baby would devastate anyone."

"It wasn't just Dad and the baby..." she said softly.

Tristan's eyebrows drew together.

"I lost..." Her chin warbled as she struggled to maintain composure. "When I went into labor, I lost so much blood. Even though the doctors tried, they couldn't save my uterus..." She closed her eyes as two tears trailed down her cheeks. "So that's the only pregnancy I'm ever going to have."

Pain sliced through him as he digested her words. She'd lost her father, her child, and her ability to bear more children on the same day. That magnitude of loss was almost unimaginable.

"And I knew you wanted more kids... We'd discussed it several times..."

"Jesus, Grace. I wanted more kids with *you*. If you lost the ability to have them, I would've accepted that and supported you through it." Sliding his fingers under her chin, he forced her to meet his gaze. "How could you doubt that?"

"After you left me alone and pregnant when I begged you multiple times not to go?" she asked, exasperation in her voice. "Yeah, I'm not sure how I ever doubted you."

Tristan gritted his teeth as frustration for his choices—and annoyance at her ability to see any nuance in them—coursed through him. "I left for good and honorable reasons, Grace. I understand now that I made the wrong choices, but you've got to give me some credit. I did what I thought was right for our future."

"I wouldn't have *had* a future if I didn't think quickly and enter into my agreement with Luthor. He's a cold-blooded man and would've killed me, Tristan. The nurses gave him access to my room because he told them he was a family friend. I'm honestly surprised I survived my time in the hospital. I'm very lucky he didn't slip something into my IV when I was sleeping and the staff wasn't present."

Tristan shook his head as hatred of Luthor coursed through his veins. He'd already hated the man with deep intensity for how he treated Jessica, but Grace's story only enhanced the sentiment.

"Thankfully, I befriended a wonderful nurse named Maria. I don't know what it was about her, but she was lovely and I trusted her immediately. As soon as I was cognizant enough to speak, I told her about Luthor and that he was a danger to me. I think she had something to do with making sure a staff member was always present when he visited my room."

"Thank god. Did she survive the EverLife crisis?"

"Yes," Grace said, her blue eyes darting between his as something unidentifiable swirled within them. "She lives in a small town not far from here called Dundore. She chose to stay away from the compounds and walled-off cities and live a quiet life."

Tristan's eyes narrowed. Grace and George had mentioned Dundore in their hushed conversation on the walk to the hotel.

A shuffle sounded outside the door, causing them to both gasp and whip their heads toward the sound.

"Did you hear that?" Grace whispered.

"Stay here."

Tristan jogged to the small kitchen area and searched the drawers for a knife. After locating a slightly rusted dinner knife, he ran to the front door, locking the knob from the inside before closing it behind him.

Searching the hallway, he strained to hear any noises. A door clicked at the far end of the hallway, and he took off after it, hoping to catch whoever had been spying on them. Tristan had become paranoid after years of living in a world without hope, and he didn't trust Solomon Grange not to betray them. After all, aligning with Luthor would give Solomon many benefits he might not receive with someone else in power.

Tristan barreled down the stairs and out to the grassy area behind the hotel. It had grown dark, but he could barely see the form of someone running into the nearby thicket of trees adjacent to the river. Gripping the knife, he entered the brush, hoping not to get ambushed.

"Hey!" Tristan grunted, grabbing a fistful of the runner's shirt before yanking him to a halt. "Gotcha!" Dragging the spy toward him, he glared down into angry brown eyes. "You're just a kid."

"Fuck you!" The boy kicked Tristan's shin, causing him to yelp and release his grip. The boy took off again and Tristan sped after him, gritting his teeth at the pain in his shin.

"Stop right there, you little jerk," Tristan yelled, catching hold of the boy's collar and forcing him to stop. The little tyrant reared his leg back and aimed for Tristan's balls.

"Hey!" Tristan said, his authoritative tone causing the kid to freeze. "I've got a knife, but I don't feel like stabbing a kid today. I'm not going to hurt you. Relax."

The boy panted from exertion as he stared at Tristan, his eyes filled with fear. Tristan noticed the shiner under his right eye, and he immediately released his grip. "You're okay, kid," he said, slipping the knife into his back pocket.

"I don't know who gave you that shiner, but I don't hit kids. Even ones who kick the hell out of my shin."

The boy's eyes darted between Tristan's as he debated whether he could trust him.

"What's your name, and who hit you?"

"None of your business—"

"Nope," Tristan interjected, shaking his head. "We're not going to do the petulant child act. If you're old enough to spy on me, you're old enough to be a man and tell me your name and who hit you. Was it one of your parents?"

"My parents are dead," he said, sending a jolt of compassion through Tristan. "They died from EverLife addiction."

"Who took care of you after they died?"

"No one," he said, kicking the ground with the toe of his worn sneaker. "I can take care of myself."

"How old are you?"

"I'll be eleven next month."

Tristan placed his hands on his hips as he regarded the kid. "I know you were spying on me and Grace. For who? Solomon Grange?"

He shrugged.

"How much is Solomon paying you? Whatever it is, I can pay more."

The boy's eyes widened. "I get unlimited access to the commissary in the main square as long as I keep the information coming. I need food more than money."

"I can give you both. Sounds like a better deal than Solomon's giving you."

The boy frowned. "I didn't say I was spying for Solomon."

"You didn't have to...?" He drew out the end of the sentence and rolled his hand to urge the boy along.

"Nathan."

"Nice to meet you," Tristan said, extending his hand. "I assume you already know who I am since you were spying on me."

Nathan nodded and shook his hand—his grip surprisingly firm for a kid.

"Did Solomon give you that black eye?"

"Yeah, but it was my fault. I snuck some food from the commissary to a Sen Force deserter I met outside the wall on one of my scouting trips."

"That doesn't sound like something that deserves punishment."

"Solomon forbids helping deserters. He thinks they're spineless, and if the rebellion fails, he wants to be able to tell Luthor he never supported soldiers who left his army."

Tristan shifted his weight, wondering what the hell to do. He'd always had a bit of a savior complex—evidenced by the fact he'd worked for Luthor for several years in an attempt to assure Jessica was safe. Whether he wanted to or not, he felt a sense of obligation toward the scrawny kid with a shiner.

Crouching down, he beckoned Nathan forward. "Here's what's going to happen, Nathan. You're going to report back to Solomon that you spied on us and didn't hear anything." Hesitating, he asked, "*Did* you hear anything?"

"Something about Dundore...and I heard Grace crying."

Tristan swiped a hand over his face. "You're going to keep all of that to yourself. Do you hear me?"

Nathan nodded.

"We're going to catalog and load all the weapons tomorrow and then head to Arthur Reyes's compound in Maryland. I'm going to pay Solomon so you can come with us."

Recoiling, his eyebrows drew together. "Why?"

"Because I don't want you to get hit anymore, and I can use a good spy. I'll make sure you're fed just like Solomon does, and we can discuss payment once I decide how I'm going to use your...*skills*. I'll need you to act surprised when I suggest you joining us to Solomon, but I also need you to agree."

"But I don't know you," he said, trepidation in his voice. "Solomon is a jerk, but I know this compound."

"Solomon isn't a good man, Nathan—"

"And you are?"

Sighing, Tristan lifted a shoulder. "Some days are better than others," he muttered. "But today, I think I'm doing okay." Offering his hand, he waited. "What do you say? Want to align with the rebellion, Nathan?"

The kid studied Tristan's hand, gnawing on his lip as he contemplated. Finally, he placed his palm over Tristan's and they shook.

"Don't be a dick like Solomon, okay?"

Laughing, Tristan nodded. "I'll try. I'm more concerned with keeping up with my ex-wife and helping her win the rebellion."

"I'm a good spy," Nathan said, his chest puffing with pride. "I'll help you."

Tristan rose. "We need all the help we can get. Go on back to town. I'll see you tomorrow when we report back to Solomon after loading the vehicles. Make sure you're there."

Nathan nodded and pivoted before jogging away. When he reached the edge of the clearing, he turned back and waved. Something about the gesture tugged at Tristan's heartstrings, maybe because it was innocent, and he could tell the kid had lost most of his innocence long ago.

But that last heartfelt wave meant there was something salvageable there.

And for some reason, Tristan felt an urge to salvage it.

Releasing a deep breath, he plodded back to the hotel to resume his talk with Grace and inform her he'd recruited a ten-year-old spy to their ranks.

Chapter 15

G race waited anxiously for Tristan to return. As the minutes passed, she washed her face and tugged on some old shorts and a t-shirt. Exhausted from the events of the day, she fought the urge to lie down. Craning her neck, she massaged the tense muscles there, her body reminding her she was a few years shy of forty and no longer bounced back as quickly as she once had.

Finally, the need to rest overtook her, and she slid into bed. She turned to her side, drawing the covers up to her chin as her knees curled into her chest. Within minutes, she was fast asleep.

Memories swam through her subconscious mind, parading as dreams that quickly turned to nightmares. The starkest memory was the blood the night she'd gone into labor...signifying all she'd lost.

Gasping, her eyes flew open as something tickled her cheek. Tristan loomed above her, looking rugged and handsome in the dim moonlight from the lone window.

"Sorry. I didn't mean to startle you, but I thought you'd want to hear what I found."

"Yes," she whispered, pushing herself up on her arm. "I was just going to lie down for a second. Damn it."

"Don't get up," he said, gently pushing her down as he sat beside her. Tenderness covered his features as he tucked a strand of hair behind her ear before softly stroking her hair.

"Tristan—"

"Old habits," he said, removing his hand and flashing a solemn grin. "I used to love watching you sleep."

Grace studied him as her heart pounded. "What did you find?"

Tristan told her about Nathan and that he'd ultimately invited him into the rebellion.

"You've been in the rebellion for one day and you've already tried to save someone," she teased, nudging his thigh with her knee from under the covers. "Your efforts to save people are noble, but I hate to tell you this, my dear ex-husband…" Biting her lip, she grinned. "They usually fail. You're very gallant, but terrible at executing your valiant plans."

"No shit," he muttered, swiping a hand over his face. "I ran off to the Middle East to save you and our marriage, and we both know how that turned out. I bent over backward to secure a job with a man I loathe to save Jessica, but she's still in his clutches."

"Luthor was dead set against hiring you, but I knew what you were up to. After failing to get on his payroll as a mercenary, I finally told him to hire you."

Tristan flinched. "You did?"

She nodded atop the pillow. "He thought it would bother me, being in such close proximity to you. I told him it wouldn't."

"Well, it was hell for me," he said, eyes narrowing. "Every time you walked into the room and kissed him on the cheek, I wanted to rip his throat out."

"All part of the show," she said, yawning.

"I know you're tired," he whispered, leaning closer and touching his fingers to her face. "But I don't want to leave. I'm still processing what you told me about losing the ability to have kids." He stroked her cheek as emotions warred inside her. "I want to comfort you."

"It happened a long time ago," she said, tears stinging her eyes as his image blurred. "I don't need comforting anymore."

"Bullshit."

Grace closed her eyes, refusing to let herself cry. Getting lost in painful memories was *not* on the agenda. She had a rebellion to lead and that was her primary focus.

"Let me hold you, empress," he said, the plea in his voice almost cracking her heart open. "Let me be there for you in the way I couldn't be before. In the way I should've been."

Lifting her lids, she stared into his gorgeous hazel-green eyes, knowing she'd already lost. She'd never been able to deny him when he looked at her like that. As if his soul was in his eyes, and he'd die if he didn't hold her.

"We have too much terrible history between us to try again," she said, the words feeling like a lie upon her tongue. "If you're expecting that, things are going to end very badly for you."

He breathed a laugh before running a hand through his hair. Rising, he kicked off his shoes and slowly removed his pants, his eyes on hers the entire time he slid them down his legs. He removed his shirt, and her eyes darted to his boxer briefs, which he left on.

"I'm very familiar with things ending badly, sweetheart, so you let me worry about that." Cocking an eyebrow in that sexy way that made her knees buckle, he asked, "So, are you going to let me hold you, or not?"

Grace felt her pulse in every cell of her body. It pounded in her throat, almost choking her as she contemplated. Finally, she lifted the sheets and invited him in.

His gorgeous smile would've been enough to soothe her frayed emotions.

But when he crawled in beside her and drew her against his warm, muscular frame, the familiar comfort of being in his arms pacified her long-suffering heart.

When he urged her cheek to his chest and pressed his lips to her forehead, Grace sighed against the scratchy hairs that tickled her nose.

And when he stroked her hair and whispered words of love and remorse, her enigmatic ex-husband soothed her tired soul as she drifted back into slumber.

Chapter 16

Grace searched the darkness behind her closed lids, zeroing in on the pleasurable feeling between her legs. Not ready to leave the dream, her eyes remained closed as her hips undulated toward the blissful pressure. Sparks of arousal heated her skin—a feeling that had been dormant for so long, but that she remembered somehow...

A low growl sounded in her ear, followed by more pressure at her core. Warm breath rushed against her neck, followed by the brush of firm lips at her nape. Awareness dawned as she realized Tristan was cupping her between her legs. They'd often slept that way in the past—him holding her most private place in an act of physical possession.

"Tristan," she murmured. Labored pants left her lungs as her breathing accelerated.

"Hmm?" he uttered into her nape, and she realized he was still half asleep. He'd always been a deep sleeper, and he'd *always* snaked around her while they were sleeping—as if he knew he might lose her one day, so he held on extra tight.

"You're cupping my..." Exhaling an exasperated breath, she felt her cheeks flush.

She felt his muscles tighten as realization took hold. His hand froze as his chest rose and fell against her back.

"Muscle memory," he said softly, his fingers warm atop the thin fabric of her shorts.

Grace struggled to breathe as they both lay still.

His hand tightened on her core, ever so slightly, and she inhaled a sharp breath.

"Do you want me to let go?"

Silence echoed in the dark room as she contemplated.

Pressing his lips to her ear, he asked, "Or do you want me to make you feel good?"

"I told you, any romantic reconciliation between us is doomed—"

"Look who's the pessimist," Tristan said, nipping her ear. "Have the tables turned? Am I the optimist now?"

A nervous laugh escaped her throat. "You're an optimist if you think having sex won't end badly for us."

"I didn't say anything about having sex." His hand flexed atop her core again, and Grace stifled a groan. "I'm just going to make you feel good, empress."

Nerves swirled in her belly as she debated whether to run or to turn on her back and let her husband pleasure her with his talented fingers. Scratch that. Her *ex-husband*, which was why this was a very bad idea...

"Look at me, Grace."

Filled with trepidation, she turned her head on the pillow to meet his lust-filled gaze. "Let me love you, sweetheart."

Unable to speak from the lump of emotion clogging her throat, she capitulated and pushed into his hand. A broad smile curved his full lips.

"Good girl. I'm going to make you feel so good, baby..."

He slipped those long fingers under her shorts, finding her cotton panties and tracing the edge. Those burning hazel irises bore into hers as he dug under the elastic to find her bare skin.

"*Oh god...*" she cried, widening her legs to allow him better access. "It's been so long..."

Tristan's fingers swirled over her sensitive skin, sliding between her folds and rubbing the tender slit. Wetness surged to her core, coating his fingers as he groaned.

"So slick and pretty while I claim you, Grace." Leaning closer, he nudged her nose with his. "You've always been so pretty everywhere."

"My body isn't the same, Tristan. They had to cut me open when I went into labor—"

"Your body is perfect, no matter how many scars you have." He continued to stroke her as he gazed into her eyes. "One day, you'll let me see them." Pressing the tip of his finger to her wet opening, he said firmly, "One day, you'll remember that you belong to me."

With an assertive yet tender thrust, he slipped his finger inside her. Grace gasped as he inched farther inside, her muscles clenching as he assessed her.

"Relax, baby," he crooned, circling his finger in her tight warmth as she slowly released the tension from her muscles. "That's it. Let your body remember me."

Oh, how her body remembered him. Her lips fell open as she gazed at him through slitted eyes, and every cell of her skin burned. Unable to control her hips, she let go, pushing into his gentle ministrations as she allowed herself a moment of pleasure.

"I've waited so long..." he rasped, inserting another finger and stretching her as he worked his hand back and forth. "I thought I'd never touch you here again."

Grace wrapped her arms around his shoulders, holding on for dear life as he claimed her all over again. He circled his fingers, coating them with her essence before sliding them up to the tiny little bud that was rapidly swelling with desire. Dousing her clit with her slick, he made sure she was ready. Trailing his fingers back down, he slid them inside her again and pressed the heel of his hand to her pulsing clit. Closing her eyes, Grace's head fell back on the pillow as she moaned.

"God, I love watching you come," he said, moving his fingers in steady strokes inside her quaking body as he rubbed her clit with the heel of his hand. "Your cheeks flush the prettiest shade of red, and your lips swell, ready to take me."

He increased the pace and pressure of his hand at her core as his lips grazed a path from her cheek to her ear. Grace shuddered when he licked the sensitive shell before whispering dirty words. "Remember when you used to take me between those sexy lips, Grace? It's my favorite memory...and my ultimate torture...knowing it would never happen again."

"You're still a pessimist," she said, joy flooding her as she teased him.

Chuckling, he pressed his forehead to her temple. "I'm always evolving. We'll see."

Grace soaked in the warmth from his strong frame, losing herself in his sandalwood scent. His smell had always enveloped her when they slept—and when they made love—and she attributed it to one of the many things that sparked their undeniable chemistry.

Sometimes, you just couldn't argue with nature. Their connection had always been irrefutable.

This is why she'd stayed out of Tristan's way in the decade she'd been married to Luthor, even though he worked for him, which meant they inevitably saw each other in passing. Staying away from Tristan was the only way her plan would work—and the only way she could protect those who needed it. Tristan had always been able to protect himself, and she knew if she allowed herself access to him, she'd jump right back into his arms.

This was clearly evidenced by the fact they'd been alone together for less than two days and he currently had his fingers deep inside her body. Jesus, she really had no control when it came to him.

"Stop thinking, empress," he crooned, increasing the pace of his skillful fingers. "We can save the world when I'm done making you scream. Come all over my fingers, baby. Let me feel you fall apart."

She released a deep breath, her muscles turning to jelly as she fully relaxed. Tristan's warm breath rushed against her ear, whispering unintelligible words as he brought her to the edge. Just when she thought her body might explode, her back arched and she dove into a blinding orgasm.

Wave upon wave of pleasure drowned her pulsing body as she cried his name. Her fingernails speared into his neck, causing him to emit a sexy growl as he cupped her deepest place. She shuddered and quaked, losing all control as he murmured words of praise.

As the high wore off, she lay limp, a sated grin on her face as she listened to the buzzing between her ears. Wanting one moment of unadulterated bliss, she relaxed in his arms, knowing she was safe.

Tristan placed soft kisses over her nose and cheeks as he tenderly stroked her sweat-soaked hairline. Eventually, he removed his hand from her core and brought his fingers to his lips.

Grace's eyes slid open as he licked her essence from his fingers, taking his time as he stared into her eyes. His tongue darted over his drenched skin, and she swallowed thickly, remembering the times that wet tongue had worked magic between her legs.

"Worth the wait," he murmured, his eyes shining with pleasure and that slight bit of cockiness that always drove her wild. "I could survive on just tasting you every day."

The corner of her lips curved. "I don't think that's very nutritious," she teased.

"I don't give a damn." Resting his head on his fist as his elbow dug into the mattress, he caressed the hair at her temple as he regarded her. "It's been ten years. A decade without touching you. I don't want to go another decade. Are you planning on marrying any other nefarious dictators I need to know about?"

Snickering, she shook her head as her hair fanned across the pillow. "No. But I am still technically married to Luthor. It's obviously a sham marriage that will dissolve once he figures out my betrayal. And he *will* figure it out," she finished with a shiver.

"Good. I hope to see the shine of betrayal in his eyes when I murder him. That will be a nice parting gift on his way to hell."

"So, you're not going to berate me for being married to someone else while we..." She bit her lip as her cheeks flushed.

"While I had my fingers inside you?" he asked, cocking a brow. "Now that I know you weren't intimate with him, it certainly makes things easier. But the marriage needs to be dissolved, Grace."

"It will be in due time," she said, gliding her fingers into his thick hair. "I thought you'd become more patient in your old age."

Breathing a laugh, he shook his head. "I'm almost forty, not eighty. But seeing you married to someone else, especially that bastard, will never sit well with me. You're *my* wife, Grace."

"I *was* your wife," she replied softly.

Frustration entered his expression as he exhaled a slow breath. "You'll be mine again. Mark my words."

Grace tamped down the spark of hope that welled in her chest. "We're different people now, Tristan, and I can't have any more children—"

"For god's sake, woman. One thing at a time. Let's defeat Luthor and then we can discuss all the excuses you're going to make for rejecting me again. I need to be fully focused so I can combat them."

Grace stroked his hair, wondering if he would feel the same when *all* of her secrets were revealed. "Tristan..."

A knock on the door interrupted them, making them both jump as their heads swiveled.

"Yes?" Grace called.

"Ma'am, the sun will rise soon, and Solomon's men are outside with our vehicles."

"Be right there."

Sighing, she ran her thumb over Tristan's lips, acknowledging she couldn't linger any longer.

"After we load the vehicles, I'm going to send everyone to Arthur's compound, but I need to stop in Dundore along the way."

Annoyance entered his gaze as he studied her. "Why?"

"I'll tell you everything on the way. Nathan can ride with us too if you wish."

He gave a curt nod before rolling off her, and stood and rubbed his chest. Grace's eyes roved over the taut skin of his nipples and the chest smattered with brown and gray hair. Desire coursed through her frame and she pressed her legs together, reminding herself they didn't have time for another round, even though her husband was incredibly hot.

Ex-husband. Sheesh. She was really having a hard time remembering that.

Extending his hand, he beckoned to her. "Ready to catalog some weapons? Let's pack those puppies up and get ready to attack that asshole."

Pressing her hand to his, she stood, ready to face the day.

Chapter 17

After a quick rinse from the jug of water in his room, Tristan donned his clothes and reconvened with Grace outside the hotel. The sun was barely peeking over the horizon, and it appeared today was going to be rain free. Tristan chose to take that as a good omen.

Hell, maybe he was evolving into an optimist after all.

They drove to the far side of the compound, where thick forest butted up against the high steel walls. Arriving at a tall mound of grass-covered earth, they exited the vehicles and George walked to the small wooden door.

"This leads into the bunker," he said, unlocking it with the keys he pulled from his pocket. "It's dark in there, so have your flashlights ready."

Tristan clicked on one of the solar-powered flashlights Solomon had placed in the vehicles. They headed inside the dark, musty bunker, and Tristan's eyes grew wide at the amount of weapons stockpiled on the various shelves. Rifles, handguns, and ammunition were just the beginning. Tristan noted several stockpiles of teargas, grenades and grenade launchers, night-vision goggles, and a few Javelin antitank systems.

"Holy shit," Tristan said, scanning the room. "You have Javelins? They're extremely effective in disarming tanks. This is a massive haul. How long have you been stockpiling weapons here?"

"For years," Grace replied, and Tristan noted the exhaustion in her tone. "Albright Industries had a production plant close to here before the EverLife crisis. George and I realized Luthor was growing more unhinged after the government indicted him for falsifying the EverLife clinical trial evidence. We realized he might try to stage a coup on the government and figured it was a good idea to stash some weapons here in case we had to make a run for it."

"You two have been colluding that long?" Tristan asked, pointing between them.

"Yes," Grace said with a nod. "How do you think the government knew he falsified evidence?"

"You were the whistleblower?" Tristan asked as his eyebrows lifted.

"I thought it would be the perfect opportunity to bring him down and finally enact my plan. I didn't expect the world to become addicted to his drug, making him the most powerful man on the planet. No one cared that he overthrew the government. They just wanted their precious *drug*." She spat the word as if it were poison.

"At that point, Grace was stuck in the marriage with him," George said. "There was nothing we could do, and we debated having her make a run for it."

"But I wanted to finish the job," she said, lifting her chin. "Little did I know it would take me so long. I've been planting the seeds of rebellion for a long time. It took years for me to find people I could trust and sow dissent. And now, we're finally ready." She waved her hands over the weapons, reminding Tristan of Vanna White—if Vanna were a high-end arms dealer.

"Everything is converging nicely," George said, shifting his weight as he balanced on his cane. "Arthur Reyes's willingness to shelter Danica Lawson and support her creation of a cure means we have solution to EverLife addiction. The fact that Luthor's troops didn't breach his walls means Arthur's militia is competent."

"They have Arianna Lawson, and that woman is fierce," Tristan said. "I wouldn't want to be on the other side of a war against her. Dominic and Maverick are capable soldiers too."

"Then I like our chances," Grace said. "We have some spies inside the walls, and I anticipate you have some too." She arched an eyebrow at Tristan.

Tristan thought of all the people he paid to funnel information, including Deandra and Ron, the deli owners in LeDroit Park who were experts at mining data from Sen Force soldiers who frequented their establishment.

"Yeah, I've got a few."

"And we have a sneaking suspicion that Arthur secretly converted the young Major Anthony Martinez to his side when they attacked the compound. Lieutenant Colonel Jackson died in battle, and Anthony assumed command and retreated early the next morning. They had all the firepower; all the tanks. Why would they retreat otherwise?"

"We're going to find out when we reach Arthur's compound," Grace said, stepping into the center of the room to face everyone. "Tristan and I are going to make a stop along the way. Zayne, I expect you to protect George as you all journey to Arthur's compound."

"Yes, ma'am," Zayne said with a nod.

"Thank you. Let's get to work. George has a notebook, and we're going to catalog everything in this bunker. We won't be able to fit everything into our vehicles, so take what's most valuable and document what we leave behind too. If we fail, at least we'll have a small stockpile left."

On that ominous note, the team got to work cataloging the weapons.

Around six p.m., after the weapons were categorized and the vehicles were loaded, the team drove back to the compound headquarters. Solomon sat in his makeshift throne atop the faded marble stairs as Tristan, Grace and George approached. The rest of the team stood behind them with Zayne in front.

"We're packed and ready to depart after sunset," Grace said.

"Are all four vehicles driving the same path?" Solomon asked. "Because my friend Nathan here informed me you just exited Tristan's truck. I assumed you'd ride with George to Cumberland."

Tristan glanced at Nathan, who stood beside Solomon. His eyes were downcast, and Tristan wondered if he was showing contrition since he'd spied on them again.

"George, Zayne and I need to ride in separate vehicles," she said assertively. "We can't chance being ambushed, and someone needs to lead the rebellion if I die."

"So, you'll take separate paths," Solomon said. "I find that interesting."

"I'm not sure what you're hinting at, but I'd rather you just come out and say it," Grace said. "I don't have time for guessing games."

"I just find it strange that small settlements still exist along the Susquehanna River and wonder if you'll pass them on the way," he said with a shrug. "It would be better for them if they moved into my compound. We always need skilled laborers. Cooks, nurses, seamstresses... Well, you get the drift." He circled his hand. "My spies tell me there is a woman who lives in Dundore who has a magnificent plumbing system even though she doesn't seem to possess any plumbing skills. I wonder how that's possible? Has someone been helping her? I've decreed that no one can help citizens who live within a hundred-mile radius of the Scranton compound. Dundore sits just inside that radius."

"I have no idea." Exasperation laced her tone as she lifted her hands. "My only goal is to get to Arthur's compound so we can begin the next phase of the rebellion. The time to attack Luthor is now, so I won't be stopping for any late-night sightseeing along the Susquehanna River."

Tristan's lips curved at her grit. She'd always been someone who stood up for herself and carried herself with confidence. But this woman—the one who stood with squared shoulders and lied with conviction to a man who most certainly had a gun holstered at his waist—was fierce.

A low-toned chuckle left Solomon's lips as he rubbed his chin. "All right, my dear. As you know, I must remain skeptical of any information I receive from my spies."

"Speaking of spies," Tristan interjected. "I had the pleasure of meeting Nathan at our hotel last night." His tone held an undeniable note of sarcasm. "He's fast, but I was able to question him before he squirmed away. You'll be proud to know he didn't divulge your secrets."

Fury flashed in Solomon's eyes as he gazed at Nathan. "Is this true, boy?"

Nathan nodded as he kicked the ground with his toe.

"I can tell you're pissed he didn't tell you," Tristan continued. "I asked him not to, and I know this will displease you, so I want to offer a solution. We need a spy capable of crawling into small spaces for the rebellion. I would like Nathan to be that spy."

Solomon's eyes narrowed as he debated.

"Nathan told me he has no family left. It would be one less minor for you to take care of and one less mouth to feed."

"Fine," Solomon said, flicking his hand. "Go on, boy. And remember my benevolence. Most spies who betray me are murdered on the spot."

"Yes, sir," Nathan mumbled before joining Tristan. The boy glanced up at him with fear-filled eyes.

Wanting to soothe him, Tristan rested a hand on his shoulder as Grace retook control of the conversation. "I was hoping you'd feed my team one last meal before we depart. We left a corner of the bunker stocked with weapons as payment for your hospitality and alliance."

"The school on the next block has a cafeteria, and my cooks are already preparing the meals. I wish you luck on your journey, Grace."

"We don't need luck," she said, straightening her spine. "We need strategy, firepower, and the art of surprise. Thankfully, once we meet up with Arthur's team, we'll have all three. I won't forget your help when we win. Thank you, Solomon."

"I'm counting on it, Grace. Safe travels."

With a nod, Grace pivoted and led her men out of the post office. The team marched down the battered street, arriving at the school and locating the cafeteria.

After eating the best meal he'd had in a while, Tristan joined the others at the vehicles. They loaded inside, George and Zayne entering separate SUVs, and Tristan slid behind the wheel of the pickup truck.

Nathan hopped in the passenger side and slid beside him before Grace claimed the passenger seat. There were a multitude of weapons in the bed of the truck, covered with a tarp and rope to secure them.

"Ready?"

"Ready," Nathan and Grace said in unison.

Under the cover of night, they exited the compound walls and set off on the two-hour drive to Dundore.

Chapter 18

As they drove, Grace inwardly admitted she'd offered for Nathan to ride with them because it gave her an excuse to draw out the inevitable. Having a little boy sandwiched between them didn't lend to a heartfelt discussion during the drive.

Biting her nail, she stared anxiously out the window into the darkness. Most of the roads had deteriorated, but the highways were navigable enough. Eventually, they would exit old Interstate 80 onto Highway 11, and Tristan would have to weave the windy roads to Dundore.

"You two married?" Nathan asked, pointing between them.

"Why do you ask that?" Grace replied, grinning.

"Because you stare at each other weird. All gooey-eyed and stuff." He bugged out his eyes and made a silly face. "It's kind of gross, but whatever."

Tristan glanced over at her and smiled. "We used to be married. Maybe we will be again one day. I'm working on it."

A flash of light beamed in the passenger side window, and Grace leaned forward to focus on it. "Shit! We're being followed." Looking at Nathan, she said, "Sorry, kid."

"I've heard curse words before, lady."

"Someone's following us," she said, gripping the handle.

"I'm going to get off the highway and try to lose them," Tristan said. "You've got the handgun I gave you?"

Grace nodded and patted the holster at her belt. Zayne had trained her how to shoot over the past year, and she felt confident wielding a weapon.

"I need a gun too," Nathan said.

"Nope, but I'm sure you have a knife or some other weapon on you. You're too wily not to."

Nathan pulled the Swiss army knife from his sock and beamed. "I can stab someone's eyes out with this."

"Okay, Hannibal Lector," he said, pushing Nathan's arm down to lower the knife. "Put that back in your sock." Lifting his gaze to Grace, he instructed, "Keep an eye out and let me navigate the side roads."

Tristan weaved and navigated down dirt roads as long minutes passed. Every so often, Grace saw a flash in the side mirror, indicating the perpetrator was still on their tail.

"Screw this," Tristan said, pulling off the road into the forest. "I'm going to throw on one of the bulletproof vests and go on the offensive. You two crouch down and stay in the truck."

"Tristan—"

"They're not going to stop, Grace," he warned, exiting the truck. "Stay inside and stay down."

Grace threw her arms around Nathan and huddled in the seat. She wasn't religious, but she closed her eyes and whispered, "Please let him be okay."

Tristan grabbed a rifle from the bed of the truck. He also tossed on a pair of the night-vision goggles, acknowledging his good fortune at having a truck full of weapons.

Headlights approached on the nearby road, stopping in front of the thicket where he was now parked. Tristan had left the parking lights on. He didn't see any reason to keep running and wasting gas—if he wanted to take the offensive, he needed to lead the enemy to them.

The car stopped and two men emerged, their silhouettes lit by the headlights. Aiming for the first man's neck, he closed one eye and pulled the trigger.

The man gasped, clutching his neck before he fell to the ground.

The other man ran behind the car, taking cover before he began to spray a barrage of bullets into the forest. Cursing, Tristan ducked behind the truck and prayed that Grace and Nathan had followed his directive to stay down.

Steeling himself, Tristan gathered his courage to take the offensive. Leaving the shelter of the truck, he stealthily moved through the trees, taking shots at the car as he advanced. Every time his assailant rose and sprayed a round of bullets, Tristan ducked behind a tree to shield himself.

Eventually, he approached the tree closest to the road, understanding that was the last cover the forest could give him. Attempting to negotiate, he yelled, "I don't want to shoot you too. Come out and let's try to find a compromise."

"The time for compromise is over, Tristan," a familiar voice called. "Luthor has been trying to locate Grace for weeks and wants her back immediately."

Tristan closed his eyes and sighed. "I can tell that's you, Tom. What the hell?"

"You're the one who defected, buddy," his old friend and comrade said. "You were Luthor's top mercenary, and when you disappeared, he needed a replacement."

"Glad to hear you were there to step in," Tristan muttered.

"I always liked working for you, Tristan, although people seem to die around you a lot. I'd hate for Grace to die too. Give her to me and I'll let you go."

"No can do, *friend*," Tristan said, gritting out the word as he peeked around the tree. He could just make out the top of Tom's head behind the trunk of his car. Tristan certainly hated to kill him, but he would to protect Grace at all costs.

But first, he'd try another tactic. Aiming his rifle, he shot both driver's side tires.

"Damn it, Tristan!" Tom cried. "We're in the middle of nowhere. Are you serious?"

Tristan noticed him rise slightly, allowing him a glance at the top of his shoulder. Thinking quickly, he aimed and pulled the trigger.

Tom wailed in pain, grabbing his shoulder as he fell to the ground.

Seizing the moment, Tristan sprinted toward him, locating Tom's gun beside him on the ground thanks to the night-vision goggles. Grabbing the gun, he tossed it into the woods before planting his feet and aiming his rifle at Tom, who was writing in pain on the gravel road.

"You son of a bitch!" Tom hissed. "You shot me."

"You're lucky I didn't kill you." Aiming at the passenger side tires, he shot them both, ensuring the car was incapacitated. Then, he searched the car, finding the shortwave radio and dropping it on the ground before stomping on it to destroy it. "Hope you've got a first aid kit in there, and good luck getting back to DC with four flat tires."

"Luthor is obsessed with squashing the rebellion," Tom said, panting as he clenched his teeth. "He won't stop until he finds Zayne and rescues Grace."

Relief swished through Tristan that Luthor didn't know Grace was leading the rebellion. For now. It was only a matter of time before the truth came out, but Tristan would take every advantage possible.

"I hope you don't bleed out, man," Tristan said, shaking his head as he backed away. "You're on the wrong side of history. If you want to have a future, I'd suggest leaving DC. There's a war coming, and you don't want to be inside the wall when it erupts."

Pivoting, Tristan jogged back to the truck and yanked open the passenger side door. "You guys okay?"

"Yes," Grace said, stroking Nathan's hair as she held him. "Are you?"

Nathan nodded, and Tristan shut the door and rounded the truck. After depositing the goggles, rifle and vest back in the truck bed, he hopped in and closed the door.

"I'm going to drive quickly and continue to take back roads. Hold on tight. It's going to get bumpy."

Revving the engine, he eased back onto the road before hightailing it out of the area and toward Dundore.

Tristan did an excellent job navigating the side roads, and they managed to avoid any other vehicles—as far as Grace could tell. She directed him to drive along the river to a small cottage with a stone chimney. Since it was mid-October and still rather warm, no smoke exited the chimney, but Grace knew they used it often in the winter.

After parking the truck, they climbed out, and Grace crouched down and cupped Nathan's upper arms. "I want you to go knock on the door. A lady named Maria is going to answer. Tell her Grace and Tristan are outside and you'd like some stew. She always has a pot of stew brewing." Smiling, Grace rose and urged him inside. "Sit down at the table and enjoy it. I need to talk to Tristan before we head inside."

Nathan nodded and walked to the front door. Maria appeared, introducing herself to Nathan in the light that shone from inside. Her eyes met Grace's, and Grace held up a hand, splaying her fingers to let her know she'd be inside in five minutes. Nodding, Maria ushered Nathan inside and closed the door.

Tristan approached her, looking so handsome in the dim moonlight. His hazel eyes sparkled, the gold flecks simmering with unanswered questions. Tears welled in her eyes as she realized this might be the last moment he ever loved her. Wanting to cherish it, she cradled his face in her hands as two tears trailed down her cheeks.

"What the hell, Grace?" he whispered, palming her face and swiping away the tears with his thumbs. "What are you not telling me?"

"He was going to kill me, Tristan," she said, the words warbled from her tears. "And he was going to kill her. And I couldn't let him. She's our baby."

His chest rose and fell with labored breaths as his eyes darted between hers. "Grace..." he growled as murky awareness glowed in his eyes. "What the fuck are you saying?"

Suddenly, the front door swung open and a little girl darted out. "Grace!" she called, running toward her and jumping into her arms.

Grace enveloped her in a tight hug, burying her face in the girl's soft blond hair as emotions warred within. Joy at holding her again. Despair at the loss of Tristan's trust...and possibly his love.

After one last squeeze, she set the girl on her feet and straightened her spine. Swiping away her tears, Grace faced the man she'd loved since the moment they met.

"Tristan, I'd like you to meet—"

"Raquel," the girl said, extending her hand.

Tristan audibly inhaled as his gaze bore into Grace's. "You didn't... You couldn't have..." he said, disbelief in his voice.

"I *had* to," she pleaded, shaking her head. "I'm so sorry."

Crouching down, Tristan slowly slid his palm over Raquel's. Grace's heart shattered into a thousand pieces at the sight of his broad hand holding their daughter's.

"Hello, Raquel," he rasped, emotion lacing the words. "It's very nice to meet you."

Chapter 19

B lood pounded in Tristan's ears, making it hard to balance as he crouched before the girl. She stared back at him with hazel-green, golden-flecked eyes, and he knew she was *his*.

As he gazed upon her, speechless, he admitted she was a perfect amalgamation of him and Grace. She had Grace's golden hair and pert nose, and his hazel eyes and strong chin. Overcome with emotion, he struggled to process the fact his daughter, whom he thought dead over a decade ago, was *alive*.

"Sweetheart, Tristan and I need to talk out here. We're probably going to have a little argument, although we won't yell because we don't want anyone to hear us." She shot him a pointed glare, warning him not to scream at her even though he wanted to rail at the damn universe.

"Run on inside," she said, smoothing a hand over Raquel's hair. "And tell Maria we'll be in soon."

"Okay. We have stew when you all are ready." Turning, she jogged to the house and closed the door behind her.

Tristan stood and flexed his fists at his side several times, closing his eyes as he told himself to remain calm. Although he wanted to strangle his ex-wife, yelling would only attract notice, and that was something they needed to avoid.

Facing her, his nostrils flared as he stared into her eyes.

"You fucking bitch."

"Yes," she said, bracing for his anger. "I'm a bitch and deserve every ounce of your hate. You can curse me out as long as you want. I knew this day would come, and I won't deny it was a huge betrayal."

"Betrayal?" he hissed, trying like hell not to scream. "You told me our daughter died. I *mourned* her. And she's been alive all this time?"

"Thanks to me," Grace said, lifting her chin in that haughty way he sometimes found sexy. At the moment, it made him want to throttle her. "I overheard Luthor speaking to his head of security on the phone when he visited my room after I went into labor. He thought I was sleeping." Wringing her hands, she started to pace. "He had everything planned out. He was going to inject my IV with something that wouldn't be detected by the staff, and then he was going to kill Raquel in the NICU. He was just biding his time until there was a slow night shift where he wouldn't be discovered."

"Why would he need to kill a helpless baby in the NICU?"

"Um, have you *met* Luthor Cromwell?" she asked with an exasperated flail of her hands. "The man responsible for the deaths of millions of people and the collapse of society?"

Scoffing, he ran a hand through his hair. "Of course, he's a fucking tyrant, but why—"

"She was my father's heir and he wanted Albright Industries. Owning his own CDMO was the next logical step in getting his nefarious drugs to market. The government would never let him purchase one, but if the board gave their approval, he would inherit my father's company upon his heirs' deaths. Namely, mine and Raquel's."

"But George Luddington would've stopped him, right?"

Sighing, Grace shook her head. "He would've tried, but Luthor was quickly becoming the most powerful man in the world when Dad died. The other board members would've wanted his approval, and they would've voted to give him control of Albright Industries."

"So you lied to me for ten fucking years?"

"I did the only thing I could," she exclaimed. "I enlisted Maria, who was our NICU nurse, to help fake our daughter's death. I was still very weak, so George helped me too. They were able to secretly transport Raquel out of the NICU late at night in a special chamber. Maria brought her to a clinic in Scranton, and George paid handsomely for a private room under an alias.

"Before they transferred Raquel, Maria brought a body up from the morgue to replace her in the NICU." Gripping her chin, Grace recounted the terrible memories. "I wasn't able to help transport her because I was terribly incapacitated, but by some miracle, they pulled it off."

Tristan planted his hands on his hips, angrily tapping his foot as he digested the horrific story. "So, you lied to me about losing your uterus?"

"What? No. Of course not. Why would I lie about that?"

He elicited a frustrated laugh. "Excuse me if I'm having trouble discerning truth in all the lies, Grace. Jesus Christ. You looked me in the eye when I returned from deployment and told me she died." Closing the distance between them, he gripped her arms and shook her. "You told me you couldn't forgive me and wanted a divorce!"

A sob leapt from her throat as remorse clouded her features. "I didn't see any other way. I had no idea when you would be home. I couldn't get in touch with you, and you told me they could extend your deployment—"

"I told you that was unlikely."

"How was I to know? It was a black ops mission and you were unreachable." Sighing, she shook her head. "It's so easy to see my mistakes now, but I was despondent and heartbroken, and I made decisions under intense pressure to protect myself. To protect *her*." She pointed toward the cabin.

Tristan searched her eyes for any hint of malice, but all he saw was deep regret and pain.

A puff of air escaped his throat as he shook his head. "Fuck, Grace," he said, loosening his grip on her arms. "What a goddamn mess."

"I had days in that hospital to plan my revenge," she said, frowning as she recalled the past. "My father had been murdered before my eyes. My child had been born prematurely, and I'd lost my ability to ever have another one. I was a target, along with my baby daughter. The man I loved more than anyone in the world wasn't there to fight with me, and I had to take matters into my own hands."

"Don't do that," he said, dropping her arms and recoiling. "Don't say you loved me when you kept this from me. When you kept *her* from me." He angrily jabbed his finger at the cottage.

"Saying it or not saying it doesn't make it less true." She sliced her hand through the air when he opened his mouth to argue. "But I won't say it again. I understand you must hate me. But our daughter is safe, and no one but you, me, George and Maria know she's alive. And it's going to stay that way until we defeat Luthor."

Tristan studied her, unable to reconcile the shocking twist of events. Opting for a brief moment of reprieve from the argument, he said, "And Nathan."

"What?"

"Nathan knows she's alive too. Somehow, we went from childless people to having two kids to take care of in twenty-four hours."

Her lips formed a heartbreaking smile as she nodded. "And Nathan. Your latest attempt to save someone. It's very noble." Stepping forward, she lifted her face to his. "*You're* very noble, Tristan. I know you try to play both sides of the fence; to be the morally gray mercenary. But I've always known who you are deep inside. You deserved to know she was alive, and I knew I couldn't tell you if I wanted her to live." Swallowing, she whispered, "I'm so sorry."

Tristan rubbed the back of his neck, uncomfortable at the genuineness in her tone. "She called you Grace. Why didn't she call you Mom?"

"Because she doesn't know I'm her mother," she said, squeezing her eyes shut at the painful admission. "She would never have been safe if she'd known. Kids let things slip too easily."

"Unlike their dishonest mothers," he droned, arching an acerbic brow.

Her eyes snapped open. "I told you. I was committed to my plan. Marry Luthor, observe his immoral business practices, and blow the whistle so he'd go to jail. Unfortunately, that plan failed and I wasn't able to prevent him from destroying the world." She lifted her finger. "But I eventually regrouped and began to plot the rebellion, and it took me *years*, Tristan. Years where that little girl was raised to believe her parents died after she was born, and that Maria was their family friend who took her in."

Glancing toward the house, she exhaled a defeated sigh. "Years where I visited her sporadically and claimed to be a friend of her dead parents. I visited her every so often to make sure she was okay, and to ensure she knew me in some capacity. It was difficult to do so without Luthor knowing, but I pulled it off."

An owl hooted in the distant trees, and Grace rubbed her arms to ward off the chill.

"I don't even know how to process this," Tristan said, anchoring his fist on his hip.

"Solomon has been mentioning Dundore in recent conversations, which means Raquel isn't safe here. We'll take her with us to Arthur's compound, where she'll be protected while we continue the rebellion. After we defeat Luthor, we can tell her we're her parents."

"And then what?" he asked, lifting his hands.

"And then, we'll see if you can forgive me. If you can't, I'll accept that and we'll figure out a way to co-parent where you'll never have to see me."

"Or I could just take her and you'll never see her again," he said, the anger rising again. "I was a special ops soldier. If I want to disappear with her, I can make it happen."

Her gaze lowered to the grass, her shoulders hunching with defeat. "You won't need to do that. If you truly don't want me to see her, I won't fight you." Her chin wobbled. "I hope it doesn't come to that, but I'm so tired of fighting, Tristan. Once we defeat Luthor, I just want peace. So, you do whatever the hell makes you happy. I won't stand in your way."

Longing surged deep in his gut, and he took a moment to acknowledge the truth: He didn't want to fight with her either. If he were honest, what he truly wanted was to marry her all over again and try like hell to live the life they were meant to live before they'd both made disastrous decisions.

In the deepest corners of his heart, he wanted to raise their daughter together and create the life they both deserved.

And yet another part of him wanted to punish Grace. Wanted to deny her any right to see Raquel as he'd been denied all these years. That vengeful part of his soul warred with the hopeful side, and he had no fucking idea which one would ultimately win out.

"You couldn't bring yourself to tell me our daughter was alive when I was literally inside you this morning? Who the fuck lies to someone like that, Grace?"

She grimaced. "Don't be crass. I've wanted to tell you every time I saw you for years. That's why I was distant and did my best to avoid you. Laying the foundation for a rebellion against an evil dictator isn't easy. I had to stay focused, and you're the one person on the planet who destroys my focus."

Tristan scrubbed a hand over his face before hanging his head. "Fine. We'll wait to tell her we're her parents until we defeat Luthor." Stepping closer, he jabbed his finger as he spoke. "But you listen to me, Grace. I won't tolerate any more lies. If there's anything else I need to know, tell me now."

"That's it, I swear," she said, honest conviction in her eyes as they darted between his. "And I know you might not ever forgive me, but I can't have your anger changing the way you treat me in front of our team. I need to project strength, so I hope you'll keep your ire private." Her lips formed a heartbreaking smile. "When we're alone, you can take your anger out on me. But in front of our men, I can't allow it."

Cursing his traitorous heart, he acknowledged the desire to comfort her vastly outweighed his anger. Yes, he was furious at the secret she'd kept for so long. But staring at her in the moonlight, reminiscent of the night they met so long ago, all he truly wanted was to pull her into his arms and soothe her.

Even after her vicious betrayal, he longed to confirm she was okay. It was stark confirmation that he still loved her deep within and always would.

But pride was a bitch, and it was pride that held him back from embracing her. Backing away, he gave a curt nod. "Okay. The team won't know." Glancing toward the house, he grinded his teeth in frustration. "Is that place big enough for us to sleep?"

"Maria and Raquel can sleep in the bed. There's a sofa and loveseat, so you and Nathan can have those. I'll offer to sleep on the floor, but Maria and Raquel will probably let me in the bed too. It's a king, so I think we'll all fit. We should leave for Cumberland at four a.m. It will take about three hours to get there, so we'll arrive around dawn."

Exhausted, Tristan nodded and walked toward the house, wanting to be done with the conversation. He needed time to process and had so many questions about his daughter.

Was she happy? What were her favorite things? What were her dreams?

"There will be time to get to know her," Grace said softly, following behind him. "She's an amazing little girl."

Tristan squeezed his hand on the cottage doorknob, wondering if he might crush it from the weight of his fury. *Ten years.* The two words repeated over and over in his mind. He'd lost ten years with his daughter.

Filled with regret and rage, he walked inside, inhaling the fragrant aroma of simmering stew. Allowing himself to compartmentalize, he acknowledged his growling stomach and sat down at Maria's small table to have dinner.

Chapter 20

T ristan inhaled the stew, sating his voracious hunger as Raquel and Nathan sat on either side of him. He'd pretty much been rendered speechless by the news that the hushed conversations referencing Dundore had actually been about his *daughter*. Raquel had no trouble filling the silence, and she chatted away while the five of them sat at the tattered wooden table.

"Did you go to school in Scranton?" Raquel asked.

"I went before my parents died," Nathan mumbled as he finished the last spoonful of stew. "But after they put up the wall, we didn't have school anymore."

"I can study with you if you want," she said, looking at Maria. "I'm at a seventh-grade level for reading and math, right?"

"Yes, dear," Maria said, patting her hand. "Raquel spends several hours each day on her studies, and she's blazing through the textbooks Grace brought during her last visit."

"That's fantastic, sweetheart," Grace said, pride glowing in her eyes as she smiled at Raquel.

"Did you bring more books this time?"

Grace shook her head. "I had to leave my home very suddenly, so I couldn't bring any supplies. I've tried to keep you stocked up here, but you might be too fast for me to keep up with."

Raquel beamed, and something in Tristan's heart cracked wide open. Her cheeks glowed in the same way Grace's did when she was happy or excited about something. Their resemblance was uncanny.

"I can share my textbooks with you," Raquel said to Nathan. "We can study together at the Cumberland compound."

Nathan shot her a wary glance. "I'm going to spy for Tristan. I might not have time for schoolwork."

"You're a great spy, buddy," Tristan said, grinning, "but when we go to DC to fight for the rebellion, you'll have plenty of free time on Arthur's compound. You can study with Raquel. It wouldn't hurt for you to resume your schooling."

"Whatever," Nathan muttered. "It won't matter anyway if you're leaving."

"Hey," Tristan said, cupping his shoulder. "I'm leaving to fight for the cause. But when we win, I'm coming back and you're stuck with me, kid. We bartered a lot of weapons to Solomon in exchange for your surveillance skills, and I need you."

In truth, Tristan needed a ten-year-old kid with a chip on his shoulder about as much as he needed to lose a limb, but he liked Nathan and wouldn't abandon him as his parents had.

Relief shone in Nathan's eyes above that smattering of freckles.

"And how about you, Maria?" Tristan asked, pushing the empty bowl away as he leaned back in his chair. "Are you coming with us to Cumberland?"

"I recently turned sixty-eight and don't move as well as I used to," she replied, shaking her head. "I'm comfortable in this little cabin and don't want to leave. I always told Raquel that I'd grow too old one day to take care of her, and that Grace would be the one to take the reins. I'm sad that day has come, but I trust Grace to take care of my Raquel." She patted Grace's arm before encircling her wrist and squeezing.

Tristan observed the gesture as he noted Maria's slight Spanish accent. She had long dark hair with several gray streaks and deep brown eyes, and he found himself wondering what her story was. Perhaps he would hear it one day—the backstory of the kind woman who'd raised his daughter. Although he was seething at Grace's secret, he couldn't deny the woman was very nurturing and compassionate.

"Maybe you two can take care of these kids together," she continued, her almond-shaped eyes sparkling as she addressed Tristan. "Combining forces is easier than going it alone."

Tristan remained silent since he'd much rather scream at his ex-wife at the moment than discuss raising multiple children with her.

"Maria says you'll be able to give me even more books when I live with you, Grace," Raquel said, her eyebrows lifting. "That's really cool, but I'll miss the cabin. We can come and visit, right?"

"You'd better," Maria said. "I'd miss you too much if you didn't."

Raquel smiled before breaking into a yawn.

"Well, I think it's time for bed," Maria said. "Grace, you can crawl in with me and Raquel."

"Are you sure? I don't want to crowd you."

"I'll get everything ready," Raquel said with excitement. "We still have running water in the bathroom next to our room from the well and plumbing you had installed, Grace. Everyone can use it to brush their teeth."

"Thank you, sweetheart," Grace said. "Why don't you and Nathan go ahead and brush first. Do you have an extra toothbrush for him?"

"We have extras. Come on, Nathan. I'll show you."

The kids headed to the bathroom that adjoined the master bedroom, leaving the adults at the table.

"You've done such a wonderful job with her, Maria," Grace said, her eyes shining with emotion. "Are you sure you won't come with us?"

"This old lady needs to rest," she said, relaxing in her seat. "I'll miss that little girl something fierce, but it's time you save the world and raise her like you were meant to."

Lifting her gaze to Tristan's, Maria harumphed. "So, I guess you're mad as a hornet at Grace. I don't blame you, young man, but I hope you understand she made hard choices to protect Raquel."

Tristan's eyes narrowed. "I appreciate you taking care of Raquel, but you're part of the deception, so forgive me if I'm not up for a fireside chat about choices."

"Ohhh, you've got firecracker there," Maria said, rising and patting Grace's shoulder. "So growly and angry. He'll come around, dear. Maybe show a bit more of this." She placed her finger on the V of her shirt and tugged to show the curve of her breasts. "And remind him how strong and manly he is. Men love hearing that."

Tristan scowled, thoroughly unamused.

Maria's face softened as she gripped the back of her chair. "And then remind him that he's your *querido* and that you never stopped loving him. That should help as well. Good night."

She sauntered into the bedroom, leaving him alone with Grace.

"What does *querido* mean?"

Grace formed a sad smile and stood. Trailing to stand beside him, she slid her hand under his jaw. "It means 'sweetheart,'" she said softly. Leaning down, she pressed a tender kiss to his head. "Good night, Tristan."

His cheeks puffed as he released a slow breath. All these years and the woman still tied his stomach in knots. As she sashayed to the bedroom, he watched the sway of her ass, still craving her even after her treachery.

Thoroughly done with the events of the day, he marched to the couch and tore off his boots. Lying back on the soft cushions, he threw his arm over his eyes and prayed tomorrow would hold no more secrets.

Tristan awoke and stared into a pair of eyes that mirrored his own. Blinking slowly, he waited for Raquel to come into focus in the dim light.

"It's four a.m.," Raquel whispered, looking over to where Nathan was still sleeping. "Grace said to wake you up because we're already late."

Stretching his legs atop the faded couch, he nodded. "Can I get one of those extra toothbrushes you have lying around?"

She smiled, and Tristan noticed she was missing her canine on her right side.

"I want to make sure I don't lose my teeth like you did," he teased.

"I'm *supposed* to lose my teeth so my adult teeth can grow in."

He squinted one eye and contemplated. "That *sounds* like a valid excuse…"

Opening her mouth, she tugged on her other canine. "I'm going to lose this one soon. Maybe you'll see it fall out when we reach Cumberland."

"My dad used to tie a string to my loose teeth and wrap it around the door before slamming it shut. That yanked them out real fast."

Raquel's features squished. "Ew."

Laughing, he sat up and mussed his hair, trying to straighten it out since it was tousled from the scratchy couch pillow. "It's not so bad. If that one doesn't fall out soon, we can try it."

"Okay. I'll leave a toothbrush on the bathroom counter for you."

She headed back into the bedroom, passing Grace, who was leaning against the doorframe. Her arms were crossed as she gazed at him with reverence.

Striding toward her, he waited until they were so close their bodies almost grazed. Staring down into her eyes, he said, "Don't do that."

"Do what?" she asked, her voice breathless as the pulse in her neck fluttered.

"Don't look at me with those gorgeous, traitorous eyes while I'm talking to our daughter." His tone was ominous as he lightly gripped her chin. "I'm still fucking furious at you."

Her throat bobbed as she searched his eyes. "I know. But I couldn't help watching you with her. It's sweet—"

"Save it," he interjected, unwilling to soften—for the moment at least. He'd slept well on the lumpy couch, but there hadn't been nearly enough time to process everything that had happened in such a short time. "I'm not interested in your opinions on my interactions with her, Grace. So just fucking save it."

Yanking her chin from his hand, her eyes flashed with fire. "I know you're pissed at me, and you have a right to be, but you can go fuck yourself if you think I'm going to allow you to treat me like shit."

Sighing, he rubbed the back of his neck. Hell, he was barely awake and he'd never been a morning person. Anger had gotten the best of him, and he'd lashed out at her.

"I need coffee," he mumbled, shaking his head to rid it of the haze of sleep. "Does Maria have any?"

Her features softened ever so slightly. "You always were a bear in the morning. Yes, I'll make coffee while you use the restroom and get ready. We can take it with us on the drive."

"Make it strong," he said with a nod before trailing to the bathroom. Maria was helping Raquel stuff clothes into her backpack from the dresser at the foot of the bed. Stepping into the bathroom, he noticed the toothbrush Raquel had laid out for him on the counter.

Gazing into his reflection, he told himself to get his shit together and focus on the rebellion. Being mad at Grace was justified, but it wouldn't accomplish anything.

But if they didn't win the rebellion, it wouldn't matter whether Raquel was alive or not. The world would continue down its path of death and destruction, and she would have no future at all.

For the good of his daughter, he vowed to tuck away the anger and focus on saving the world. After that, he could figure out what to do with his treacherous wife—the woman who consumed his every thought.

Chapter 21

Luthor Cromwell sneered at the wounded man on his couch. Tom had shown up an hour ago, severely injured from a gunshot to his shoulder. He'd driven his car on rims for ten miles before locating an abandoned one he could hotwire—one that actually had air in the tires.

Now, he was sitting on Luthor's pristine leather couch in his penthouse office, and Luthor found himself more concerned about the leather than the man.

"Tell me again," Luthor said, crossing his arms as he paced. "Grace was in the truck with Tristan?"

"It was dark, but I'm sure I saw her, sir. Zayne was nowhere in sight."

Rubbing his chin, Luthor contemplated. "So...this can only mean one thing. My wife is a part of the rebellion. She must be working with Zayne."

"I believe they're all heading to Arthur Reyes's compound," Tom said. "They most likely took different routes so they wouldn't be ambushed together. Tristan was following a path along the Susquehanna River, and the bed of his truck was loaded with weapons."

"Interesting." Walking to the high glass windows, Luthor peered out, clenching his teeth to keep his seething anger from surfacing. Unable to control it, he strode to the cart that held his expensive liquor and grabbed a glass. Heaving it, he shattered it against the wall. Striving to regain his composure, he tugged his suit jacket before turning to face the room.

"It's futile to attack Arthur's compound again," Luthor said, addressing Colonel McGrath and Dr. Ziegler as other members of his team stood still, their eyes wide at his enraged actions. "If they want a war, they can come to us. The DC Sen City is my fortress, and I'm prepared to face them here. How are the two hundred men we injected with the super-serum doing?"

Dr. Ziegler cleared his throat, and Luthor's nostrils flared at the nervous gesture. If the man weren't so intelligent, he would've exiled him from the city long ago. He missed working with Danica Lawson, who was the most brilliant and dedicated scientist he'd ever known. Unfortunately, she wasn't on board with his methods, which was absurd. Yet another person who couldn't see the big picture.

"Seven of the men have died, sir, but the rest are doing well. Their muscle mass is increasing as the serum releases in their system. The injection will slow-release for three months and then they will need another round."

Luthor could tell by their expressions that some of his security team were appalled that seven men had died from the serum. Of course, they couldn't understand that sacrifice led to ultimate gain. One had to make hard choices to create a world that would thrive.

"Excellent. Colonel McGrath, make sure the injected soldiers are ready to protect the outer rim of the city. If they're stockpiling weapons, it's only a matter of time before Arthur and Zayne combine forces and attack us. The soldiers who received the serum will meet them outside the city, and I doubt the rebellion militia will be able to fight them effectively. If they do make it into the city, we'll have the regular battalions ready."

"Yes, sir," Colonel McGrath replied.

"And as for you," Luthor said, approaching Tom as he winced on the couch, holding his arm. "Get out of my office and come back when you can do the job without getting injured. I don't have time for subpar performance."

"I did my best, Mr. Cromwell—"

Luthor sneered and rested his hand on the holster that held his gun. "I'd suggest you follow my orders, Tom, or it's not going to work out well for you."

Tom rose swiftly and exited the room.

Turning to his men, Luthor lifted his chin and spoke with confidence. "I won't accept failure. I should've killed Anthony Martinez when he returned with his tail between his legs, but I let him live at your insistence that his death would impact morale for the troops." He gestured toward the door. "Tom barely escaped death due to his incompetence. Let this be a reminder that I am benevolent, but I also want results. Are we clear?"

"Yes, sir!" the men echoed, and Luthor flicked his hand, urging them to leave.

Once he was alone, Luthor sat at his large mahogany desk. Resting his elbows on the table, he steepled his fingers and recalled the day Grace asked him to marry her.

"I have a proposal for you," she said, her skin still so pale from her recent health trauma. "Tristan and I are over. I won't ever forgive him for not being here when I lost the baby. I know you wish to take over Albright Industries, and as the new owner of the company, I can make that happen."

Luthor had been shocked. He'd thought her and Tristan madly in love, even if the man was gutter trash far beneath her station.

"I want to propose a marriage between us," Grace said. "I'll give you the company in exchange for your protection. We'll present a united front to the world." Lowering her gaze, she rubbed her hands over her sides in a nervous gesture. "After the trauma of losing my uterus, I'm no longer interested in...sexual relationships. Our marriage will be platonic, and you can have as many women on the side as you like. All I ask is that you're discreet."

At the time, Luthor had thought it the perfect plan. Grace was wounded and wanted protection. He would gain control of Albright Industries, allowing him to get his drugs to market faster and with much less red tape. And the little chit didn't want him to fuck her, which was a relief since he found her bland and boring.

Now, sitting at the helm of the once-great empire he created, he tapped his fingers against his lips as he contemplated.

Several years into his marriage with Grace, someone had blown the whistle on the clinical trial data he'd been falsifying to the FDA for years. It was the catalyst that had caused the US government to investigate him and what drove him to ultimately take down the government and create his own. One that wouldn't stifle his plans with red tape and investigations.

Luthor had never discovered who blew the whistle, but he figured it was someone who worked at Sendaxa. Had it actually been Grace? Had she been deceiving him the entire time they were married?

Recalling their interactions since he walled off the city and took power, he remembered how much Grace lurked in shadowed corners when he had important meetings. She was always interrupting to place a kiss on his cheek and ask what he wanted for dinner...and then she would linger and pour a drink while he carried on his business.

He'd never suspected the little bitch could deceive him.

But now, as realization washed over him, he recognized that underestimating his wife had been a grave mistake.

Grace had been gathering intel all along.

Roaring with fury, Luthor slammed his hand on the desk.

His wife had been plotting against him for years, and he'd let her into his inner circle, right under his nose.

Standing, Luthor trudged back and forth over the soft carpet. She must've seen him kill Robert all those years ago. He'd always suspected she had, but she'd never admitted it.

"Of course she didn't, you fool!" he hissed. "How could I have overlooked this? Goddamnit!"

Resting his palms on the desk, he blinked rapidly as he accepted the truth.

Grace Albright, his wife and the woman he'd never known at all, was spearheading the rebellion.

Somehow, she'd stockpiled a ton of weapons and was aligning with Arthur Reyes to bring down his empire.

"Well done, my dear," Luthor said, his tone menacing as he clenched his jaw. "All these years, you've secured access to me and tried to bring me down."

Stalking to the bar cart, he poured two fingers of scotch and lifted his glass in a salute. "To you, my duplicitous bitch of a wife," he said, then chugged the drink and relished the burn. "I can't wait to murder you like I did your father. May you drown in your own fucking blood."

Seething with rage, Luthor poured one last shot before he returned to the task of saving the world he'd created in his image.

Chapter 22

Tristan observed the Cumberland compound come into view shortly after dawn. Raquel sat on Grace's lap while Nathan was sandwiched in the middle. Once they were parked in front of the imposing compound wall, Tristan ordered them to stay in the truck while he approached the front doors.

He walked forward and the large doors swung open. Two men stepped outside, each armed with rifles.

"Please ask your companions to exit the truck, sir," one said, and Tristan waved for everyone to join him.

They were instructed to line up and lift their arms. The two men did an efficient frisk as Tristan frowned.

"Do you really need to frisk the kids?"

One of the guards pulled Nathan's Swiss army knife from his sock and held it high. "It would seem so," he said, cocking a brow.

Tristan couldn't argue with him there, so he remained silent.

Once they'd confiscated Tristan and Grace's handguns, one of the guards banged his fist on the compound door. It swung open again to reveal Arthur Reyes on the other side.

"Tristan," he said, extending his hand. "It's nice to finally meet you in person. Come inside the walls. It's not safe out here."

They all entered the compound, one of the guards driving Tristan's truck inside before locking the gate behind them.

"And you must be Grace Cromwell," Arthur said, shaking her hand. "I must say, you've surprised us all. Your team arrived last night and their armaments are impressive. Well done, ma'am." He saluted her. "I'm grateful and indebted to you."

"I'm glad we've finally reached this point," she said, smiling. "With my weapons, your militia, and Danica Lawson's antidote, we might just win this thing."

"We have no choice, so we'd better," Arthur said. "It's time for your husband's reign to end." Crouching down, he smiled at Nathan and Raquel. "And who do we have here?"

They introduced themselves and Arthur stood, his eyes narrowing on Grace. "Is she your—?"

"She's the daughter of family friends who have long passed," Grace interjected. "It's a boring story I'll be happy to tell you in private."

"Not that boring," Tristan droned, scowling. "But a private conversation is certainly best."

"We've prepared some rooms for you in the old sixth grade ward of the school that Danica, Maverick, Arianna, and Dominic are staying in. My men put some beds in there, and there's running water in the boys' bathroom."

"Ah, heaven," Grace said with a smile. "Thank you, Arthur. We'd like to freshen up and then we need to meet with you, Danica, and the others."

"I've already set a meeting for ten a.m. The children can play with Chris, Jenny and their crew while we talk. They have a wiffle ball game set for ten as well." Leaning down, he rested his hands on his knees. "Do you two like wiffle ball?"

"Never played," Nathan murmured, his eyes downcast.

"Me neither, but I can try," Raquel chimed in.

"Good." Arthur patted them both on the shoulders. "Chris and Jenny are great kids and will be happy to show you the ropes. Go ahead and follow Mike to the school in the truck. Once you arrive, he'll drive the truck to unload the weapons."

"Are you already confiscating our ride?" Grace asked, lifting an eyebrow.

"My compound, my rules," he said, showing his palms. "But I assure you, you're still the rebellion leader. I don't want a power war here, Grace. We can lead our teams together. It will only make them stronger."

"I agree."

Arthur smiled and gestured toward the truck. "Go ahead and get settled in. You'll probably run into Danica or the others at the school. We'll meet in the old home economics room at ten."

Tristan slid back behind the wheel as the others climbed inside. Mike took off in his car, and Tristan followed him to the school, ready to see Danica Lawson again.

Hope welled in his heart that she'd truly created a cure. If so, a brighter future was possibly on the way for Jessica and countless others.

They had obstacles ahead, but for the first time in so long, Tristan could feel the tide beginning to turn, ever so slightly. Gripping the wheel, he hoped his fledgling optimism wasn't misplaced. Vowing to ensure it wasn't, he prepared for the next phase of the rebellion.

Dr. Danica Lawson-Ward lifted two vials, the contents milky as she stood in front of their unified team.

"The EverLife cure has proven effective on everyone in the compound." She shook the vial in her right hand. "The workers Arthur assigned to me have helped me create three hundred vials. That's all I can produce until I get access to a factory."

Arthur nodded from his seat at the circular table. He was flanked by Arianna, Dominic, and Maverick to his left, and Grace and Tristan to his right as Danica stood before them. "The first factory we'll take over is Luthor's EverLife factory inside the DC Sen City's walls."

"He's not going to just let us in the front door, so he'll need to be dead for that to happen," Arianna said acerbically.

"That's the plan," Tristan said. "I can't wait to wipe that bastard off the planet."

"I think we're all in agreement the world will be a better place without him here," Dani said diplomatically. She shook the vial in her left hand. "This vial holds the super-soldier antidote. Thanks to the stash that Ari stole, I was able to discern what's in Luthor's serum and create something that will dull the effects."

"That's my woman," Dominic said, cupping her shoulder.

"I'm not anyone's woman," Arianna muttered, brushing his hand away. Dominic grinned, and Tristan felt his lips twitch. Those two were damn near perfect for each other. Dom knew exactly how to handle her mulish demeanor, and he honestly seemed to revel in it.

Glancing at Grace, his eyes skated over her profile as she listened to Dani. Had they ever been a perfect fit? They'd certainly been tethered together by an undeniable chemistry and had fallen deeply in love. But there was so much betrayal and heartbreak between them. Could they truly ever recover?

"I've prepared three hundred vials of this as well," Danica said, lifting a dart gun. "The militia will be armed with dart guns and our minimal supply. It's imperative they shoot Luthor's soldiers in the neck for full effect. I know gaining this type of proximity to soldiers injected with strength serum is difficult, but it's necessary. It's possible the soldiers might also go into cardiac arrest shortly after injection. Just preparing you if you see them collapse during battle."

"My wife, the badass scientist," Maverick said, glowing with pride.

"It takes a village, and I appreciate all the people you've assigned to help me with this project, Arthur. I've done my best. Now it's time for you all to kick ass."

"Let's go over the plan again," Arianna said, straightening in her chair. "Dom and I will go to DC first since we did a pretty good job sneaking in last time." She flashed a smile his way.

"I've been connecting with my tech whiz, Bodie, on a secret radio channel while I searched for Grace," Tristan said. "I can instruct him to loop the cameras at the same spot. The guards were most likely embarrassed they were ambushed, so I would guess they stayed quiet. No one wants to fail in Luthor's regime."

"That's helpful," Arianna said. "And maybe he can keep an eye out if that spot is compromised and direct us to another one."

"He can," Tristan confirmed. "I'll make sure to hop on the frequency we use before you two leave so you can communicate with him directly."

"We're going to surveil the soldiers who've been injected with the serum as they train," Dominic continued. "I want to see if we can identify any weaknesses. We're hoping Deandra can give us their training location. She's a master at overhearing Luthor's soldiers' conversations in her deli."

"Zayne, our team and I have spent years cultivating the seeds of rebellion in the city," Grace said. "If you see anyone who has an X drawn on their wrist, it means they're sympathetic to the rebellion."

"How many sympathizers do you think live in the city?" Arianna asked.

"Can't say for sure, but there's lots of dissention in the tent cities amongst the addicts. Recently, Zayne and I have noticed more graffiti and signs of unrest like bonfires popping up in the more safe and affluent places too. It's probably why Luthor sent a battalion here several weeks ago. He feels his power slipping."

"Good," Arianna said. "I hope he enjoys the last tastes of power, because we're going to douse it."

Leaning forward, Dominic rested his forearms on the table. "We'll continue to communicate with you on the secret radio channel, Arthur. We're going to head to the city tonight, and you and Maverick will lead the militia to the city in two days and arrive after sunset."

"Correct," Arthur said with a nod. "I want to train everyone on the dart guns and the new artillery before we attack. Maverick has agreed to help me, although the soldiers will miss taking orders from you, Arianna. You've whipped them into shape, and they're more loyal to you than anyone at this point."

"I look forward to helping lead when we reconvene in DC," she said with a salute. "We'll try and stay in the same hotel as long as we can bribe Devon again. We need two gold bars—one for a room and one for his silence."

Arthur pointed toward the door. "Mike is setting aside weapons and gold for you to take with you. Please be safe. We need you to win this war, Arianna. And you too, Dominic."

"Yeah, he comes in handy sometimes," Arianna teased, patting his arm as he scowled.

"Tristan, I'd love your help training the militia on the weapons too. We're fortunate to have a special ops soldier in our ranks."

"No problem," Tristan said. "I think Grace should stay here with the women and children to protect the compound while we attack—"

Grace cleared her throat and shot him a withering glare. "While we appreciate your thoughts, Tristan," she interjected, "I'm the leader of the rebellion and will join my men in battle."

Facing her, he frowned. "You're not a soldier. I don't want you to get hurt."

"That's not your decision. And I would argue I'm the stealthiest soldier of all. My planning and steadfastness led us here. I've surreptitiously stockpiled weapons for years and recruited trustworthy soldiers who can fight with us. I've sowed the seeds of uprising in the city, and I *will* be on the battlefield with you all."

Anger and fear collided in his gut as he regarded her stubborn expression. It was ridiculous for her to fight since she wasn't a skilled soldier, but neither were many of the men and women in Arthur's militia. They were just citizens of a broken world who wanted to fight for a better future. Although he was terrified for her to get hurt—or die—he couldn't deny she'd earned her chance to fight too.

"I want to do some extra training with you," he said, crossing his arms, his tone growing more serious. "If you're going to put yourself in danger, you need to be as prepared as possible."

"Fine. We'll carve out some time this afternoon and to-morrow morning."

"Fine," he said, clenching his jaw.

"*Awkwarrrrrrd*," Arianna chimed, grimacing before she stood. "You two going to be able to stay united with all that weird tension between you? If you want some advice, you should probably just bang it out. That helped me when this one was driving me crazy." She jerked her thumb at Dominic.

Dominic stood and nipped her thumb. "Let's not dispense romantic advice, sweetheart. We've got our hands full with our own shit."

Blinking rapidly, she formed a sarcastic smile. "Call me sweetheart again in public and you're really going to have some shit to deal with."

Dominic rolled his eyes and playfully scrunched his features at her. "I told Chris we'd stop by the wiffle ball game before they're done. Come on." Encircling her wrist, he tugged her toward the door.

"I think the plan is set," Arthur said, rising, "but I'll be available for any last-minute questions."

Maverick approached Dani and plopped a kiss on her cheek. "I was totally checking you out while you were schooling us on antidotes, Dr. Lawson-Ward." He waggled his eyebrows. "I think I need some private lessons."

"Mav," she said, biting her lip. "We just welcomed Tristan and Grace onto the compound. Can you wait a few more minutes before we dive into our weird flirting ritual? I need them to think I'm a serious scientist."

Tristan rose from his chair and walked toward the two vials. Lifting the EverLife cure, he studied it with wonder. "My sister is addicted to EverLife," he said solemnly. "I can't thank you enough for creating this, Dani. Sorry I fucked up your break-in at the lab, but I had a plan and it ended with us standing right here. Thank you for giving me hope."

"You're lucky I can only remember about half of everything that happens," she teased. "I think I was probably pissed at you in the lab, but I appreciate you sheltering my sister in DC. I wish her life hadn't ended so tragically. Hopefully, I can ensure your sister's won't."

"That's very kind. I hope we can save her too."

"Let's go watch some kids crush a wiffle ball, slugger," Maverick said, extending his hand. Dani picked up the two vials and they exited the room, leaving him and Grace alone.

"I'm so happy there's a cure for Jessica," Grace said, gliding over to stand beside Tristan. "And while we're here, I wanted to suggest something to you."

Tristan lifted his eyebrows.

"I think it would be nice if you spent some time with Raquel. Dani told me there's a large pond behind the school and it has a nice walking trail around it. You two could take a walk and get to know each other a bit."

Resting his hip against the table, he smiled. "I'd like that. Did she tell you about her loose tooth?"

Grace nodded. "She's so cute when she talks about it."

Aching to touch her, he held himself back. "She looks just like you," he whispered.

"But with your eyes." Lifting her hand, she traced a finger under the curve of his eye.

Tristan grabbed her hand, holding it immobile as they stood frozen.

Her lips parted, and his gaze lowered to her wet tongue, slightly visible beneath those pretty pink lips.

"Even when I hate you, I want every piece of you," he whispered. "It's maddening."

Sadness overtook her expression. "I hope you can learn not to hate me one day," she said softly, her eyes darting between his.

"We'll see," he murmured, releasing her hand. "And I'll take Raquel for a walk along the pond after lunch." Scratching his head, he squinted. "What the hell do I talk about with a ten-year-old girl? I'm a morally gray mercenary with zero redeeming qualities."

Breathing a laugh, she bit her lip. "I think you have lots of redeeming qualities. And just be yourself. She's a talker, so she'll lead the way." She patted his arm supportively. "If you'd like to train this afternoon, I'll take you up on it. Zayne showed me how to shoot a handgun, but I'd like to practice with a rifle."

"Okay. Let's plan on three o'clock. Maverick and Arthur will be training the troops on the field, but we can find a place nearby so I can focus on thoroughly teaching you. I want you to know the ins and outs of using a rifle so you don't hurt yourself."

"The woman you profess to hate?" she asked, arching an eyebrow.

"Regardless of your deception, I don't want you dead."

"Well, that's comforting," she sighed, backing away and rubbing her forehead. "Want to go catch the end of the wiffle ball game? We can see how Raquel and Nathan are getting along with the other kids."

"Sure."

He followed her from the room, yearning to draw her back and tell her his words were a lie. That he could never truly hate her.

As they walked to the baseball field, he remained silent, allowing his anger to stifle the sentiment. There would be time for reconciliation when they defeated Luthor.

For now, Tristan's main concern was keeping his ex-wife and daughter alive.

Focused on that goal, he mentally prepared for some alone time with his little girl.

Chapter 23

That afternoon, Tristan walked beside the pond with Raquel as she chatted away. She told him of her love for butterflies and her wish to have a puppy one day. She recounted growing up in Maria's cottage and how much she loved the kind woman.

"Maria seems like a good soul," Tristan said, thankful his daughter had been safe and sheltered all these years. "What type of puppy do you want?"

"Don't care," she said, shrugging. "As long as it likes to play. Maria always said I have too much energy, so I need a puppy who can keep up with me."

Chuckling, he gazed at the top of her golden head. "You're taking the news of leaving the cabin well. I know you'll miss her."

"She told me I'd have to leave one day and live with Grace. Once she got too old to take care of me and the dictator who rules the world is gone."

"Maria told you about Luthor Cromwell?"

"Yes. She said not to be scared because Grace and her friends would beat him one day." Staring up at him, she asked, "Are you and Grace boyfriend and girlfriend?"

"Why do you ask that?"

She grinned. "Because you look at her like she's the only person in the room."

"Grace and I used to be married," he said, figuring that was common knowledge and didn't need to be kept secret.

"You're not married anymore?"

"Nope. We couldn't make it work."

Raquel's soul seemed to shine in her eyes as she gazed up at him. "Why? Grace is awesome, and she's pretty too. Maybe you should ask her to marry you again."

"I'm not sure we'd make each other happy. We didn't do a good job of it before."

"You had to be happy *sometimes* to get married," she said, as if he were daft. "Otherwise, you never would have done it in the first place."

Tristan couldn't contain his grin. "I guess we were sometimes, especially in the beginning before things got hard. We did all sorts of fun stuff together."

"Like what?"

"We went to the garden by my house that had tons of butterflies, and we always laughed at how silly the world was. When she got her tattoo—"

Raquel gasped. "Grace has a tattoo?"

Shit. Was he supposed to keep that a secret?

"Yes, but I'm not sure I'm supposed to tell you that. Don't tell her, okay?"

"What does she have a tattoo of?"

"A dragon."

"That's so cool," Raquel whispered, her eyes wide. "I want a tattoo."

"Maybe one day," he said, smoothing his hand over her hair. "Let's beat Luthor first and have you grow up just a bit more."

They continued down the dirt trail before turning around and heading back toward the school.

"Grace is going to be okay, right? I heard her say she's going with you and the others to fight."

Crouching down, he held her upper arms and stared into her hazel eyes. "I'll always protect Grace and would give my life before I let her get hurt."

Raquel's lips formed a broad smile. "You love her."

"I do. Keep that secret too. You've got two secrets now," he said, holding up two fingers. "I'm trusting you."

"I won't say anything." She made an X over her heart, the gesture cementing a new, tentative bond between them.

Straightening, he held out his hand, and she slipped hers into it so naturally it caused something to shift in Tristan's soul.

Love washed over him as he tightened his grip and led his daughter back to the school.

Grace stood at the window in her makeshift room, watching Tristan lead Raquel back from the pond. He held her small hand in his, and Grace allowed the tears to well. God, they'd all missed so much time together. Guilt gnawed at her, and she pushed it away. She'd learned long ago that guilt was a vengeful, angry companion, and it wouldn't serve her. She'd made hard choices, and her daughter was alive because of them.

Sighing, Grace changed into the sweatpants and t-shirt Dani had loaned her. Apparently, they had lots of extra clothing in the clinic from people who'd passed away. They'd all been freshly washed and were used by those remaining on the compound.

Smoothing her hand over the soft shirt, she reveled in the small pleasure of being safe and comfortable, if only for a moment. For so long, she'd been a prisoner in a marriage where she was plotting revenge. Arthur's compound offered refuge, and she'd take joy in it until they left to continue the fight.

"To *end* the fight," she vowed.

"You talking to yourself?" Tristan's voice echoed from the doorway.

Turning, she smiled and nervously rubbed her arms. "Yep. Did you have a nice walk with Raquel?"

"I did. She loves butterflies as much as you. Oh," he said, lifting a finger, "and she wants a puppy."

Grace's eyebrows lifted. "Wow. That's a lot to deal with when we're trying to save the world."

"Seriously. I told her she'd have to wait a bit." Crossing his arms, he leaned against the doorframe. Grace's eyes roved over his lanky frame, and she licked the suddenly dry roof of her mouth. Maybe it was seeing him with their daughter; maybe it was how well he filled out his black tactical pants. Whatever it was, she was suddenly flushed and craving his lips on her skin again. Anywhere would do, but the lower the better.

Tristan's eyes lit with desire, and she could tell he sensed her attraction to him. Hell, she'd never truly been able to hide it, so why start now?

"I know we were going to do rifle practice in the woods by the pond," he continued, "but Maverick is giving a tutorial on all of the weapons to the militia in a few minutes on the training field. Why don't we attend that so you can learn about the arsenal? After dinner, we can practice by the pond."

"Will there be enough light?"

"For a while." He straightened and sauntered toward her, stopping until there were only inches between them. "You scared to be in the dark with me, empress?"

Her lips curled. "The opposite. I'm afraid I might do something reckless. Secluded woods by a pond? We have a pretty awesome track record in that scenario."

Lust flared in his eyes as he emitted a soft growl. "Skinny dipping in the lake by my old apartment was definitely one of our favorite nighttime activities."

"Are we too old to skinny dip? I haven't done that since I did it with you."

A reverent look crossed his features, and she tilted her head. "What is it?"

"Raquel was asking us if we were happy when we were married—"

"I guess that cat's out of the bag," she muttered.

"It's common knowledge, so I saw no reason to hide it from her."

Grace nodded, urging him to continue.

"She asked if we were happy, and I told her we had some good moments. Skinny dipping in the lake was definitely one of my favorites."

"Mine too," she whispered, her body straining toward him as she physically held herself back.

"If you learn how to use the rifle properly, maybe we can take a dip."

Grace arched a sultry eyebrow. "A reward for my hard work? I'm going to wield that rifle like a pro once you're done with me."

"Okay, G.I. Jane, take it easy," he teased, patting her shoulder. "I just want to make sure you know how to use it well enough that you don't blow someone's head off."

"Except Luthor's," she said, lifting a finger.

"By all means, if he's in your line of vision, blow the bastard's head off."

Grace tilted her head toward the next room where he was staying. "How's the room?"

"It's fine. Nathan and Raquel claimed the room on the other side." He pointed toward the hallway. "It has two cots and he gave her his extra blanket. He's a good kid."

"I'm happy they get along and think they complement each other nicely. She can bring him out of his shell a bit, and he's street smart. She needs more of that in her life. She was sheltered with Maria, but it was the only way to keep her safe."

"I'm glad she was sheltered," he admitted, even though he hated the deception around it. "I wouldn't have wanted her near the death and destruction we've seen over the past few years."

"Me neither."

They gazed at each other for another beat before Tristan turned and headed toward his room. "See you on the training field. If you want to walk together, I'll be ready in ten minutes."

She observed his broad shoulders retreat as anticipation welled deep within. Could he possibly lower that angry shield when they trained later? Intrigued by the challenge, she sat down to slide on her shoes and anticipated skinny dipping with her husband under a star-filled sky.

"*Ex-husband*, Grace," she scolded. "Sheesh."

Accepting that he would always be her one true husband deep in her heart, Grace tied her hair into a ponytail, ready to study the hell out of some fancy, but deadly, weapons.

Chapter 24

G race enjoyed Maverick's artillery lesson under the bright afternoon sun. He was thorough and patient as he moved through each of the different types of weapons that had been stockpiled by Grace and George over the years.

Arianna and Dominic helped as well, and by the end of the two-hour hands-on session, Grace felt their militia had a much better understanding of how to wield their powerful armaments.

"We've made a list of the sharpest shooters in the militia, and those soldiers will be on the front lines with the dart guns holding the serum that will immobilize the super-soldiers who've been injected," Maverick said, holding up a piece of paper. "We'll post this list in the cafeteria on Main Street where you all gather for meals. If your name is on it, please show up at sunrise tomorrow morning for an additional training on the dart guns."

"Yes, sir!" the soldiers responded.

Arianna stepped forward. "Dominic and I are leaving for DC tonight. We're going to surveil the city, and hopefully the soldiers, and try to pass along as much information to Arthur and Maverick before you all attack. Tomorrow will be your last training day, and you'll advance on DC in two days. We'll be there to meet you, and look forward to taking back the city."

Dominic gave a solemn nod of agreement as he stood beside her, feet planted in the short grass.

"You've all trained very hard and I'm honored to fight with you." Arianna saluted, and Grace's lips curved as the militia saluted her back. It was obvious the troops deeply respected her, and Grace was proud to have her, Dominic, Maverick and Danica on their side.

A small kernel of hope bloomed in her chest, and she had the stinging suspicion they just might win.

After the weapons tutorial, Grace and Tristan joined the others for dinner at the huge cafeteria on Main Street. It was an old restaurant that had been converted into a mess hall after the compound was sealed off and had rows of tables where everyone sat to enjoy the meals that Arthur's staff prepared.

"It's very altruistic to feed everyone," Grace said to Arthur as he sat beside her in the loud dining hall. "Solomon still makes the residents of his compound purchase or barter for food."

Arthur pursed his lips as he contemplated. "Solomon has a right to run his compound the way he sees fit, but hunger leads to dissention, and dissention leads to crime and addiction in my experience. Why not feed everyone and prevent that?"

"Spoken like a generous leader. I also assume it will be a great campaign message when you assume temporary leadership of the new government we create before running for office."

Smiling, Arthur studied her. "Do you not want to lead? After all, you sowed the seeds of rebellion for years and stockpiled the weapons that will make our attack possible."

"God, no. I just want peace, and there's no peace in politics. I'll certainly support your government and help you in any way I can, but I have no desire to lead."

"Maverick, Dani and the others have said the same thing. Perhaps I'm a masochist for wanting to take over the new government, but I truly feel I can help people."

"Then you're the perfect person to be our new president." She covered his hand. "I'll certainly campaign for you."

Chuckling, he tipped his head. "I'm counting on it."

After dinner, Grace and Tristan headed back to the school to make sure Raquel and Nathan were situated in their room before they headed to the pond to train.

"I can train with you guys if you want," Nathan said, a slight yearning in his eyes. "I'll have to learn to use a rifle eventually."

"I need you rested in case I need your surveillance skills on the fly," Tristan said, noticing the boy stifling a rather large yawn as he lowered onto his cot. "Maverick and Dani are in the old guidance counselor's office down the hall if you need anything. We'll be in the rooms next door when you wake up tomorrow."

"Have fun and don't fall in the pond," Raquel said from behind the book she'd propped on her chest as she lay on her cot.

They exited and Grace gestured down the hallway. "I just need to hit the restroom and we can head out."

"Me too. Be ready in ten."

As Grace washed her hands in the old boys' bathroom, she felt the anticipation building in every cell of her body. Tonight would be the first time she and Tristan were truly alone since he'd discovered Raquel was alive.

Although he planned to train her on using a rifle, there were other issues that needed to be addressed and hard conversations that needed to be had. Staring into her eyes in the reflection, she reminded herself to be open and honest. He deserved that, and she was done with all the deception and lies.

She hoped the next chapter of her life would finally embody the happiness she craved, if she was lucky enough to survive long enough to begin a new chapter.

And she hoped more than ever that Tristan would be part of that future. As with all things in their dystopian world, only time would tell.

Chapter 25

An hour later, Tristan stood behind Grace, subtly adjusting the rifle in her hands.

"You want the butt of the rifle firmly in the pocket of your shoulder," he said, sliding it up slightly so it was better positioned. "Now, fire again."

They were in a secluded area of the forest that lined the pond, and Grace squinted one eye before firing another round. Tristan didn't want to waste ammunition, so he'd told her to go easy, but she seemed to be enjoying obliterating the hell out of the bark of the nearby trees.

"Good," he said, placing his hand on her shoulder so she'd release the trigger. "You're a natural. Are you imagining me as your target?"

She smiled up at him, her blue eyes sparkling under the rising full moon and the last remnants of dusk. "I'm imagining Luthor. I've wanted to punch him in the face so many times over the past decade. He's a misogynistic, narcissistic asshole."

"Uh, yeah. I don't think that's breaking news." Tristan slowly eased the rifle from her arms. "I think you've got the basics down. I'm going to make sure you've got a bulletproof vest and bulletproof pads on your legs under your pants when we attack. They won't protect against everything, but at least they'll help."

She formed a sad smile. "Promise me you'll take care of Raquel if I die. Luthor will certainly kill me if we make contact in the city."

"I won't let that happen."

"You can't control everything," she said, shaking her head. "And I know it's not fair for me to ask you to take care of her, but I need to know you will."

"Of course I will," he said gruffly. "She's our daughter."

Remorse swam in her eyes as she studied him. "I'm sorry. I know words are terribly inadequate, but I owe them to you."

Sighing, Tristan set the rifle on the ground and slid his hands around her waist. Drawing her close, he rested his forehead against hers. "I've been so filled with regret and rage for years," he murmured, lifting a hand to stroke her hair. "And I'm tired too—of all of it. It takes so much energy for me to pretend I hate you, when we both know that will never be the case. I might as well expend the energy somewhere else."

"That's very pragmatic," she said, nudging his nose with hers. "And very evolved. I wouldn't blame you if you hated me."

"I understand why you did it." Running his hand down her face, he cupped her chin. "Luthor is laser-focused when he wants something. If he threatened to kill her, you had to ensure he believed she was already dead."

Grace nodded, her expression laced with deep emotion.

"And attacking him from within was brilliant. It led us to this moment. But I'm still proud, Grace, and I'm not going to profess feelings to a woman who's still married to a man I detest, whether the marriage was a sham or not."

"I understand," she whispered. "I'm sorry I hurt you. It was a very regrettable side effect of my master plan."

"Once this is over, and if we both survive, we can talk about the future. When Luthor's dead and we have the ability to see past tomorrow."

Grace shivered and he pulled her closer. "I hope we make it. I'm not ready to die. There are so many things I want to do with Raquel. So many ways I want to love her and give her the life she deserves."

"Let's hope the universe gives us some clemency." Tightening his hands on the swell of her ass, he squeezed. "And to be completely clear, as much as I want to fuck you, I'm not going to fuck Luthor Cromwell's wife. When I'm inside you again, you'll only belong to *me*."

Gliding her hands up the back of his neck, she plunged her fingers in his thick hair. "I've only ever belonged to you."

Tristan growled and nipped her lips.

Slowly disengaging, she backed away and gripped the hem of her shirt. Eyes cemented to his, she tugged it from her body, tossing it on the grass before unbuttoning her pants. After kicking off her shoes, she threw her pants to rest atop her shirt.

"I assume *skinny dipping* isn't off limits with Luthor's wife—right?"

Tristan's mouth went dry as he gazed at her in her beige bra and black underwear. Her skin glowed in the murky light, beckoning to him as he flexed his fingers. His eyes roved over every inch of her skin, taking it all in before they rested on the scar that covered her lower abdomen.

"It's horrendous," she said, covering it with her hands. "I should've prepared you. The birth was traumatic, and they had to take drastic measures to save her."

A wave of compassion and shame washed over him. He should've been there for her, holding her in the worst moment of her life. Instead, he'd been off in the Middle East, convinced *his* way was the only way he could save their marriage.

Closing the distance between them, Tristan gently encircled her wrists and drew her hands away. Lowering to his knees, he placed his palms on the sides of her abdomen before tugging down the hem of her underwear to see her scar. He tenderly caressed the discolored skin with his thumbs as he reveled at her strength.

"Tristan..." she whispered, threading her fingers through his hair.

"We both made so many mistakes," he rasped, exploring the faded laceration as his fingers trailed over the coarse skin. "I'm sorry too, Grace. I'm so fucking sorry."

"I know," she warbled, tears lacing her voice. "All I ever wanted was to be with you. To be *happy* with you."

Something caught his eye in the moonlight and he shifted his hand over, lightly tracing the newer tattoo on her hip. "You got another tattoo. A butterfly." He grinned as he lifted his gaze to hers.

"That one's for Raquel," she said, her fingers massaging his scalp in pleasurable motions as her lips curved. "You're my dragon, and she's my butterfly. Those are the only two I ever got, to remind me when times were hard of what I was fighting for."

Tristan pressed his face to her scar, nuzzling the skin that had healed long ago...unsure if their hearts would ever find time to truly heal...

Grace slid her fingers under his chin, reclaiming his gaze under the rising stars. Her smile was gorgeous as she backed away, edging toward the pond as she silently beckoned to him.

She stepped into the water and sucked in a breath as she grimaced. "Holy crap, that's cold!"

Laughing, Tristan rose and began to tug off his clothes. "It's October, empress. Still warm for fall, but not ideal skinny dipping weather."

"I don't care," she said, lowering into the water. "I want to do something reckless. I've been so damn restrained for all these years."

Tristan stripped down to his boxers, loving the flare of desire in her eyes. "You left your underwear on, so you're technically cheating," he teased. Throwing caution to the wind, he removed his underwear and tossed it aside. Seizing the moment, he steeled himself for the cold and rushed into the water.

Grace floated in front of him, a gorgeous mermaid under the twinkling stars. Tristan swam toward her, capturing her in his arms. She wrapped her legs around his waist, causing him to grow instantly hard, even though the water was frigid.

"We didn't think this through," she said, mirth in her tone as she shivered in his arms. "It's fucking freezing."

Tristan tossed his head back and laughed, overcome with unabashed joy at holding her once more. "Then we'll have to keep each other warm."

She tightened her limbs around him, spearing her fingers in his hair and drawing her mouth to his.

Tristan plunged his tongue inside, swiping over every crevice of her wet mouth. Tasting...nibbling...devouring...

She purred into his mouth, setting him on fire as he swallowed the sexy sound. As their tongues slithered over one another, she glided her hand to his swollen cock. Moaning with lust and desire, she encircled his length, gently squeezing as he groaned.

"Jesus, Grace," he hissed, pushing into her hand. "That feels so good, baby."

"I missed touching you like this," she breathed into his mouth, capturing his tongue again as she sucked it deep between her swollen lips.

Tristan closed his eyes, overcome with the pleasure of his wife sucking his tongue in slow, fluid strokes as she jerked her palm over his straining shaft.

Of course, she was his *ex-wife*, but hell, how was he supposed to remember that when she was the only woman he knew he'd ever love?

"I understand why you won't fuck me," she crooned, stroking her hand up and down his cock in a pleasurable slide that would soon send him over the edge. "We're not ready for that yet. But I can make you feel good too."

Tristan undulated into her palm, reaching for the ultimate pleasure as he enveloped her mouth in deep, ravenous kisses. "*Yeah, empress...*" he gritted, biting her bottom lip before sucking it between his lips to ease the sting. "Just like that... So fucking good..."

Grace increased the pressure, squeezing him in a vise that sent shards of pleasure to every cell in his frame.

Pressing his face to hers, he panted into her mouth as the base of his spine tingled.

"Going to come..." he uttered, eyes closed in sweet agony. "*Oh god...Grace...yes, baby...*"

Suddenly, his spine snapped and he lodged into a blinding orgasm. Jets of release pulsed into the water as Grace continued to stroke him, driving him mad. "No...more..." he gritted, his body jerking as he groaned her name.

Grace's hand stilled, holding his sensitive flesh as he relinquished all control. She buried her face in his neck, kissing a trail along his heated skin as he sighed.

Eventually, he softened in her hand, but she refused to let go. She held his sated length as she burrowed into his repleted body.

Tristan held her, thankful her legs were wrapped around his waist since his muscles had turned to jelly. Trailing his lips down her cheek, he pressed them to hers in a soulful kiss.

Their lips toyed and played with each other, soft and tender, as he recovered from the blissful release.

"Didn't expect that when I promised you rifle practice."

Grace broke into jubilant laughter, her throat exposed as she tossed her head back. Unable to resist, he pressed his lips to the glistening skin, dying to taste every inch of her.

After thoroughly kissing her neck, he fisted his hand in her hair and forced her to meet his gaze. "You're shivering," he said softly.

"It's really cold," she said, biting her lip. "But worth it."

Tristan tightened his arms around her. "Hold on." Praying his exhausted muscles could support them both, he carried her out of the water, placing her on her feet once they were back on the soft grass.

They dressed in comfortable silence, each shivering as the cool air hit their wet skin. Tristan reached for her hand, thrilled when she laced her fingers with his. After retrieving the forgotten rifle, he led her back to the school.

Once inside, they headed toward the shower stall in the boys' bathroom that had running water. Tristan took his time, running the soapy cloth over her body, worshiping her with his strokes as she gazed upon him.

After she returned the favor, they slipped on the clothes Danica had left in their rooms. Although they each had a room with a couch that Arthur had provided, Grace tugged him toward her room and pointed at the pull-out bed.

"There's enough room for both of us."

Tristan debated, understanding it would be difficult not to hold her as they slept. Or, perhaps, that was what she wanted.

"Please don't go," she whispered, reminding him of all those years ago when she begged him not to deploy.

His heart cracked at the intense sadness in her melodious voice. Unable to deny her, he nodded and slipped into bed beside her.

She doused the lone lamp and turned on her side, snuggling into the mattress as he lay on his back beside her. She faced away from him, and he closed his eyes, overwhelmed with the need to hold her.

Expelling a defeated breath, he rolled to his side and glided an arm around her waist. Throwing caution to the wind, he hooked his leg over her thighs and pressed his face to her nape.

She shimmied into him, her soft skin a contrast to the spiky hairs that lined his skin.

Reveling in her scent, his eyes drifted closed.

Her fingernails grazed over his arm, soothing him in long, pleasurable strokes as he faded into darkness.

For a moment, he forgot about the end of the world...and war...and death.

And he was just a man, holding his wife...the woman he loved with every ounce of his soul.

Chapter 26

G race awoke to the sight of Raquel's cute grin as the girl studied her. "Are you awake?" she whispered.

Breathing a laugh, Grace nodded. "I am now."

Raquel's gaze traveled to Tristan, who was clutching Grace as he snored against the back of her neck. Mischief entered the girl's eyes as she observed them.

Grace decided to let it rest since she was nowhere near ready to have a discussion on the birds and bees with her daughter. "Where's Nathan?"

"He's getting dressed and then we're going to head to the mess hall. We wanted to see if you're hungry."

"I am, and we have lots to prepare for before leaving for the DC Sen City tomorrow." Looking over her shoulder, she jabbed Tristan's arm. "Wake up. It's time for breakfast."

"Mmm…" Tristan murmured, sliding his hand to cup the sensitive place between her legs under the sheets. "Let me play with you first, empress…"

Clearing her throat, Grace jabbed his arm again.

"Ouch!" He lifted his head, and recognition lit his eyes as he gazed at Raquel. "Oh…good morning," he mumbled.

"Morning!" She was as chipper as he was drowsy. "Nathan and I are starving, and we wanted to see if you were hungry too."

"I'm definitely hungry, but breakfast wasn't what I had in mind."

Grace shot him a droll look at the double entendre.

"Let me get dressed, and we'll meet you at the mess hall," he said. "You and Nathan can walk together, and we'll be there in a few minutes."

"Okay. We'll save you some seats." She pivoted and breezed through the door.

Leaning on his fist, Tristan's lips curled. "Where does she get that energy from? We're both pretty fucking reserved."

Laughing, she shrugged. "Not sure. My mom was a talker and loved all the fancy parties Dad took her to. Maybe she inherited it from her."

"Maybe." His expression grew serious as he traced a finger over her cheek. "You're still my favorite thing to see when I wake up in the morning." Bumps rose along the skin of her arms as he gently traced her nose. "How are you so pretty?"

"I used to be pretty," she said, frowning. "I have wrinkles now. Luthor used to offer to inject me with tons of crap that would make them go away, but I always found a way to refuse. Thank god. His drugs are toxic."

"The wrinkles aren't so bad," he said, touching the skin beneath her eye. "I've got them too. We're old now."

Pushing to sit, she swatted his chest. "Don't put me out to pasture yet. I've still got some life in me."

"If we win, what do you want for your future?" He rolled to his back and laced his hands behind his head as he waited for her answer.

I want to marry you all over again. The words flitted through her brain as she rose and began to dress. "I want to be happy. I have no idea what that looks like, but hopefully I can figure it out."

He sat up and yawned while he rubbed his chest. Grace's eyes darted over his toned pecs and the mix of gray and dark hair that covered them, reminding herself that daydreaming had no place in her agenda.

"I'll meet you in ten minutes once I hit the restroom and get dressed," he said, rising.

He sauntered out of the room, and she all but drooled at his confident gait and broad shoulders.

"Get it together, Grace," she muttered to herself as she dug for the hairbrush in her bag.

Ten minutes later, they strolled to the mess hall and joined Raquel and Nathan. After inhaling her eggs and bacon, Grace waved to Chris, who appeared to whisk the kids away to wiffle ball practice.

Dani and Maverick strode over, and Grace asked, "Did Arianna and Dominic get into the city okay?"

"They were able to infiltrate, thanks in part to communication with Bodie," Maverick said. "Thanks for your help, Tristan."

"Hopefully, they'll get some intel for us," Dani said, sliding her arm around Maverick's waist. "I'm going to spend the day preparing the last of the vials while you all train. I'm impressed at your willingness to fight, Grace."

"My inability to bring Luthor down before he destroyed the world is my greatest failure," Grace said, pushing the plate away and rising. "I'm determined not to fail this time."

Maverick kissed Dani on the cheek before the three of them left her behind to walk to the training field. Grace spotted Zayne and her small team of men, and excused herself to approach them privately.

They formed a circle at the edge of the field, and Grace looked each of them in the eye as she addressed them. "We've worked and plotted for so long to get here," she said, her tone filled with determination. "I'm honored to fight with you and appreciative of your hard work."

"When you approached me and told me about the rebellion, I was initially suspicious that you were spying for Luthor," Zayne said, grinning. "I couldn't believe the mild-mannered woman I helped protect had concocted such a brilliant plan. He never suspected you." He tipped his head in acknowledgment. "Well done. I'm proud to be on your team."

"Thanks for taking the fall and posing as the leader," she said, patting his arm. "Luthor has probably figured out my deception by this point, but you took one for the team. I appreciate it." Glancing at the others, she spoke with reverence. "You all are brave and on the right side of history.

Know that if we fail, we'll at least have failed doing what's right and just."

"Hear, hear," the men chimed.

George Luddington hobbled over, full from a hearty breakfast at the mess hall. "Just stopping by for one last huddle before you all go save the world," he said, balancing on his cane. "Arthur put me up in a cozy little house two blocks from the mess hall, but I'm ready to reenter the city. I miss the luxury of hot showers. Living on jugs of water isn't going to cut it for me."

Grace acknowledged that living outside of the conditions he was used to would be a shock, especially since he wasn't in great health. Wealthy people rarely understood the real world, but she didn't fault him for that. He'd been born into one of the richest families in Virginia, and Grace had known him her whole life.

"You've supported me for all these years," she said, squeezing his upper arm. "I could never have done this without you, George. Thank you."

"I *might* forgive you for making me pretend to like that husband of yours," he chided, his eyes sparkling. "If I ever have to go on another fishing trip with Luthor, I'll probably dive in the water and end it there."

"Hopefully, those days are over. Our deception worked perfectly. My *husband*," she emphasized the word, showing her distaste, "always believed me a vapid aristocrat without two brain cells to rub together. I guess I showed him."

Chuckling, George nodded. "You certainly did, my dear."

Grace wound down the impromptu meeting, and George meandered off the field. She and her men joined the others to prepare for tomorrow's attack.

Although the future was uncertain, they were finally taking matters into their own hands. If all went as planned, they would accomplish their goal and change the course of history.

In a matter of days, they would know for certain, and Grace was ready, whatever the outcome.

Arianna and Dominic stealthily moved through the city, making sure the deli wasn't crowded before entering. Arianna wanted to ensure Deandra had time to speak to them alone.

"What can I get you?" she called, turning to face the register and sticking a pencil behind her ear. Her eyes grew wide when she recognized them. "Well, hello. If it isn't my favorite badass couple, back from exile. How are you?"

"We're good," Arianna said. "Back to order lots of sandwiches." She slipped a gold bar across the counter.

"By *sandwiches*, I think you mean information, but Ron will make you some food anyway. What'll it be?"

"Two bagels with eggs, and he'll have ham on his too," she said, pointing at Dominic.

"She's ordering for you now?" Deandra teased before repeating the order to Ron, who confirmed it as he worked the grill.

Leaning forward, Dominic whispered conspiratorially, "I let her think she's in charge and then she lets me kiss her wherever and whenever I want—"

Arianna planted a hand on his face and pushed him behind her. "I *am* in charge, and he might get to kiss me if we can stay alive long enough to end the nightmare we're all living in."

Chuckling, Deandra hid the gold bar under the counter before wrapping their sandwiches. "Fair enough." The bell chimed as two more patrons walked in. "Meet me in the park a block north from here in ten minutes."

"She can only chat with you all a few minutes," Ron called from the grill. "Last time, she left me in a lurch."

"Oh, you hush," she said, waving her hand at him. "He's a big baby who can't work the register and cook. I swear."

"Quiet, woman!" Ron called, the words softened by the loving smile he shot her.

"I'll be there in a few," she said, shooing Arianna and Dominic from the deli.

They located the park and sat on a graffitied bench to eat their sandwiches. The words *Death for Luthor* were painted on the faded wood, along with many other messages of dissention, showing how far the rebellion had spread.

"That's a good sign," Dominic said, reading the words as he ate.

"It is. Do you think Arthur will put Luthor on trial if we capture him?"

Dominic's eyes narrowed. "I think Luthor will die in the attack. Tristan seems pretty dead set on murdering him."

"He's not the only one," Arianna muttered.

"Are you worried for Dani's trial?"

Contemplating, Arianna shook her head. "I think the jury will show her deference for creating the cure. I still have hope *some* people aren't assholes."

"Me too."

Deandra approached and sat beside Arianna, opening her hand to take the discarded wrappers. After tossing them in the receptacle beside her, she leaned back and crossed her arms over her chest. "The shit really hit the fan when you all left. Luthor sent a battalion to Arthur's compound, but you know that already. They returned with only half the men, led by a young major named Anthony Martinez." She arched an inquisitive eyebrow. "It seems you turned Major Martinez to your side."

"If you know that, Luthor surely must as well," Arianna said. "And that's not good."

"From what I've gathered overhearing the soldiers' conversations as they wait for food, Luthor sees it more as incompetence because Anthony is inexperienced. I think Luthor's arrogance blinds him from believing anyone would turn against him."

"Which is why he didn't realize Grace was leading the rebellion," Dominic said.

"You don't say," Deandra said, her mouth falling slightly open. "That wisp of a woman leading the rebellion?" Chuckling, she rubbed her palms over her legs. "How very interesting. Luthor believes Zayne is the leader."

"He's aligned with Grace, but she was the mastermind," Dominic confirmed.

"Good for her. So she really wasn't 'kidnapped' at all." She made quotation marks with her fingers. "Absolutely glorious."

"We need all the info you have on the soldiers who've been injected with the strength serum," Arianna said. "How many, where they train, any weaknesses you know of."

"Well, my dear, lucky for you, I hear *everything*." She tapped her ear. "Two hundred were injected, and seven died—"

"Jesus," Arianna breathed, shaking her head.

"I'm sure Luthor sees them as collateral damage," Deandra said. "He doesn't really view the soldiers as human. He thinks most people are beneath him."

"That tracks," Arianna said, her lips flattening in distaste. "Besides enhanced strength, does the serum have any other effects?"

"It seems to allow for rapid healing. Most likely because the soldiers are taking EverLife too. Luthor keeps them pumped full of it and gives all his soldiers the cleanest version of the antidote he'll allow so they stay young and primed for fighting."

"Do you know where they train? We'd like to scope it out," Dominic said.

"They've been training in Garfield Park, close to downtown where his headquarters are."

"Deandra, you're a goddess," Arianna said, squeezing her hand. "Thank you."

"Just remember who scratched your back when you beat that crazy old dictator." She stood and planted her hands on her hips. "Ron and I love the deli, and we need lots of renovations. Maybe Mr. Reyes can find it in his heart to help us out when he rebuilds."

Rising, Dominic extended his hand. "You can count on it, Deandra."

Deandra pointed back and forth between them. "I want an invite to the wedding. Don't leave me hanging."

Laughing, Arianna nodded. "You'll be the first to know. I'd advise you and Ron to close and lock the deli tomorrow evening, and to have some protection while you stay inside."

"Yes, ma'am," she said with a salute. "Ron will protect us. That man is fiercer than he lets on. See you all once we've entered the new world. Go get 'em."

With a final wave, she sauntered away as Arianna and Dominic prepared to spy on Luthor's troops.

Chapter 27

The next day, a nervous but excited energy filled Arthur's compound. The morning was spent training before Arthur sent everyone home, encouraging them to spend time with the family they had left. The unspoken reality was that many of the militia members would be lost in the attack, but everyone was united in the cause and ready to sacrifice their life to regain freedom for those left behind.

Grace urged Tristan to take Raquel on another walk while she used the pen and paper Danica had given her to write her daughter a letter. She hoped it wasn't a goodbye letter, but if that were the case, she wanted her to know the truth.

My darling Raquel,

I write this letter to you in the hopes you never have to read it. If you do, please know it was written with love and a fair amount of tears.

My greatest accomplishment was ensuring your light wasn't extinguished in a world where so many others were. My greatest source of pride is being your mother. Yes, my darling, I am your birth mother, and I'm so very sorry I couldn't tell you all these years.

Maria did a wonderful job sheltering you, and was a mother to you in all the ways I craved. Getting to know you during the small visits we had over the years soothed my broken soul. I hid the fact that you were mine because the world was thrust into chaos, and I was determined to right that terrible wrong.

My separation from you, and the dissolution of my marriage from your father, are the only regrets I ever let myself suffer.

Tristan and I conceived you with an abundance of love and joy, and you shine so brightly with that joy every day. I continue to be amazed by your vivacious spirit, inquisitive mind and kind soul.

Please don't blame Tristan for not telling you he was your father. I lied to him in my effort to keep you safe, and all the blame falls on my shoulders. He will be a wonderful father to you, and I hope you both can build a future together if I'm no longer here.

I understand the huge betrayal you must feel and don't blame you if you hate me for the rest of your days. I hope they're filled with happiness in a long life where you never have to suffer. Even if you can't forgive me, I'll have the solace that my efforts weren't in vain if you seize each day with wonder and hope.

Some of my fondest memories are of the short months I was pregnant with you before your father deployed. He would rub my belly and speak to you, and he wanted you with all his heart. Please let him inside yours. You two have lots to catch up on and a beautiful relationship to build.

Live well, my beautiful girl. Carry the torch for so many others whose were extinguished. Show the world your humanity and let it be an example for everyone as they hopefully navigate new freedoms.

Love,
Your mother, Grace Holder

Wiping the tears that streamed down her face, Grace released a long breath and reread the letter. She'd used Tristan's surname because it was the one that held the most meaning in her heart. Afterward, she folded it several times and wrote Raquel's name on the outside.

Wanting to ensure the letter's safekeeping, she treaded down the hallway from her room to find Dani in the old science lab. She looked up from the vials she was preparing and smiled.

"Hey, Grace."

"Hi." Stepping forward, she held out the letter. "I was hoping you could hold onto this and give it to Raquel if I..." She cleared her throat. "Well, you know."

Dani took the letter and walked to a nearby cabinet. "I'll put it here so it's safe." She opened the top drawer and deposited it inside before returning to her seat behind the microscope. Pointing to the stool across from her, she silently asked Grace to sit.

Grace lowered onto the stool and circled a hand over her face. "You've got that inquisitive scientist look."

Dani laughed. "So, I'm a geneticist, and that means I'm really good at seeing genetic patterns in people." Her green eyes sparkled as she spoke. "It's pretty clear to me that Raquel is your and Tristan's daughter."

Grace nodded. "She is, but she doesn't know. That's what the letter is for." She pointed to the cabinet. "And Tristan only found out she was alive a few days ago. I told him she died during childbirth." Speaking the words aloud sent a wave of emotion through Grace, and she buried her hands in her face as she started to cry. "Oh, god. I've made so many terrible decisions..."

Dani rushed around the table and rubbed Grace's shoulder. "Hey, you're talking to the woman who created Ever-Life. I'm not sure you want to have a discussion with me about regrettable choices."

Laughter burst from Grace's throat as she lifted her gaze to Dani's. "Holy shit, you're right. You might be the only other person in the world who's made worse decisions than me."

"I could make the excuse that I don't remember half of them, but that never really works. I still feel like crap, believe me."

Grace smiled and swiped her cheeks. "It's hard because I made those choices in order to save her. Unfortunately, I thought it would happen *slightly* faster than it actually has."

Dani pulled over a nearby stool and sat down to face her. "Here's the thing," she said, swiping a hand through her shoulder-length brown hair. "It doesn't help to beat ourselves up, although I constantly want to. I just keep reminding myself that I can't change the past, but I can damn well change the future. I'm determined to cure everyone on this goddamned planet."

"That's so valiant," Grace said. "You've done amazing things here in an old run-down science lab. Imagine what you can do when you actually have a functioning lab and a factory to produce the cure."

"I imagine that every day," she replied wistfully.

Grace's cheeks puffed as she exhaled. "I'm so afraid I'm going to save the world and accomplish everything I want, only to be hated by my daughter and the man I love. I can tell Tristan wants to move on, but I violated his trust and he has every right to be angry. And Raquel..." She shook her head as she gazed at the floor. "I have no idea how she's going to handle the news that I'm her mother."

"Children are very resilient," Dani said, patting her leg. "They can also smell dishonesty and disingenuousness from a mile away. Tell her the truth—that you made hard choices because you love her. She'll understand that, Grace. I know she will."

"You make it sound so easy."

Dani grinned. "Honestly, I think it's about time something was easy. We deserve that. Let it be easy."

Grace bit her lip as she studied her. "Are you and Maverick going to have kids?"

"I hope so. As long as I'm not in prison. Let's hope the jury is lenient."

"I'll do my part to sway public opinion your way." Encircling her wrist, Grace squeezed. "Thank you, Dani. I'm not sure if you remember, but we met casually at various work events Luthor held for Sendaxa while you worked there. He held you in high regard: the brilliant scientist who would create the most important drug in history. Of course, once you figured out his nefarious tactics, his opinion of you soured. I'm not sure what you remember, but you tried to stop him. It made him livid. And that's why I know you're a good soul."

"I don't remember meeting you, but that's par for the course." She playfully rolled her eyes. "And this time, we *will* stop him. I know it."

Grace smiled, hoping they both would survive and become close friends. Dani was kind and easy to talk to, and lord knew Grace needed more friends and confidants in the world. Being married to Luthor had been a self-imposed prison, and she was ready for a new chapter of her life.

Envisioning a future without Luthor Cromwell, Grace returned to her room to prepare to depart the compound.

By the time the late-afternoon sun kissed the horizon, Arthur's militia was ready to advance on the DC Sen City. They'd packed many of the SUVs and trucks on the compound with weapons, and the remaining pickup trucks would carry multiple soldiers in their beds. All of the available gas on the compound would be dedicated to fueling the vehicles for the journey.

They would make the two-and-a-half-hour drive to DC in a caravan under the early nighttime sky for additional cover. When they reached the city, they would stop at Fort Bennett Park and quickly arm themselves. Arianna and Dominic would meet them there so they could reconvene and join the attack.

Arthur had been communicating with Major Anthony Martinez over a secret radio channel. Since Luthor had destroyed all of the bridges into the city when he erected the wall, Anthony and his men had surreptitiously hidden row boats in the woods of Fort Bennett Park over the past few weeks. Arthur's men would use them to cross the Potomac River and rush the grassy bank outside the DC wall.

Once outside the wall, Anthony's battalion would meet them there. Although his battalion was small—thanks to the men they'd lost when they'd attacked the Cumberland compound—every ounce of help mattered. They would give Arthur's militia an additional hundred or so men, some with tanks, and that would be a huge advantage.

Arthur anticipated Luthor would send the super-soldier battalion to fight outside the wall. As they fought, Arthur's men would use the grenade launchers to try to blow the wall open. If successful, they would breach the city and enter downtown. This is where Grace played a very important role.

Her proximity to Luthor for the past decade ensured she knew the location of all of his secret bunkers. As Arthur's militia advanced, Grace would lead them to his primary bunker downtown. If he wasn't there, she could lead the militia to the next bunker, and so on, until they found him.

The primary goal was to gain Luthor's surrender and take him into custody. After that, Arthur would seize control of the city and begin the long, winding path to rebuilding the government and society.

As she sat beside Tristan in the bed of one of the pickup trucks, Grace grappled with the huge task ahead. She ran her hands over her black pants, testing the bulletproof pads underneath.

"I know they're not comfortable, but I want you safe," Tristan said.

"I get it," she responded. "They're just itchy."

"Better itchy than dead."

Since she couldn't argue there, Grace stayed silent as the wind whipped her hair on the long drive.

They eventually made it to Fort Bennett Park and parked all of the vehicles under the shelter of the perimeter woods. The men and women exited the vehicles and quickly armed themselves. The superior marksmen strapped the dart guns filled with rounds of anti-strength serum to their belts while those tasked with operating the grenade launchers strapped them behind their backs. It was a clear night with a bright moon, so there was enough visibility to see, but Arthur also ensured the marksmen armed with the dart guns were equipped with night-vision goggles for better precision.

A few men had been assigned to groups of two who would transport the Javelins across the river and launch them at any tanks operated by Luthor's super-soldiers. They could also be used to blow open the wall if the grenade launchers failed.

Once they were armed, Arthur led them in search of the row boats. As Grace stomped through the thick brush, she heard a gruff voice whisper, "Over here!"

Arthur shined his flashlight toward the sound, his teeth flashing in the dim moonlight as he beamed. "Arianna. Glad you made it to the rendezvous."

"You all are loud as hell," she said, scowling as Dominic stood beside her. Thick trees surrounded them, and Grace could see the outline of several row boats stacked along the trunks.

"What she's trying to say is that she's happy to see you too," Dominic said.

Arianna shot him a glare. "Is everybody armed?"

"Yes. The intel you sent back on the super-soldiers was invaluable," Arthur said. "Maverick and I trained the soldiers with the dart guns to aim for the head and the neck. We thought their heads would be covered with helmets, but thanks to you, we know that's not the case."

"The strength serum causes swelling in the brain, and none of the helmets fit them," Dominic said. "We saw it with our own eyes, and Deandra overheard it from many soldiers who frequented her deli."

"It's a fortuitous discovery," Arthur said. "Thank you for the surveillance. Ready to kick some ass?"

"Ready," Arianna and Dominic said in unison.

Arthur gave the command to drag the boats to the river, and the militia loaded into them and began rowing. When they were halfway across, several flood lights illuminated atop the city wall.

A loud screech echoed in the silence, causing many of the men to plug their ears. Suddenly, Luthor's voice sounded over loudspeakers that must've been attached to the wall.

"Advance any further and we will consider this an act of war," Luthor said, his tone calm and sinister at the same time. "Once we declare war, I won't hesitate to use the full weight of the Sen Force army against you, Arthur. Think about your soldiers and save them now."

Arthur waved to his men, urging them to continue.

"Very well," Luthor's voice called eerily as it rang out over the horizon. "Fire!"

Bullets began to fly from the city, and Arthur held his hands up to his mouth to yell a command. "Row until you can wade in the water and continue on foot!"

The soldiers listened, many of them jumping into the water since they could stand. They would duck every so often but continued to advance toward the riverbank.

Tristan helped Grace jump from the boat, her teeth chattering as she encountered the cool water. She marched toward the grassy bank beside several other men, noticing how Tristan made sure to walk in front of her. Her heart somersaulted at the protective gesture, and she made a mental note to kiss the hell out of him if they survived...and more. A hell of a lot more if he would let her.

But now wasn't the time to ruminate on the extent of her ex-husband's possible forgiveness. Now was the time to *fight*. Grace crawled onto the shore and followed Tristan as he jogged to a nearby bush. They ducked behind it, and Grace thanked the universe that Luthor hadn't maintained the land outside the city wall. It meant there were lots of overgrown bushes to hide behind, and Arthur's men took full advantage of that oversight.

A section of the wall swung open, and soldiers dressed in Sen Force uniforms began to filter through. Thanks to the bright lights atop the wall, Grace could discern their outlines. Their bodies were thick with bulging muscles, and they wore no helmets, so she understood these were the super-soldiers.

Arthur's troops armed with the dart guns moved in, aiming for the soldier's necks. Although they were able to take down a few, the hulking men continued to advance. With the river behind them, there was nowhere for Arthur's men to go. Faced with that inevitability, he seized the moment and yelled, "Charge!"

Arthur's troops sprang forward, firing their rifles as the sounds of war ripped through the air.

"Stay behind this bush until I come back to get you," Tristan said, rising and pointing at the ground as he spoke. "I mean it, Grace. We'll need you to locate Luthor in his bunker once we blow a hole in the wall, and you can't do that if you're dead."

"Okay," she said, her voice shaky.

He gave a curt nod and gripped his rifle in both hands as he ran to join the combat. Covering her lips with her fingers, Grace watched the battle unfold with wide eyes.

The soldiers fought under the stars, Arthur's men scurrying around bushes to take cover before emerging from the other side to attack the super-soldiers' flanks. Bullets seemed to bounce off the injected soldiers' thick muscles, giving them an air of invincibility. Grace counted about ten soldiers of Luthor's who'd fallen, but Arthur's militia had already lost over twenty-five in her estimation. At this rate, they would surely lose. Would Arthur call for a retreat or have them fight to the death?

Luthor's voice boomed "Cease fire!" over the speakers, and the super-soldiers froze, awaiting their next orders.

Arthur held up his hand, signaling for the militia to halt as he assessed.

The wall swung open again and another battalion rolled through, most of them in tanks. The tanks filed to flank Luthor's soldiers on either side. A man walked through the opening and strode forward to stand beside the leader of the super-soldier regiment.

"It seems we meet again," Major Anthony Martinez said, approaching Arthur as he stood in front of his men scattered across the riverbank. "This time, you're the one who will retreat. Luthor can hear everything we're saying," he said, tapping the receiver in his ear. "If you surrender now, he'll take you and your men into custody and let you live."

"You know I can't do that," Arthur said. "Tell your commander we came here to take back the city, and we won't stop until we succeed."

Anthony paused, appearing to listen to orders in the earpiece before backing away to rejoin the super-soldier front line.

"You've made your choice," Anthony said, lifting his chin. "We will now unleash the full power of the tanks against your militia."

Grace knew this was the moment Arthur and Anthony had discussed in secret. Instead of attacking Arthur's militia, Anthony would turn the tanks on the super-soldiers and begin to fire.

Except, in that moment, everything went terribly wrong.

The super-soldier commander snaked his arm around Anthony's neck and pulled his handgun from his holster. Grace gasped as Anthony struggled before the super-soldier commander shot him in the temple. Anthony collapsed on the ground, his body lifeless as the soldier who shot him stood stoic.

"Did you really think you could turn my own soldiers against me without me knowing, Arthur?" Luthor's sinister voice called over the loudspeaker. "The entire battalion was dead the moment you sent them back to me. I don't tolerate dissidence in my regime."

Suddenly, the tanks that flanked the super-soldiers exploded in a brilliant round of fire. Grace held her ears, barely able to tolerate the ringing in them from the excruciating sounds.

When the smoke cleared, she blinked rapidly as realization washed over.

Luthor had destroyed his own tanks and the men inside them rather than allow their disloyalty.

Major Anthony Martinez and his entire battalion were now dead.

Arthur's militia had lost an entire battalion of soldiers they'd counted on to help them win.

Fear snaked up her spine as comprehension dawned, and she whispered words only she could hear...

"Holy shit...we're all going to die."

Chapter 28

Tristan observed the carnage, barely able to wrap his mind around the crazed actions of Luthor Cromwell. The man had just killed a hundred of his own men. Yes, they'd secretly turned against him, but the action was extreme, even for Luthor.

"As you can see, I armed the interior of each tank in Major Martinez's battalion with explosives," Luthor said over the loudspeaker. "I hope this shows my determination to end anyone's life associated with the rebellion."

Tristan looked toward Arthur, whose head hung slightly as he stood still on the battlefield. Losing Anthony's battalion was a huge setback, and he could see Arthur trying to formulate a solution.

"Many of your men are already dead, Reyes," Luthor said. "End this now and surrender. I'll give you a fair public trial."

Tristan scoffed. Luthor would publicly execute Arthur if he surrendered, and everyone on the battlefield knew it.

Arthur turned to Maverick, Arianna, and Dominic, and they began a hushed discussion. Tristan jogged toward them, anxious to help if he could.

"What are you all thinking?" he asked.

Sighing, Arthur shook his head. "I don't want to lose any more men, and not having the tanks to attack the super-soldiers puts us at a disadvantage. I can surrender and you all can retreat while they capture me. You'll have to lead the militia and move quickly—"

"No fucking way!" Arianna hissed. "We're not surrendering to that asshole. Let's fight. We have the grenade launchers and the Javelins. I know we planned to use them to blow through the wall, but let's use them on the super-soldiers first."

"Those weapons aren't meant to be used on humans," Arthur said, contemplating. "I hate to senselessly kill Luthor's soldiers, and it violates the basic rules of engagement. Those weapons will rip those soldiers apart, super-serum or not."

"It's terrible," Arianna agreed, "but the future of the world is at stake. I don't think we have a choice. We can't surrender. If we lose, who else will fight? We have to seize this moment."

Crouching down, she drew circles on the ground in rapid movements. "Dom and I will lead a third of the men on the left flank. Maverick and Tristan will lead a third on the right flank. You and Zayne lead the remaining third head-on. We'll give the command to fire at will and blast those fuckers."

Arthur contemplated another moment before making the sign of the cross over his head and chest. Looking to the sky, he said softly, "Lord, forgive me. I don't see another path."

Cupping his hands over his mouth, he called, "Troops! Those to my right follow Arianna and Dominic," he said swiping his arm over that flank of the riverbank. "Those here follow me, and those to my left follow me and Zayne. Charge!"

The militia gave a rallying cry and fell into step behind their respective leaders.

Luthor commanded his men to fire at will, and the fighting resumed.

Arthur's troops advanced, each soldier stopping every few feet to plant a knee on the ground, balance the grenade launcher on their shoulder, and fire the weapon.

Although it was a slow advance due to the heavy artillery, Arthur's men succeeded in making some headway against

Luthor's soldiers. Still, they were outnumbered and needed to breach the wall sooner rather than later.

"Advance to the wall and launch the grenades at it," Arthur commanded Tristan and Maverick. They led the men with the grenade launchers forward as other militia members continued the advance against Luthor's soldiers.

Tristan approached the wall, observing Luthor's men draw near out of the corner of his eye.

"Hand me the Javelin!"

He hoisted the heavy launcher on his shoulder and held it steady. Clenching his teeth, he shot the steel wall. The explosion reverberated around him, knocking him on his back as the Javelin fell to the ground. Lifting his head, he blinked to see if he'd managed to open a hole in the wall. He had, but it was small and none of Arthur's men would fit through it.

"Fuck!" he said, struggling to stand. "We must've hit a reinforced area of the wall. The hole is too small. We're going to have to launch another Javelin. Do we have any left?" They'd only had a few to begin with, and most were currently being launched at Luthor's troops.

"Maybe we can fire a grenade launcher at it," Maverick said, scanning the battlefield for a soldier who still had loaded launchers. "We've almost depleted those too."

"I can fit through it!" a voice called behind Tristan, and he whirled around to see Nathan jogging toward him.

Surprise and shock reverberated through Tristan's body as the kid spoke with excited confidence.

"I can crawl through and open the gate from the other side."

Tristan's mouth fell open as he gazed upon the kid's freckled face. "What the hell are you doing here?"

Breaking into a wide grin, Nathan puffed his chest. "I *told* you I was a good spy."

Grace felt helpless as she observed the awesome firepower being unleashed on Luthor's troops. The super-soldiers were making a valiant effort, but they were no match for the heavy artillery.

Narrowing her eyes, Grace saw a figure dart toward Tristan in the distance. Inhaling a sharp breath, she rose to her feet. "Nathan?" Afraid for the boy, she threw caution to the wind and ran to join him and Tristan at their location near the wall.

"How the hell did you get here?" Tristan asked the boy as she approached.

"I hid under a blanket in one of the truck beds with all the weapons," he said. "And when the driver parked the truck, I jumped out and hid behind a tree."

Tristan opened his mouth to say something else, but a grenade exploded in the background, causing him to cover his face with his arms. Nathan held up his arms reflexively too, and Grace fell to the ground from the reverb.

"Damn it, Grace," Tristan said, helping her up. "I told you to wait behind the bush."

"I'm going to have to get inside eventually," she said, wiping the dirt off her pants. Clutching Nathan's shoulders, she noticed his clothes were wet. "Did you swim across the river?"

Nathan nodded and pointed toward the small opening in the wall. "I can climb through it! Then I can open the wall from the inside."

"No way, kid—"

Crouching before him, she ignored Tristan. "It's really dangerous, but if you can get through that hole, there's a lever about twenty feet that way." She pointed to her left. "If you pull the lever down, it will allow that flap of the wall to swing open."

"Are you serious?" Tristan asked, arms stretched at his sides. "He's a kid, Grace—"

"I can do it," Nathan said, looking up at Tristan. "I've done much harder missions for Solomon."

Tristan lowered beside Grace. "I don't doubt your fortitude, but I don't want you to get hurt."

Nathan patted his chest. "I promise I can do it."

Grace looked at Tristan and then looked toward the battle that raged behind them. Reclaiming Tristan's gaze, she said softly, "It will allow us to open the wall. Then we can infiltrate and find Luthor. If we capture him, the fighting stops."

Tristan blew out a breath and stood. "You have to move fast. Crawl through and run to the lever. Once you push the wall open, I want you to run back that way along the inside of the wall." He motioned south with his arm. "There's a trail called Rock Creek that runs along the wall, and it has lots of overgrown trees. I want you to hide there until I come back to get you. These are orders, soldier. Can I count on you?" Tristan lifted his hand to his forehead in a salute.

Nathan straightened his shoulders and saluted back. "Yes, sir. I promise I'll hide by the trail until you come and get me."

Lowering his hand, Tristan crouched and drew the boy into an embrace as Grace's heart squeezed in her chest.

Releasing him, Tristan urged Nathan toward the opening. "Run fast. I don't want you to get shot. Now go!"

Nathan broke into a full-on sprint toward the wall. When he reached the opening, he squeezed his body through and disappeared. Grace waited for several heart-wrenching moments, hoping he would succeed. Suddenly, Arianna's voice echoed through the smoke and bullets.

"The wall is open!" she yelled. "Charge forward!"

The remaining militia members rushed the wall, fighting the super-soldiers as they struggled to enter the city.

Facing Grace, Tristan took her hand. "Ready to track down your asshole husband?"

Armed with steely determination, Grace uttered one resolute word. "Ready."

Chapter 29

Arthur's troops were able to infiltrate the city, and they scattered throughout the interior, drawing away the super-soldiers' attention so Tristan, Grace, Arianna, Dominic, Maverick and Arthur could head toward Luthor's downtown bunkers. They advanced as a team, holding rifles as Arianna and Dominic acted as lookouts. They led the way, scoping out each block ahead and ensuring it was clear before the small team moved forward. Although it was a highly precarious situation, Grace felt safe surrounded by such skilled soldiers.

They made their way down Constitution Avenue before heading north on 14th Street. When they passed the abandoned and desolate White House, Grace marveled that the once-great symbol was now an empty husk that represented days long gone.

"I always wondered why Luthor never moved into the White House," Tristan said quietly as they passed it in the shadows of the trees that lined the street.

"Because it's a symbol of a world that didn't accept his arrogance and evil," she said. "His headquarters are where he's comfortable. A sign of the new regime."

"We're approaching McPherson Square," Arianna said as they crept toward the dilapidated park. "This is his main bunker?"

"Yes," Grace said. "There's a secret doorway on the base of the statue of General McPherson. I think you all will have to blow it open."

"Dani made me some kick-ass door charges from some chemicals she found in the school lab," Maverick said, pulling them from the small pack at his waist. "We can use them to blow it open."

They moved behind a thicket of trees, assessing the Sen Force soldiers that surrounded the statue in the middle of the park.

"Ten soldiers around the base of the statue, and several scattered throughout the park," Arianna murmured.

"Confirmed," Dominic said, sliding his rifle around his shoulder and lifting it to aim. "Bet I can take out more than you, Lawson."

Arianna clutched her rifle and aimed through the leaves. "You're on."

They began to fire, each aiming for the thighs of the soldiers to hopefully wound instead of kill. Maverick and Tristan joined in, firing carefully measured shots as the officers fell to the ground one by one. They all writhed in pain as they clutched their legs, and Arthur stepped forward, retrieving a dart gun from his waist.

"I'm shooting you with sedatives, boys," he said, discharging a dart into each arm of the now-fallen soldiers as Arianna and the others confiscated their forgotten weapons. "Dani assured me it's safe. Sweet dreams of freedom," he finished acerbically.

After all the soldiers had been shot full of sedative, Maverick placed the door charges at the base of the faint outline of the bunker door. They all fell back as the charges detonated, and Maverick wrapped his hands around the stone, yanking it open.

Arthur motioned to Grace, who was still hiding in the brush, and she swiftly moved forward.

"Dom and I will lead the way," Arianna said, rifle in hand as she peered down the darkened stairs. "There's a small path of lights, similar to an airplane aisle, but that's all we've got. Stay sharp."

She stepped inside and everyone followed. Grace fell into step behind Arthur and Maverick, and Tristan walked behind.

The stone stairs were curved and led to a dark tunnel. Arthur turned on his flashlight, and they continued to advance.

They eventually reached a metal door, and Maverick pulled out another door charge. "Stand back, guys. I'm blowing this one too."

After detonation, he tugged the door open, and Arianna and Dominic rushed inside, rifles aimed. Grace entered, observing the large room, full of technology that hadn't been widely available since the world collapsed. Screens lined the walls, showing different video feeds from across the city.

A large mahogany desk sat on the far side of the room, in front of several mounted screens, and a high-backed leather chair rocked with eerily precision, indicating someone sat on the other side of the back that faced them.

Slow claps sounded from the desk, and the chair slowly swiveled. Luthor Cromwell's sinister face appeared, his eyes lit with derangement and rage.

"Well done, my friends," he said, finishing the slow clap before lowering his arms. "You infiltrated my city and are here to kill the nefarious dictator." His voice dripped with sarcasm. "I only wonder what took you so long. As the battle progressed, I decided to bunker here and wait for you. After all, running is for cowards, and I'm man enough to meet you and assume my destiny."

Arthur surveyed the bunker. "How magnanimous you are to let your men die outside the wall while you hide in a bunker and observe their efforts."

"I *saved* them!" Luthor said, standing as spittle flew from his mouth. "Every single person in this new utopia I've created. Why can't you all see that?"

"Freedom is messy and democracy is imperfect," Arthur said, showing his palms. "But they're much better than living in a regime where everyone is an addict, homeless or dead."

Luthor scrubbed a hand over his face. "You'll never understand, so I'll cease trying to reason with you. Bring in the hostages!"

Grace recognized Colonel McGrath and Dr. Ziegler as they both appeared holding two squirming hostages who were gagged and bound at their feet and wrists.

"Jessica!" Tristan called, rushing forward before Arthur slammed an arm over his chest to hold him back. "You let her go, you bastard!"

"Nathan!" Grace cried, covering her mouth as the little boy struggled in Colonel McGrath's arms.

Luthor broke into menacing laughter as he shook his head. "Ah, my doting wife. You spent so many years deceiving me, and I never suspected a thing." Perching his hip on the desk, he crossed his arms over his chest. "I've figured it all out now, of course. You were the whistleblower, all those years ago, who almost sent me to prison." He slammed his fist on the desk. "And when you failed, you plotted the rebellion until it brought you right here."

"You murdered my father!" she screamed, all the pent-up rage from years of pain and heartache causing her to lurch forward. "I vowed on that day to make you pay."

Luthor's eyes narrowed. "I always suspected you saw that. Robert was always too headstrong for his own good. Look at how he ruined your marriage to this vagrant." He gestured toward Tristan. "You did serve me well sometimes, Tristan, but your sister served me much better. I always enjoyed the times she let me go deep—"

"I'll fucking kill you!" Tristan screamed, rushing forward as Luthor held up a hand.

"They have orders to kill Jessica and the child on the spot if I'm harmed," Luthor said. "The boy sang like a bird when he was captured and defiantly told me he was '*helping the rebellion.*'" He made quotation marks with his fingers. "So, kill me if you wish, but your sister and the little brat will die too."

Tristan's expression flushed with anger as he faced Colonel McGrath and Dr. Ziegler. "Where's your humanity?

This man is a mass murderer!" He jabbed his finger at Luthor.

"Many members of Colonel McGrath's family are addicted to EverLife and need my antidote," Luthor said. "And Dr. Ziegler will surely be tried and sentenced to death for the drugs he created under my regime if I lose power. They both need me to remain the sovereign leader of this city and of the world."

"My wife, Dr. Danica Lawson, created a cure for EverLife addiction," Maverick said. "Let the boy go and I'll make sure every member of your family receives it as soon as possible."

"A cure isn't possible," Dr. Ziegler said, confusion in his expression. "I've tried and can never find the right balance."

"With all due respect, you don't hold a candle to my wife. She's fucking brilliant, and she's going to rid the world of the garbage your boss created."

"Danica is the reason we're all in this situation!" Luthor exclaimed. "She alone is responsible for the destruction. I only wanted to create a world where everyone could live long lives, free from the pains of growing old."

"You wanted power, Luthor," Grace said, her nostrils flaring. "It's why you killed my father, and why you plotted to murder me and my child who was fighting for her life in the NICU. You're a fucking monster."

Luthor emitted a harsh laugh. "You always were a simpleton, just like your father. I should've killed you when I had the chance. I regret not making it a priority. There was always someone in your hospital room, and I decided you weren't worth the effort. It's one of the few miscalculations I've made in a life full of necessary decisions."

"So, where do we go from here?" Arthur asked. "We can't kill you if we want the hostages to live. How do we solve this, Luthor?"

"It's quite simple, really." Luthor walked around his desk and retrieved a handgun from the top drawer. "You all need to die. It will squash any talk of rebellion, and I can rebuild what you've broken here tonight." Lifting the gun, he aimed at Arthur. "You were a worthy opponent, but you'll be the first to die, my friend."

"Wait," a voice called, and Grace turned to see Colonel McGrath lift his gun and aim it at Luthor. Holding it steady, he locked eyes with Maverick. "How do you know the cure works?"

"My wife tested it on all of the patients in the Cumberland clinic. They've all been cured and are in good health. She has vials ready to deploy when Arthur assumes leadership of the city."

Colonel McGrath looked back and forth between Luthor and Maverick, the debate evident on his ruddy face.

"Oh, for god's sake," Luthor droned, rolling his eyes. "I don't have time for this." Aiming the gun at Colonel McGrath, he pulled the trigger and shot the man in the neck. McGrath gasped, clutching his neck as his hold on Nathan loosened. Since Nathan was bound, he couldn't run, and Dr. Ziegler stepped in front of him as he fell to the ground. Grace watched him struggle to free his binds on the cold floor, and she ached to run to him.

"Who's next?" Luthor asked, wielding the gun while a crazed expression lined his face. "Or do you want Jessica to die, Tristan?"

Tristan stood frozen, his chest heaving with deep breaths as he assessed the situation.

"I hate to make the call, but it's her or humanity," Arianna said, aiming her gun at Luthor. "I'm sorry, Tristan—"

"No!" Tristan yelled. "There has to be another way—"

A gunshot reverberated throughout the room, causing everyone to duck. Grace slowly opened her eyes to see Dr. Ziegler inhale a sharp breath as a red dot appeared between his eyes. Blood oozed from the red circle before he slumped and fell in a heap on the floor.

Turning to face the door, Grace observed a tall Black man step inside.

Luthor aimed his gun at the man, and Tristan lifted his to aim at Luthor at the same time. They both fired as the room erupted into chaos. Rushing toward the desk where Luthor had taken cover, Tristan advanced, ready to fire another round.

"You son of a bitch," Tristan snarled, slowly circling the desk. Luthor lifted his gun, and Tristan kicked it out of his hand, sending it crashing across the floor.

A sneer curved Tristan's lips as he loomed above Luthor, his gun aimed square between his eyes. "Well, well. The moment I've longed for has finally arrived. Any last words?"

Luthor reached for the knife at his belt in one last frantic attempt to save himself. Tristan's jaw ticked as every muscle in his body tensed. "Burn in hell, you fucking bastard."

And then, Tristan Holder kept the vow he'd made for so many long, wretched years.

There, in a cold bunker under a broken city, he pressed the muzzle of his gun to the evil dictator's temple and buried a bullet in Luthor Cromwell's brain.

Chapter 30

"**D**amn, Ron!" Arianna exclaimed, rushing toward the tall man and throwing her arms around him in a rare show of affection. "Deandra told us you fought in Kuwait in the nineties, but that's some sharp shooting. Thanks for the assist."

"You're welcome," he said, returning the hug before releasing her. "Deandra's got some excellent surveillance skills, but I prefer old-fashioned hand-to-hand combat. When she passed along your advice to lock ourselves inside and wait out the advance, I just couldn't do it. I needed to help if I could. For my son, Carter, who died from Luthor's horrible drug, and for all the others who also lost the ability to fight back."

"Thank you, Ron," Dominic said, extending his hand. "We're grateful."

Grace rushed over to Nathan, removing his binds and gag as Tristan did the same for Jessica. Grace pulled the boy into a smothering embrace, kissing his hair as he trembled in her arms.

"I'm sorry I got caught," he mumbled, causing her heart to shatter. "I promise I was hiding by the trail."

"You're not in trouble, buddy," Tristan said, reaching over and cupping his shoulder as he held Jessica in his arms. "You did a great job opening the wall. I'm proud of you."

Pride glowed on Nathan's face, demonstrating how important Tristan's approval was to him. Glancing at Jessica, Grace smiled. "You okay, Jessica?"

Her bloodshot eyes met Grace's, full of pain from her addiction and terrifying brush with death. "I don't know if I'll ever be okay," she whispered. "I tried to tell you all to let me die, but I was gagged. I'm not worth saving if you can save the world instead."

"Hey," Tristan said, gently shaking her. "I don't want to hear you talk like that. Of course you're worth saving. We're going to get you on Dani's cure, and you're going to be good as new. You hear me?"

Tears streamed down her face. "I'm so tired, Tristan."

"I know," he said, releasing a ragged breath. "We all are, Jess. But I'm here now, and that bastard is gone." Drawing her head to his chest, he stroked her hair as he gazed into Grace's eyes.

Grace stared back, allowing him to see her relief, and her pain...and her *love*. All the love she'd never stopped feeling for him, even after things had gone so wrong.

I'm sorry, she mouthed, caressing Nathan's hair.

He lifted her free hand to his lips and pressed a kiss to her palm as butterflies fluttered in her stomach. "No more apologies, empress. It's time to start a new era."

Jessica lifted her head to look at Grace. "I'm sorry about...*being with* Luthor, Grace. It was the only way I could get EverLife and the watered-down antidote."

"Oh, don't apologize to me," she said, grimacing. "I'm sorry you had to endure that. What he put you through was awful."

Jessica lowered her gaze to the floor, and Grace understood she had a long road ahead of her full of physical and mental healing. Hell, they all did after the nightmare they'd experienced with Luthor.

"I need a team to stay here with me as I assume temporary leadership," Arthur said, addressing the room. "Dominic, Arianna, and Zayne, would you be willing to hang back for a few days?"

"Absolutely, as long as Ron throws some bagel sandwiches in the mix," Arianna said.

"Done," Ron said with a salute.

"I'm going to send the rest of you back to the compound so we can prepare for the next phase. Maverick, please have Danica treat Jessica with the EverLife cure, and then prepare the vials we have for transport to the city. I'm going to set up clinics where we can receive the addicted patients, especially the homeless ones, and begin to cure them. I'll recruit any of Luthor's soldiers willing to pledge loyalty to a new democratic government. Any who remain loyal to him will have to be incarcerated until we can have a fair trial for them."

"Will do," Maverick said with a nod.

"I'm also going to visit the factory in Northeast DC where Luthor produced the majority of the EverLife supply. We need to begin production on Dani's cure immediately."

"I know she'll be excited to ramp up production," Maverick confirmed. "What about her trial?"

"We'll get to it," Arthur said, "but let's have her heal a couple thousand people first. I think that will go a long way toward obtaining a not guilty verdict from a sympathetic jury."

Grace could see the hope in Maverick's eyes as he nodded.

"Let's task some of the remaining militia to gather the bodies of the fallen and cremate them outside the walls," Arthur continued. "We prepared the families they left behind that we wouldn't be bringing bodies back because we have no way to properly store them. Can you take care of cataloging the names of the men and women who didn't make it? We'll have a military funeral for them and honor them in a formal ceremony in a few weeks once we have a handle on things."

"I can do that," Maverick said, extending his hand. "You sure you're ready for this, Arthur?"

He lifted his eyebrows as he shook Maverick's hand. "Whether I'm ready or not, we've got to blaze a new path. But yeah, I'm ready."

"What do you want me to do with Luthor's body?"

Arthur glanced over to Luthor's lifeless body on the cold floor. "Burn it first."

Armed with a plan, the members of the fledgling new government got to work.

Grace and Tristan returned in the caravan to Cumberland. They arrived just before dawn and as the withdrawal symptoms were setting in for Jessica.

"We're almost there, Jess," Tristan soothed, holding her trembling body in his lap as they sat in the back of one of the pickup trucks. He'd wrapped her in a blanket, and Grace admired the protective gesture. He was going to be such a good dad. She just hoped he allowed her the chance to be a mom alongside him. Although he'd declared no more apologies were needed, they had an important talk ahead of them.

When they pulled into the compound, Tristan asked the driver to take them directly to the clinic. He jumped from the truck and rushed Jessica inside, calling out for a nurse.

"I'm a nurse," a woman said, approaching them. "Is she on EverLife?"

"Yes," he nodded. "We need the cure ASAP. Is Dani here?"

"She's at the school," the nurse said.

"I can go get her," Nathan offered.

"Thanks, buddy. I appreciate it."

Grace stayed by Tristan's side as he followed the nurse, Rikina, into a triage room with a vacant bed. He lay Jessica on the crisp sheets as her teeth chattered.

"I'm going to die," she moaned.

"You're going to be okay," he soothed, rubbing her sweaty forehead. "We made it, Jess."

"Be right back with the cure," Rikina said, rushing from the room and returning a minute later with a syringe. She urged Tristan to step back, and Grace held his hand.

"Let her work, Tristan," she said, squeezing his fingers. "You've done your part."

Jessica gasped as Rikina injected the cure into her arm. Dani rushed into the room, picking up a stethoscope from the counter and plugging it in her ears.

"Status?"

"Injected with three cc's of EverLife cure-serum," Rikina stated.

Dani lifted the small light from her pocket and clicked it on. Lifting Jessica's eyelid, she examined one pupil and then the other.

"Name?"

"She's my sister, Jessica," Tristan said from the foot of the bed.

"Hey, Jessica," Dani said, observing her enlarged pupils. "You're doing great. This stuff's going to cycle through your veins, and you should start to feel better in a few minutes. My name's Danica and I'll be right here."

Grace watched their interplay, imagining how many people would soon go through the same process. "We have so many people to heal. How can we possibly do it?"

Tristan threaded his fingers through hers. "One person at a time."

"How very optimistic of my ex-husband."

His lips twitched before they fell silent, holding hands as they observed Jessica relax on the bed. Dani approached and looked at her watch. "She's going to need hours to rest and will most likely fall asleep. Rikina will monitor her. In the meantime, you must be hungry and exhausted. The mess hall just opened for breakfast."

Grace's stomach grumbled, confirming Dani's statement.

"Go on," she said, shooing them from the room. "We've got this. Go get some food and then some rest. And you probably have a lot to discuss, so I'll make sure Nathan and Raquel don't disturb you in your rooms."

Tristan glanced at Grace. "Does she know...?"

"She knows," Grace said. "She figured it out."

"Your secret is safe with me, but maybe it won't be a secret any longer?" Dani flashed a cheeky grin. "Anyway,

Maverick informed me that Luthor is dead, but I'm dying to hear the whole story. Great job kicking his ass."

"It's just the first step on a long, winding path to rebuilding," Grace said.

"But at least we have something to rebuild." Dani lifted a finger. "Now, go on. If Jessica falls asleep, I'll head over and grab some breakfast. If I don't see you there, I'll assume you're *talking*." She waggled her eyebrows. "Have fun!"

Tristan spared Jessica one last look before leading Grace out of the clinic.

Chapter 31

Although she was starving, Grace wanted to remove the tactical gear and bulletproof pads. She and Tristan stopped by the school to change clothes before heading to the mess hall. They found Raquel there, chatting away with Nathan, Chris, Jenny and the other kids. When she saw them, her eyes lit with excitement and she ran across the room straight into Grace's arms.

"Hey, sweetheart," Grace said, squeezing her until her arms trembled.

"I'm so proud of you guys," Raquel said. "Maria knew you'd kick Luthor's ass one day."

"Since we just saved the world, I'll overlook the use of that word, young lady," Grace said, her tone equal parts scolding and teasing.

Raquel turned to Tristan and enveloped him in a hug. "Maverick said you all were awesome. He told us everything."

"He fought valiantly," Tristan said, pressing a kiss to Raquel's forehead. "Is he here?"

"He said he has to take care of some things, but Dani is going to come and play wiffle ball with us today. It might be our last day because Maverick said some people are going to leave the compound and move to DC now that it's safe." Tilting her head, she looked between them. "Are we going to move to DC? If we do, can we bring Maria?"

Laughing, Grace ran a hand over her hair. "These are great questions that Tristan and I need to discuss, but we're starving."

"Oh! You can come and eat. Nathan's over there. He said he snuck into one of the trucks and helped you guys! That's badass—" She glanced toward Grace. "I mean, it's really cool."

"He was an excellent soldier," Grace said, pointing at two open seats at the long table. "Save these for us."

She and Tristan loaded up their plates and sat with the kids while they ate.

A few minutes later, Grace patted her stomach and sighed. "I'm in a food coma. Time to shower."

Tristan's eyes bore into hers as he cocked a brow. "Want to conserve water, empress? I need a shower too."

Breathing a laugh, she shrugged. "I mean, why not do our part to save the environment?"

Tristan's eyes blazed with lust, and his chair scraped as he stood. "Okay, kids. Have fun at wiffle ball. Grace and I are heading to shower and nap."

As he led her back to the school, Grace noted his quick, determined pace.

"Slow down there. You're dragging me like a caveman heading back to his lair."

"I feel like a caveman right now," he gritted, leading her inside the school. "But I'll restrain myself...for now."

A jolt ran down Grace's spine, and she realized it was anticipation. After so many long, lonely years, she was finally going to make love to Tristan again. Nerves swirled in her belly as they approached their rooms.

They grabbed the towels Dani had left out before walking to the stall in the boys' bathroom that had running water. Sunlight streamed through the faded windows as they slowly removed their clothes. Tristan drew her under the spray, which was lukewarm thanks to the small generator Arthur's men had set up, and bumps rose on her skin as the water sluiced over her.

Tristan picked up the bar of soap on the small shelf and lathered his hands before soothing the bumps on her arms with the suds. Turning her to face the spray, he moved his hands along her back, running them over the swell of her backside, before crouching to wash her legs.

When her back was clean, he stood and slowly turned her to face him.

He lathered his hands again before placing them over her collarbone. Fingers spread, he gazed at her lovingly, washing her neck and the swells of her breasts as her eyes drifted closed.

"Tristan..."

"I almost forgot how pretty you are here," he murmured, cupping her breasts in his hands and gently massaging them. "How these sexy little nipples are so much pinker than the rest of your skin." He tenderly pinched each nipple before running his thumb over the taut nubs to ease the sting.

Grace gasped, every cell in her body tingling from his proximity and the ministrations of his fingers.

"You always loved when I played with you here." He squeezed her nipples again as her head fell back.

"*Oh god*...I want more..."

Tristan growled before lathering his hands again and quickly washing his body. Grace observed his rapid movements and bit her lip to stifle a laugh. Lowering her gaze, she noticed his cock springing from the nest of hair between his legs, hard and ready to claim her.

The urgency in his movements ignited something deep inside, reaffirming he still craved her as much as she yearned for him.

When they were finished, they dried off and wrapped the towels around their bodies. After reaching Grace's room, Tristan closed the door and turned the lock.

Grace sent him a questioning look.

"No one's coming in here for *hours*," he said, tossing away his towel before hooking his fingers over the top of hers as it hugged her body. "I mean it, empress. I'm going to fuck you in all the ways I couldn't over the past ten years." He yanked the towel from her body and threw it on the floor. "You ready?"

Her nipples pebbled in the cool air as she backed toward the bed. When the mattress hit the backs of her knees, she sat and leaned back. Resting one heel on the bed, and then the other, she spread her legs, inviting him to look his fill.

A slow, drawn-out breath escaped his lungs as he stared at her slick core. "Fuck yes, you're ready. Look at that sweet, sexy pussy..."

Striding forward, he dropped to his knees and pressed his palms to her inner thighs, spreading her legs wider. "This pussy wants to be touched..." Resting his cheek on her leg, he stared into her eyes as he kissed a trail from her knee to her thigh. "And it wants to be played with," he rasped, placing his fingers at her drenched core and circling them in the wet essence.

"Yessss..." she cried, pushing into his fingers.

"And it wants to be kissed..." he said against the skin of her thigh before his lips moved to her drenched folds. He swiped his tongue over her deepest place, growling in approval as she groaned. "And it wants to be tasted, doesn't it, baby?"

A tremor shot through her body as her clit ached for his lips...for his *tongue*...

"Yes, Tristan...*please*..."

He took pity on her, burying his face in her core and lapping at her honey. His lips nibbled and tasted her sensitive flesh, setting her on fire as her skin flushed.

"Sweeter than I even remembered," he breathed against her wet skin. "So fucking sweet..."

Grace undulated into his mouth, unabashed and unashamed as he loved her. His mouth generated torturous pleasure, reverberating through her whole body as it quivered. Tristan placed his lips over her clit, sucking the swollen bud in smooth, fluid motions as he slipped a finger inside her.

She gasped, unused to the pressure after years of abstinence.

"Take it, sweetheart," he murmured against her clit, inserting another finger and moving them back and forth. He circled the tight vise, gathering her honey as he prepared her for more. "That's it. Open up for me." His tongue flicked her clit, sending her ever closer to the edge as he worked his fingers deep inside her.

"Oh...*fuck!*" she cried, spearing her fingers in his thick hair. "I'm going to come...Tristan!"

Her back arched; her muscles straining as she squeezed her eyes closed. Bursts of gold and yellow exploded behind her eyelids as she began to come. Greedy and wanton, she pushed into Tristan's skillful mouth and fingers, emitting a joyous laugh as she drowned in bliss.

Tristan's motions slowed, his fingers stilling as he pressed kisses to her wet flesh. Grace felt his soul in each tender kiss...felt his *love* as he reveled in her pleasure.

Her body fell lax on the bed as she released a deep breath. "*Ohmygod...*" she whispered, grinning as her eyes remained closed. "So fucking good..."

Tristan hummed against her core, his palm caressing the soft skin of her thigh in long, languid strokes. Forcing her lids open, she stared at him through half-lidded eyes.

He gazed up at her, his cheek pressed against her inner thigh as he nuzzled her core. The flecks in his eyes burned with unchecked emotion, and her heart slammed.

"I want you inside me," she whispered, trailing the backs of her fingers over the stubble that lined his jaw. "I missed you so much..."

Tristan rose, placing his arms beneath her and repositioning her so she lay flat on the mattress. He crawled over her, lithe as a predator, and positioned his muscled body between her legs. Balancing on his forearms, he slid his fingers into her hair, tugging slightly in the way she'd always loved...

In the way he still remembered.

His eyes bore into hers as his cock glided through her wet folds, searching for the place it had always belonged.

"Tell me again," he rasped, his eyes searching hers as his cock probed before testing...easing slightly inside as she gasped.

"I missed you," she said, clutching his hair as her eyes stung with tears. "I'm so sorry..."

"None of that, remember?" he said, easing deeper inside as she opened herself, allowing him to claim her. "If we keep apologizing for the past, we'll never have a future." He pushed deeper, groaning as his fingers tightened in her hair. "And I want a future with you, Grace. God help me, I love you. You're the only woman I'm ever going to love, empress."

Tears streamed down her cheeks as he surged deeper, filling every crevice as she clung to him.

"*Shhh...*" Pressing his lips to her cheek, he sipped her tears, swallowing the salty essence that represented all their past pain and heartache. "Just feel me, sweetheart. Let me make you mine again."

He drew back, gazing into her eyes before heaving forward, asserting his claim in one long stroke. Grace wanted to say the words back, but her throat was clogged with heavy emotion, making speech impossible.

Tristan worked his hips, increasing the pace as he fucked her in long, pleasurable strokes. His breath grew shallow and rapid, his skin heating as he filled her over and over...

"Your body is *mine*, Grace, and I'm never letting you go again," he crooned, pressing his forehead to hers as he spoke against her lips. "Do you hear me?"

She captured his lips, unable to speak but dying to stake her claim too. She thrust her tongue inside his mouth, swirling and tangling with his as he moaned. Sweat dripped from his skin, mingling with hers as they moved in tandem. Their bodies danced in a rhythm both remembered, connected and pulsing as their breath mingled.

Tristan slid his hand under her leg, drawing it high and balancing it against his arm as he pressed his palm flat to the mattress...opening her wider...stretching her as she chortled with pleasure.

"Fuck, Grace," he rasped, his hips hammering against her as he neared the edge. "You're going to suck everything from me, aren't you?"

She purred, arching her back to allow him greater access...wanting him as deep as possible. The blunt head of his cock pressed against the spot only he knew, reigniting the tiny fires in every nerve ending of her trembling body. Gripping his shoulders, she speared her nails into his flesh, reveling in his desire-laden hiss as he slammed into her.

"Oh...*god!*" he rasped, his body lurching as he dove over the cliff. Grace joined him, sliding into the pleasurable abyss as they clung to each other. Aching to possess him, she bit his lip, holding him in her grip as her body quaked beneath him. He used to love it when she bit him during sex, and he growled with unguarded lust.

Clenching her hair, he drew her head back, baring her neck. "You fucking bit me," he rasped, raking his teeth over her skin. "Fuck, you know I love that."

Burying his face in her neck, he shuddered several times, emptying everything into her ravaged body. His muscles jerked...shaking against her own...until he released a heavy breath and collapsed against her sated frame.

Grace ran her fingernails over his scalp in the long caresses he loved. He emitted a satisfied "*Mmm...*" against her nape, causing her lips to curve. God, the deep grumble of his voice against her sweaty skin was so sexy. Wrapping her legs around him, she held tight, wanting to hold him inside her as long as possible.

Time melted away as they lay entwined. Tristan's hand searched for hers, lacing their fingers as they rested atop the bed.

His breath slowed against her nape, and he lifted his head to gaze into her eyes. Resting his head on his fist, he released her hand and touched his finger to her lips. Hazel eyes stared into blue ones filled with emotion as he slowly traced her lips.

"I'm humbled you can still love me after keeping Raquel from you," she whispered against his finger. "I probably don't deserve your forgiveness."

His lips twisted into a grin. "You probably don't. But I've just survived a decade where I was fucking miserable, and I'm smart enough to get out of my own way so I don't repeat the cycle. That's what you always told me to do, right? Get out of my own way."

Breathing a laugh, she nodded. "Yes. Sometimes, you just have to have faith and let everything else go."

"I have faith in *you*," he whispered, his tone so reverent it almost broke her heart. "And I have faith in us. I don't want to be an angry person who pushes away the person I love. That will only ensure I remain miserable." Kissing her, he drew back and smiled. "Of course, that means you have to love me too. I'm waiting, empress."

Laughter leapt from her throat at his cocky demand. "I was having trouble speaking since you were banging my brains out. And I..." Struggling to voice the words, she shook her head on the pillow. "I'm a different person from that girl you loved all those years ago. Maybe you still love her, and if that's the case, this might not work."

"We've both changed, but that doesn't mean we're doomed. Maybe we both just grew into the people we need to be to make it work this time."

Grinning, she ran her thumb over his lips. "You've *definitely* become an optimist. It's so weird."

"It's weird for me too, but it feels pretty good." The creases at the corners of his eyes deepened as he smiled.

Reality began to creep back in, and her expression grew more serious. "I can't give you any more children. It's something I want so badly, but I can't..." Her nostrils flared as wetness clouded her eyes.

"Hey," he said, cupping her cheek as his eyebrows drew together. "That's okay, Grace. I mean it. We have Raquel, and I'm pretty sure we've both fallen for Nathan too. He's a great kid."

"He is. Are you open to adopting him? I'd love to raise him and give him a family."

"I'm open." He pressed a kiss to her lips before continuing. "I have no idea how to be a dad, but I guess I'm about to get a crash course in parenting. We both are."

"You're great with them. I'd be honored to raise them with you."

"And if you want a baby after we figure it out, we can adopt one," he said, stroking her cheek. "Lord knows there are lots of kids who need parents in this world."

Grace's chin wobbled as she realized she might finally get the opportunity to live the life she'd sacrificed for so long. "I think I'd like that," she whispered.

"Okay, sweetheart. We'll discuss it once we figure everything else out. I mean, don't get me wrong. We still have a *lot* of shit to figure out."

"Well, first, you need to marry me again. I'm finally free and want to be Mrs. Grace Holder again."

"Damn, woman!" he exclaimed, feigning exasperation. "That's the second time you've demanded I marry you. I let you get away with it the first time, but this time, I'm going to give you a proper proposal. I just need a damn minute."

"I think I'd like a proper proposal. I've been married twice and never really gotten one."

"I'm not going to take the blame for you showing up in the pouring rain and demanding I marry you all those years ago." He nipped the tip of her nose. "You were so determined, sputtering and wet. You wouldn't take no for an answer."

"Because I was madly in love with you," she said, shaking her head on the pillow.

He studied her, his lips curved into a satisfied grin as he waited. "Go on, empress. Tell me now if you're going to tell me. Otherwise, we're at an impasse. I can't do this if you don't love me back. I need you to be half as obsessed with me as I am with you, or my pride is going to suffer some serious setbacks."

"Tristan..." she warbled, struggling to speak over the swell of emotion in her chest and throat. "Of course I love you. I've always loved you, even when you left and I swore I'd never forgive you." She placed her palm over his heart. "I love you in hidden corners of my soul I didn't even know existed. You showed them to me when we first met, and they'll only ever be inhabited by you."

He covered her hand against the scratchy hairs atop his chest and squeezed.

"I loved you when I made hard decisions that hurt us both, and I love the man you've become. You're complicated and enigmatic, but also deeply loyal and caring...and sexy," she finished with a grin. "I want to spend every day I have left with you, if you'll have me."

He squinted one eye. "Umm, yeah, I think I'll have you."

Tossing her head back, she laughed with joy. "Well, thank goodness. I was hoping you wouldn't reject me when you're *literally* inside me."

"Speaking of that..." Tristan slipped from her as he lifted and balanced his weight on his arms. "Let me get something to clean us up." He stood and grabbed a cloth from the dresser before pouring some water from the nearby jug into a basin. After soaking the cloth, he strode over and commanded softly, "Open those pretty legs, baby."

Grace complied, gazing upon him as he cleaned away the evidence of their loving. He returned to the basin, ringing out the cloth before cleaning himself. After spreading it over a nearby chair to dry, he walked toward her and Grace swallowed thickly, overcome by his confident gait and his sinewy muscled body.

"If you keep checking me out like that, I'm going to be back inside you in a matter of minutes," he said, sliding in beside her and drawing her to his side.

Grace curled into him, tossing her leg over his thighs as she held tight. "Well, you *did* say you were going to fuck me to make up for lost time."

Laughter rumbled in his chest underneath her ear as she snuggled against him. "I am. Just need a few minutes to recover..."

His fingers lazily stroked her hair as they drifted, their muscles slowly relaxing as exhaustion claimed them.

Grace knew he would make good on his promise to make love to her several more times before they rejoined the rest of the world. For now, she allowed herself to fall into slumber, free from the evil and heartache that had pervaded her life for so long.

Chapter 32

That evening, after lots of exertion balanced with peaceful napping, she and Tristan cleaned themselves up and headed to the mess hall for dinner. She and Tristan entered to find Dani and Maverick sitting with Raquel and Nathan.

"Well, well," Dani said, her eyes alight with mischief. "Looks like somebody had a *very* good nap."

"Uh, yeah," Grace said, feeling her face turn several shades of red as she rubbed the back of her neck. "It was really nice."

"*Pfft*," Tristan said, pulling out the seat for Grace. "I think it was more than nice."

"Okay, I'll let you off the hook since kids are present. But good for you," Dani said with a wink.

Grace faced Raquel and Nathan. "Tristan and I want to talk to you both in private after dinner. Raquel, we'll speak to you first, and then we'll bring Nathan in. We can talk by the pond."

"Okay," Raquel said as Nathan mumbled in agreement.

Grace could see the slight bit of fear that crossed his face, and she ached to soothe him. "It's nothing bad, sweetheart," she said, encircling his wrist. "I promise."

He nodded, and they proceeded to eat one of their last meals on the compound.

Afterward, Grace asked Nathan to hang back with Dani and Maverick for a few minutes before joining them by the pond.

The three of them walked toward the water, Raquel chatting in between them as they held her hands. Grace glanced over her head toward Tristan, smiling as her heart threatened to pound from her chest.

When they arrived at a soft patch of grass on the bank of the pond, they lowered to sit in a small circle.

Grace cleared her throat and nervously rubbed her hands over her thighs. "Sweetheart, there's something Tristan and I need to tell you. It's a secret we couldn't tell you for a long time, but we're ready now."

"Why couldn't you tell me?" she asked, her eyebrows lifting.

"Because the dictator we fought in the city—"

"Luthor Cromwell," Raquel interjected.

Grace nodded. "Luthor was a terrible man, as you already know. Because of his relationship to me, he threatened to hurt you."

"What relationship?"

"Luthor was partners with my father before the world collapsed. During those years, he threatened my father, and eventually me and...you." Clearing her throat, she ran her hand over the soft grass. "I couldn't let him hurt you, so I hid you from him with Maria so he wouldn't find you."

Confusion marred her features as her eyebrows drew together. "Maria told me she rescued me because my birth parents died."

"She did rescue you, sweetheart, but your parents weren't dead. That was something Maria and I told you to protect you." Tears filled her eyes as she scooted closer and placed her hand over Raquel's thigh. "It was something I never wanted to hide from you, but I didn't know any other way to keep you safe."

Her eyes searched Grace's as realization set in. "Are you my mom?"

A sob tore from Grace's throat as she nodded. "I am, and I love you very much. I know you might be mad at me for not telling you, and if you are, I understand—"

Raquel jumped into her arms, hugging her as emotion washed over Grace in overwhelming waves. Clenching her daughter tight, she allowed the tears to steam down her cheeks as she rocked her in her lap.

"I'm so sorry, sweetheart," she whispered. "I wish we hadn't lost so much time."

Drawing back, Raquel wiped away Grace's tears. "I'm not mad. You don't have to cry. Honestly, sometimes I wondered if we were related and you just didn't want to tell me. We look a lot alike."

"We do," Grace said, smoothing her hair. "And I'm so proud you're my daughter, Raquel. You're the best part of me."

Raquel slowly looked toward Tristan. "Since you were married, does that mean you're my dad?"

Grace saw the sheen of wetness in Tristan's eyes. "Yes, sweetheart."

Raquel reached for him, and he scooped her into his lap, squeezing his eyes as he held her.

"And there are some things we want to talk to you and Nathan about," Grace said, looking over the horizon. Sure enough, Nathan trudged over to them, his shoulders slightly slumped as if he were expecting bad news.

"You said to come out in ten minutes," he said, crossing his arms. "If you're not ready—"

"We're ready," Grace said, patting the ground beside her. "Sit here."

He lowered beside her, and she cupped his shoulder. "We want to talk to you to tell you something good, Nathan. Well, we hope you'll think it's good."

His eyebrows lifted as he waited.

"Tristan and I had a child ten years ago we couldn't keep." She smiled at Raquel. "Raquel is that child and we just told her."

Nathan glanced between them. "Okay. That's cool. Are you all going to live together now?"

"We are. We've decided we're going to move to the city and help Arthur rebuild. They have technology there, and we feel it will be the best place for you all to go to school."

"You want me to come with you?"

"Of course we do," she said, tilting her head. "We think you're very special, Nathan, and we'd like to adopt you if you want to be part of our family."

His eyes darted between Grace and Tristan's, searching for insincerity.

"What do you say, buddy?" Tristan asked. "Want to stay with us?"

His chin trembled as he nodded. "I was scared you were going to send me back to Solomon."

"One of these days, you're going to trust us, kid," Tristan said. "I know trust is hard to come by in this world, but you're family now."

Nathan studied them as the news set in. "Where will we live in the city?"

"There's a rowhome in Dupont Circle that I think would be perfect for us all to start over. It's owner recently passed and I inherited the property." In fact, she was now the owner of several new properties thanks to her husband's recent demise. "It's close to the capital where Arthur is going to rebuild, so it's an ideal location."

"Is there enough room for Maria?" Raquel asked. "We have to convince her to come with us."

"We're going to do our best. We've decided we're going to leave the compound once Jessica is better, and we're all going to return to the city. We'll stop in Dundore on the way. I'll need you to turn on that killer smile and convince her to come with us," Grace said.

"I can do it!" Raquel said confidently.

Tristan grinned. "I mean, who can resist that endearing determination? Maria doesn't stand a chance."

Grace leaned back on her hands and inhaled a deep breath. "It's a new beginning for all of us. I'm excited for our future."

There by the pond, under a dusky sky, the fledgling family solidified their tentative bond, hopeful for the days ahead.

Part III

The Future

Chapter 33

One year later

"Dr. Danica Lawson-Ward, will you please stand for the reading of the verdict?"

Dani looked over her shoulder, wiping her sweaty palms on her pants as she looked at Maverick. Her husband stared back, an abundance of love and support shining in his eyes, and mouthed, *I love you.*

Releasing a deep breath, Dani stood to face the repercussions of her actions.

The courthouse had been rebuilt after Arthur assumed power, and he had appointed himself judge for Dani's televised trial. Technology was slowly being reintroduced across the country—and the world—and people from every corner of the globe were watching Dani's trial if they had access to Wi-Fi.

A jury of twelve of Dani's peers stood to her right, six on the bottom row of the jury box and six above them. She recognized a few as recovered addicts she'd cured with NewHope, the proper name that had been given to her EverLife cure.

NewHope was also a callback to Star Wars, an epic tale with its own rebellion who eventually defeated the dark side. The name had been chosen by voters in the first election of the reformed government. It was a provision on the ballot, along with the vote at the top of the ballot, where Arthur Reyes ran for president.

Now, almost a year into his term, he had proven himself as a man of the people. He, Dani, Maverick, Grace, Tristan and others on his team had worked tirelessly to heal the sick and destroy every last vial of EverLife on the planet. Although stashes of black-market EverLife still existed, Dani had faith that those would eventually be destroyed. Arthur had created a special ops division of the new army specifically trained to hunt down the remaining EverLife dealers and drug makers.

One day, the scourge would be eliminated for good.

"Foreperson, please read the verdict," Arthur said from his perch at the judge's bench, drawing Dani away from her musings.

"We, the jury, find the defendant, Dr. Danica Lawson-Ward, guilty of involuntary crimes against humanity."

A collective gasp buzzed through the room, and Dani reminded herself to remain calm. This is the verdict she'd expected, and it was an honest summation of her crimes. Making eye contact with the foreperson, she gave an understanding nod.

The foreperson, a middle-aged Black man with salt and pepper hair, returned a sympathetic smile and handed the verdict to the bailiff, who then handed it to Arthur.

Arthur took the verdict in his hands and read it over to confirm. Lifting his gaze to Dani's, he spoke with firm clarity.

"Dr. Lawson-Ward, you have been found guilty by a jury of your peers. Do you understand this verdict?"

"Yes, sir."

Arthur pursed his lips as he formulated his next words. "I chose to serve as judge for this trial because it gives me the opportunity to impose a sentence. One that is just and takes into consideration the substantial effort you've put into healing our society."

Dani licked her dry lips as her heart raced.

"You arrived at the Cumberland compound and dedicated yourself to creating a cure. You fought alongside your husband and the rebellion to remove Luthor Cromwell from power. In the year since, you've worked tirelessly to cure addicts in DC while also traveling the country and the world to cure others. Your sentence must reflect the effort you've already expended and your future efforts."

Arthur rose, and Dani's lips twitched at his slight flair for the dramatic since the trial was being streamed. The next election would be held in a year, and he knew this moment would get several million replays before then.

It was a savvy political move, and Dani admired it.

"People of the new America," he said, lifting his hands. "I understand the desire many of you still have to blame Dr. Lawson-Ward for the EverLife crisis. Although she played her part in the downfall of society, as the charges state, I truly believe it was involuntary. Luthor Cromwell was the evil mastermind, and the majority of the blame will always lie with him."

"Dr. Lawson-Ward," Arthur said with a nod, "I hereby sentence you to ten years of servitude to the new American government. You will donate your time, knowledge and expertise to creating a cure for cancer and other terminal illnesses. You will not receive payment for this work, but the government will fund your labs and research. I look forward to you continuing to improve society with your fastidious brilliance, and believe your contributions to humanity over the next ten years will come to outshine the damage from the EverLife crisis."

Dani's chin trembled as she nodded. "Thank you. I want nothing more than to discover a cure for cancer, and I will do my best to contribute to the improvement of society."

"Very well. The bailiff will escort you out to process the paperwork. You will be required to stay in DC for your ten-year sentence unless you obtain approval to leave from your probation officer. I can assign an ankle monitor, but I don't think we need that. Do you?"

Dani breathed a laugh. "No, sir. If you build a lab for me in DC, I'm a workaholic who won't ever leave it. Ask my husband." She pointed over her shoulder to Maverick.

A chuckle spread through the court at the moment of levity.

"I look forward to working with you, Dr. Lawson-Ward. Court is adjourned."

Covering her heart, Dani expelled a deep breath. Maverick rushed over, enveloping her in a hug before the bailiff could drag her away.

"Great job, slugger."

"I'm going to create my cancer cure," she said, staring into his eyes as her own filled with tears. "Finally, Mav."

"I never doubted you, sweetheart, and know you'll succeed." He cupped her face before the bailiff called her name.

"Ma'am, I need to take you to process the paperwork."

"Of course. You'll be here when I'm done?" she called to Maverick.

"I'll always be here, babe. See you in a bit."

Hope rushed through Dani's frame as she filed down the hallway to the processing room. She felt the sentence was just and couldn't wait to get started on her mission to save people from the intense pain she'd felt when her mother died.

The road to creating her cancer cure was winding and jagged—and nowhere near finished—but she was excited for the days ahead.

Her memory had mostly returned, although she still had dark spots and bad days that were a struggle. Thankfully, her husband was always by her side, steadfast and strong, helping her cope.

She would forever live with the guilt of the destruction her efforts had wrought. But now, with a firm resolution in place, perhaps she could balance the guilt with the pride she would feel when she cured the world of cancer, diabetes, Parkinson's and the many other terminal illnesses she would spend the next ten years trying to eradicate.

Dr. Danica Lawson-Ward was ready to save the world, and this time she wouldn't fail.

Arianna Cavalleri stood on the wooden porch of her home in the mountains of West Virginia. Staring across the expansive valleys, she spotted a hawk flying in the distance. Majestic and regal, it reminded her of Dani's face as Arthur imposed her sentence earlier that day. She was extremely proud of her sister, and grateful she would finally get to complete the work she'd yearned to fulfill for many years.

Clutching the wooden post on the porch of the home her husband had built with some local contractors, she inhaled the fresh air, thankful to be far away from the city. Arianna had helped Arthur and his team rebuild for several months, but then her circumstances had changed and she'd craved an escape from the technology the world was reembracing.

Call her old-fashioned, but the one thing she'd liked about the end of the world was not having to be tethered to technology every damn minute of every day. There was freedom in watching a brilliant sunset against the backdrop of ancient mountaintops without being interrupted by a phone ringing or a car horn blaring in the distance.

The front door creaked behind her, and Dominic's footsteps sounded. He sidled up behind her and covered her distended abdomen, caressing it in slow, smooth circles.

"How's our little terror doing in there?" he teased, resting his chin on her shoulder.

"Kicking up a damn storm," Arianna said, covering his hand and moving it over the spot where the baby was seemingly practicing the lambada. "She's going to be a squirrely little thing."

"We still don't know it's a girl since you refuse to go to the hospital for a proper checkup."

"Dani has checked on me during her monthly visits. I trust her, and after the past few years, I don't trust most of what happens in the healthcare industry. Talia is amazing," she said, referencing the midwife they'd hired to help Arianna when she gave birth in a few weeks. "She's all I need."

"I know you're tough, but I worry," he said, kissing her nape. "If something goes wrong during labor, we're an hour away from the closest hospital that's reopened."

"I'm going to be fine." Turning to face him, she slipped her arms around his neck. "I don't know how to explain it, but I just *feel* this is the right path. That I'm supposed to have her here, with you and Talia by my side, and that everything's going to be okay." She flashed a grin. "Since I'm a morbid pessimist, you should probably take the win on this one. I'm actually positive and hopeful about something."

Rich laughter leapt from his throat. "That's very true." Resting his forehead against hers, he swayed as the last rays of light surrounded them. "My grumpy wife, the love of my life and eternal doom-monger."

"Ohhh, I like 'doom-monger.' Let's make that nickname official. It has a nice ring."

Dominic just chuckled and shook his head. Drawing back, he formed an empathetic smile. "Dani looked good when we streamed the verdict today. I know you wanted to be there, but she was adamant you shouldn't travel this close to your due date. The sentence was what we expected."

"She's going to be just fine," Arianna said. "She's tough as nails and smart as hell. With a government lab and unlimited funding, she's going to accomplish so many amazing things. Mom would be proud."

Staring into her eyes as they swayed in a slow rhythm, Dominic asked softly, "So, you're happy?"

Arianna's nostrils flared as tears stung her eyes. "So fucking happy. Sometimes I wonder if it's all a dream, and I'm going to wake up in that goddamn farmhouse in a world that's still ravaged by death and destruction. This is real, right? I hope it's real..."

"It's real, sweetheart." He brushed a kiss over her lips. "And I'm happy too, in case you were wondering."

She barked a laugh. "I *do* wonder sometimes, but I think I'm afraid to ask. We're really secluded out here. That's always been my dream, but I know it's not yours."

Dominic cupped her chin and moved closer, his eyes boring into hers. "*You're* my dream, Ari. If you're happy, I've done my part."

A stupid tear slipped down her cheek, and she scoffed as she brushed it away. "Damn hormones. Stop making me cry. It's annoying."

His lips curled as he traced his thumb over the wet path on her cheek. "You love it. You love *me*. Stop pretending you're not obsessed with me, woman."

"*Pfft*. Go back inside. I was watching the sunset in peace before you interrupted me." She tried to extricate from his grasp, but he just turned her so she faced the mountains once more. Aligning his front with her back, he placed both palms on her belly and rested his temple against hers.

His hands slowly cradled their child as the half-moon peeked behind the horizon. As night gradually replaced day, Arianna observed the stars twinkle, wondering how many other beings were standing in their own seclusion, so far away, staring back from a world with its own problems, fears, injustices and hopes.

Eventually, the air turned chilly, and her husband threaded his fingers through hers, leading her inside to the dinner he'd prepared. It turned out that Dominic Cavalleri was one hell of a cook, and she added that to the long list of things she loved about him.

Once they'd eaten and the kitchen was clean, they slid into bed. Dominic positioned the pillow under her belly in the way she preferred as she lay on her side. He spooned behind her, wrapping his thigh over hers as he held her.

Within minutes, the familiar sound of his snores echoed in her ears as his warm breath hit her neck. Closing her eyes, she whispered to the child she already loved with a voracity she'd never known.

"Your dad is sleeping, and it's time for me to sleep too." She rubbed her belly, hoping her daughter would get the message. "Calm down in there, sweetheart. Just a few more weeks and then we're going to meet you. I can't wait."

Ignoring the wetness that clung to her eyelashes, she blamed the hormones again and exhaled a relieved breath when the baby stopped kicking.

Snuggling into Dominic's warm body, she closed her eyes and allowed him to protect her as she plunged into dreams.

Two months later

Grace smoothed her hands over the white satin dress, reveling in the silken fabric against her palms as she gazed into the full-length mirror.

"Absolutely beautiful," Maria said, her eyes shimmering with tears as she fidgeted with the veil hanging from Grace's hair. "Tristan might faint when he sees you."

"I'm not sure he'll faint, but I'm excited to have a formal wedding this time. The first time we eloped in a local courthouse, and it was a bit *rushed*, to say the least."

Maria chuckled as she nodded.

"And when we had our civil ceremony after we defeated Luthor, it was very"—Grace wrinkled her nose—"*practical*. Tristan promised me a grand wedding celebration once we helped Arthur rebuild and Dani began to disseminate her cure."

"You had the civil ceremony so you could officially become a family and start over," Maria said, cupping Grace's shoulders. "That was very understandable. But today is purely for celebration, and I couldn't be happier for you. And once today is over, you and Tristan can discuss adopting a baby. I know it's something you've wanted since we returned to the city."

"Yes. Once everything returns to normal after the wedding, we're going to discuss it at length." Leaning forward, she muttered, "Maria, this is definitely my last wedding. Please remind me of that when my husband is being surly and I want to strangle him."

Maria's melodious laughter filled the room. "You two don't fight often, but when you do, it's passionate and purposeful. That's a good thing, my dear. It means you both care. When you no longer fight with passion, the love is truly lost."

Grace thought of all her years locked in a lonely marriage for the sole purpose of defeating a man she loathed. "Tristan and I never lacked passion. I was drawn to him from the moment we met, and that tether between us has never truly broken."

"Then you're very lucky," Maria responded.

Grace took her hands and squeezed. "I'm so glad you chose to live with us, Maria. When we came to ask you to join us after we defeated Luthor, I could see the hesitation in your eyes. But my daughter is very persuasive." She flashed a grin. "You were doomed as soon as she began to plead with you."

"I was," Maria said. "I had reservations about living in the city, but I adore your family and it's been wonderful. Thank you for taking me into your home."

"Are you kidding? Thank you for saving me and Raquel all those years ago, and for raising her to be the amazing woman I know she'll become. I'm so grateful to you, Maria. You're family and a second mother to me." Pulling her into an embrace, she spoke against Maria's dark hair. "I love you."

Maria sniffled before drawing back and pulling a tissue from her dress pocket. "Don't make me cry. My makeup is done, and I'd like it to be presentable to Jack when I see him at the wedding."

Jack was Ron's brother, who'd moved back to DC after it was liberated. Ron and Deandra had introduced him into their circle, and he'd quickly become smitten with Maria.

"He's very handsome, and you look stunning, so he won't stand a chance."

"That's the plan, my dear," Maria said, her eyes sparkling.

After some final touches on her dress, they walked to the basement level of the rowhome Grace had converted into their permanent home. The house held four stories, which afforded more than enough room for their family and any visitors. Arianna and Dominic had accepted their wedding invite, which slightly surprised Grace since Arianna and Tristan weren't exactly best friends. But in the end, they'd come together for the common cause, and a bond had been cemented by everyone who'd fought together.

Arianna had also recently given birth, so Grace thought that might preclude her from traveling, but she had RSVP'd with an email representative of her brash personality.

Hi Grace,
We received your invitation and are thrilled you thought of us. Baby Cynthia is doing well, and I think my husband is going a bit stir-crazy. Therefore, we'll take you up on the invite and your offer to stay at your home.
We'll travel with everything necessary for the baby, but I'll warn you I can't cook. Dominic can, so if you want us to prepare some meals while we're there, I'll wrangle him into paying his dues for your hospitality.
I am, however, an expert at washing dishes. Feel free to put me to work. Lawsons carry our weight, and we'll only feel comfortable staying if you allow us to do so.
Also, tell your husband not to be a jerk or boss me around. He really pisses me off when he tries to tell me what to do.
Looking forward to it.
Arianna

The Cavalleri family had arrived a few days ago, and Grace had given them the entire third floor for their two-week stay. It allowed them some privacy and things had gone well so far. Arianna and Tristan had even spent a late night playing poker together, and Grace was thrilled at their comradery. She figured saving the world together could make even the greatest adversaries bury the hatchet under the right circumstances.

Grace approached the double doors that led to her home's expansive back yard. The soft sounds of the four-piece orchestra sounded, and she faced Maria to place one more reverent kiss on her cheek.

George Luddington stepped forward and handed his cane to Maria. "I can't properly walk Grace down the aisle with this thing. Please keep it for me until I sit."

"Will do," Maria said, winking before she strode through the doors to take her seat amongst the guests.

"You are truly magnificent, Grace," George said, taking her hands. "Robert would be proud."

"I miss him," Grace whispered, blinking away tears. "I know our fallout stemmed from his need to protect me, but I wish he could've seen the man Tristan was." She glanced toward the altar, where Tristan stood waiting. "The man he's become. He forgave me for terrible transgressions and is such a good father. I love him so much, George."

"I know, sweetheart," George said, patting her arm. "Robert became stressed and unable to see things clearly at the end. His association with Luthor wore on him, and I think you were unfortunate collateral damage. But his love for you was unwavering, and I know he's watching this from somewhere, elated you're happy."

"I hope so." Inhaling a deep breath, she faced the doors and wrang her hands at her sides. "Okay, enough dwelling on the past. I worked hard to get to this moment, and I only want to look forward."

George offered his arm. "My dear, I wholeheartedly agree."

Grace straightened her spine as the two doors swung open, thanks to the ushers on either side. The orchestra stilled before breaking into "Here Comes the Bride" as George led her down the carpeted aisle atop the soft grass.

Grace smiled at Dani and Maverick, Arianna and Dominic, Arthur, Deandra, Ron, Jessica and others as she slowly paced. Her lips twitched at the sight of Dominic, with his huge frame and imposing scar, lovingly holding his wisp of a daughter in his arms. It was a poignant sight, representative of the futures they helped shape for so many, and a surge of pride swelled in her chest.

She had helped save the world.

Her efforts in studying Luthor and planting the seeds of rebellion had created a new world where people could thrive once more.

Their team had been small but mighty, and she couldn't imagine working with more caring and capable souls.

They would be bonded together for the rest of their lives. Their shared remembrance of darker times would help them advise future leaders and make society a place where their children would thrive.

Or, at least, Grace hoped that was the case. The future was still uncertain as they continued to build their fledging new world.

Grace finally lifted her gaze to Tristan, her heart skipping a beat when she observed his immaculate tuxedo beneath his stunning hazel eyes. Their children stood beside him, and Grace winked at Raquel, who looked so lovely in her violet dress.

"You look pretty, Mom," she whispered, offering her hand as Grace took it.

"Thank you, sweetheart. So do you."

She handed the bouquet to Maria, who promptly took it before returning to her seat beside Jack.

George released Grace's arm and shook Tristan's hand. "Let's make this one stick," he teased as Tristan breathed a laugh.

"Agreed. Thank you, George."

George lowered into his seat beside Maria, and Grace slipped her hand into Tristan's. Craning her neck, she smiled at Nathan, who stood to Tristan's right. He was endearingly handsome in his black suit and tie, and she took a moment to appreciate the sheer joy of holding hands with her family in front of the people she loved.

"Dearly beloved," Arthur said, smiling as he stood under the altar. "We are gathered here today to celebrate the union of Grace and Tristan. As many of you know, the happy couple technically married over a year ago in a small ceremony I also had the pleasure of officiating. The world was just beginning to dig out from its harrowing nightmare, and there wasn't time for a formal wedding. I see this ceremony as a celebration of the future we paved, and am delighted to officiate once more. However, since this is Grace and Tristan's third wedding, I assume it will be the last."

"Oh, it's *definitely* the last," Grace teased as the onlookers laughed.

Tristan squeezed her hand, his expression filled with mirth. "I've been assured my wife has no more secret rebellions up her sleeve, so we should be all set."

"Very well," Arthur said as the crowd's chuckles ceased. "You've both requested I keep this short so we can enjoy this beautiful day, and I aim to do just that. Grace, please repeat after me..."

True to his word, Arthur kept the ceremony under ten minutes as Grace and Tristan spoke reverent words of love and devotion to each other. They exchanged rings, and Tristan kissed his bride against a backdrop of raucous cheers.

When the ceremony was complete, they removed the chairs, and the orchestra was replaced by a playlist Raquel and Nathan had created together. It was comprised of upbeat songs the guests could dance to while enjoying the passed refreshments and complimentary drinks from the bar.

Grace enjoyed the ceremony immensely, secretly admitting she'd always wanted a lavish wedding. It had taken years, but she'd finally managed to have the wedding of her dreams. Her gaze wandered to Tristan, as he shared a cigar with Arthur, Maverick, and Dominic, and butterflies flitted in her stomach at his intense hazel gaze, filled with desire and love.

After all this time, her body still reacted to him just as intensely as the night he'd approached her on the moonlit balcony—the enigmatic man who'd stolen her heart and left no room for anyone else.

Eventually, the guests all returned home, with Dani and Maverick being the last to leave. They hugged Arianna and Dominic before Dani took Cynthia in her arms one last time to say goodbye.

"Aunt Dani's going to be back tomorrow, and we're going to walk in the park," she exclaimed, rubbing the tip of her nose against Cynthia's. "I'm going to tell you all about your Aunt Raquel and your Grandma Cynthia, who you were named after. How does that sound?"

Cynthia crooned in her arms, and Grace could see Dani's heart melt in her eyes.

"Are you and Maverick trying?" Grace asked, sidling up to Dani and playfully rubbing Cynthia's arm with her finger. "You've obviously got baby fever."

Dani nodded as she handed Cynthia back over to Arianna. "We were waiting until the verdict to make sure I didn't go to prison." She lifted an acerbic eyebrow. "Thankfully, since my servitude will entail just continuing to be a geeky scientist who creates cures and antidotes in a lab, we're good to go. I want to give Cynthia a cousin as close in age as possible."

"That's wonderful," Grace said. "We're also going to adopt as soon as things calm down from the wedding."

"Oh, Grace, I'm thrilled to hear that!" Dani threw her arms around her and squeezed. "We can have playdates together!"

Laughing, Grace stroked her back. "I can't wait. Arianna and Dominic will always have a place to stay with us, and I hope they'll visit often."

"She loves that cabin they've built in the mountains, but understands Dominic needs to rejoin society every once in a while. I've made her promise to visit no less than three times per year." Dani lifted a finger. "Everyone thinks she's the tough one, but when I put my foot down, it's the law. She's already planning possible dates to visit next year."

"The brilliant and resolute scientist," Grace said, grinning. "I love it. I'll help you hold her to it."

Once Dani and Maverick left and the house was quiet, Grace and Tristan stood in the kitchen, sharing a piece of wedding cake.

"*Ohmygod*," Grace moaned, taking the second-to-last bite. "This is so good. I was starving."

Tristan chuckled and speared the last piece with his fork before stuffing it in his mouth. "So fucking good. I loved seeing everyone, but that was a lot of entertaining for me."

Grace gently patted his cheek. "I'm very proud of my churlish husband for being cordial. Thank you."

His eyes narrowed. "I'm not sure I like your tone, Mrs. Holder." Taking the empty plate, he set it on the counter and hauled her over his shoulder. "It's time for me to take back control in this damn house."

Grace lightly pounded his back with her fists as she kicked her legs, the dress billowing around them. Tristan marched up the stairs as she squirmed, loving his strength as he wielded her atop his shoulder.

When they reached the second floor, he stopped in front of Raquel's room and set Grace on her feet so they could check on her. She snored softly surrounded by the posters of galaxies and quasars she'd hung on the wall. Their daughter had developed a love of space since enrolling in the reopened school system, and Grace had a hunch she would eventually end up in the newly revamped space program one day.

Tristan slowly pulled the door closed before stopping at Nathan's room to check on him as well.

When they entered the master bedroom, Tristan softly closed the door and turned the lock.

"Tristan!" Grace scolded. "We have guests. What if they need something—?"

Tristan snaked an arm around her waist, aligning his front with hers. "No *one* is getting your attention until tomorrow morning." He nipped her lips. "You're *mine* and it's time I reminded you of that, empress."

She slid her arms around his neck as her lips curved. "We have been consumed with the wedding and all the visitors, haven't we?"

"Yes. If it didn't make you happy, I'd kick them all out and tell them to rot in hell—"

"You would not," she exclaimed, swatting his chest.

"Don't tempt me." Cupping her chin, he ran his thumb over her lips. "But now it's just us, and I aim to keep it that way."

Desire curled deep in her belly as the flecks of his irises shimmered with hunger and emotion. "Well, okay then. I think my husband means business."

Tristan's hands gripped her waist, turning her so she faced the mirror atop their dresser. Cementing his eyes to hers in the reflection, he pressed his lips to her ear and murmured, "Sweetheart, you have no fucking idea..."

Tristan felt his wife shudder in his arms at his possessive words. Dying to touch her soft skin, he began unfastening the tiny buttons that lined the back of her dress. She gazed at him in the mirror through half-lidded eyes, her cheeks reddening in anticipation. Once he'd released the buttons, he pushed the dress to the floor, leaving her in a strapless bra and silky thong.

Grace stepped out of the dress as it pooled on the floor. Resting her hands on the dresser, she leaned forward, offering a salacious view of her backside. Tristan hissed, placing his hands on the globes and caressing as she pushed into his palms.

"Don't pretend you're not greedy for me to fuck you, baby," he rasped, hooking a finger in her thong and dragging it down her legs. He tossed it aside and removed her bra, baring her breasts to the cool air. Her nipples pebbled and Tristan grew rock hard, ready to remind her that she belonged to him. She'd always been his wife in his heart, even when she'd almost broken it, and he longed to solidify his possession of her.

It was something he would continue to do for the rest of their days. To remind her that she was always his first, and now she was his forever.

"You looked so beautiful in your dress," he said, gliding his hands up her sides to cup her breasts. "But you look like a goddess right now. Your skin blushes the prettiest shade of red when I play with these sexy nipples." He tweaked them between his thumb and forefinger before circling them as she moaned. "You like that, don't you?"

Her head fell back on his shoulder as she whispered his name. "Why are you still dressed?"

"Because I needed to look at you before I fuck you, just to remind myself this is real."

She slithered in his arms, turning to face him and flashing a sultry grin. "Darling, nothing has ever been more real."

Her fingers tore at the buttons of his shirt, all but ripping it from his frame before she pushed him toward the bed. Tristan fell on his back, huffing a laugh as his wife tugged his pants and underwear off.

They loved each other, heatedly and passionately, physically cementing the bond they'd reaffirmed earlier that day. When they both reached their peak, Grace's joyful laughter surrounded them as their bodies melded into one.

Tristan emptied everything into her—every piece of his soul and the love he'd thought unrequited for so many long, lonely years. As the last shudders abated, he threaded their fingers together beside her golden hair on the bed.

Panting and sated, they stared into each other's eyes for several poignant heartbeats.

When Tristan began to slip, he withdrew from her warmth and reached for a tissue. Gazing lovingly at his wife, he wiped away his release, marveling at the sight of the milky essence on the smooth skin of her inner thighs.

"I love seeing my mark on you," he murmured as he slid the tissue over her skin. "It's proof that you're *mine* and always will be."

Grace sighed, closing her eyes as her body relaxed upon the bed.

Tristan lifted her and pulled back the covers to place her on the cool sheets. She reached for him, her expression one of yearning as she waited.

Overcome with love for her, he slid beside her and drew her front against his. She glided her leg over his thighs, drawing him closer as they shared a pillow. Gazing into her eyes, Tristan noticed the sheen of tears.

"Hey," he whispered, tenderly caressing her cheek with his thumb. "That was supposed to make you happy, not make you cry."

A warbled laugh escaped her throat. "I'm crying *because* I'm happy. We finally made it here. I knew on the first day we spent together—the first day we fell in love and got tattoos—that we'd end up here. I just didn't realize it would take us *quite* so long."

"I, on the other hand, felt we had so many obstacles against us. I never should've doubted us."

"You shouldn't have. It broke my heart that you ever believed I loved Luthor." Cupping his jaw, a tear fell down her cheek. "How could you believe I ever loved any man but you? It's not possible, Tristan. I love you with every part of my soul."

"I was a stupid fool, and still a kid in so many ways. I wasn't sure I deserved you."

"And now?"

"Now, I realize I'm probably the only man who can put up with you. You're tempestuous and headstrong, and you'd probably drive any other man crazy."

She scoffed and playfully hit his shoulder. "You'll pay for that."

"See what I mean?" he asked, pulling her closer and resting his forehead against hers. "You drive me mad, woman, and I love you more each day. And now that I'm pretty sure you don't have any other secrets to reveal, we can build the life we always wanted. Together."

Grace pressed her lips to his, drawing him into a soulful kiss as their bodies relaxed. Eventually, she rested her head on his chest, and he stroked her smooth hair until her breathing grew slow and measured.

Closing his eyes, Tristan recalled the first time he'd held her this way, all those years ago when she had a fresh tattoo on her hip and the world had been vastly different.

Vowing to protect her and their children as they blazed their future, Tristan clutched his sleeping wife and pledged to be the man she deserved in the moonlit darkness of the city they'd saved.

Arthur Reyes had a fantastic time at Tristan and Grace's wedding. He'd been honored to officiate both their civil ceremony last year and their official wedding in the back yard of their lovely home. Officiating celebratory ceremonies was one of his favorite activities as president of the newly formed government, and he aimed to continue to find opportunities to do so.

It made him a man of the people, and if he were honest, he also understood it was good politics. As much as he'd promised himself he'd never turn into a slimy politician, being a leader meant you had to play the game at least some of the time.

He'd danced with Jessica Holder at the reception, quietly admitting his attraction to her as she swayed in his arms. Although he had no time for romance now, he wouldn't be president forever and would eventually want to settle down. Was there a future for him with Jessica? The answer was uncertain, but he looked forward to exploring it down the road.

Frowning at the thought, Arthur sat at his desk in the newly rebuilt White House, eyeing the papers in front of him. There would be an election soon, and several candidates had declared their intentions to run. Arthur was extremely popular with the people, thanks to the successful mission he led to defeat Luthor Cromwell. But popularity often waned, and people were fickle. Would a new leader be able to continue to build their fledgling government, or would it throw the world back into chaos, opening the door for another dictator like Luthor to take over?

And if that happened, wouldn't it be better if Arthur retained control, if only for one more term, to ensure the people were safe?

It wasn't about remaining in power. Arthur told himself this repeatedly. No, it was about doing what was right for the world, with the leader the people deserved. The leader who knew what they needed.

Zayne Danvers appeared at the door, and Arthur waved him in.

"Good to see you, Zayne. Sorry to call you so late on a Saturday. Please sit."

He sat in the chair on the opposite side of Arthur's desk, a curious expression on his face. "I'm always happy to help, sir. What do you need?"

"I'm still awaiting confirmation that the last stash of unauthorized super-soldier serum was destroyed in Scranton. I was appalled to learn that Solomon Grange got his hands on several doses thanks to his secret communications with Luthor."

"It was a disturbing discovery, sir," Zayne said. "Although Solomon has accepted the new government for now, we hear rumors that his management of the city is less than kind. He's armed every Scranton citizen with handguns and holds regular trainings to ensure they're capable with the weapons. He justifies this by stating he wants his people protected if someone like Luthor rises to power again, but many believe he might eventually convince his citizens to form a militia and assume power of the new government for himself."

Arthur sat back in his chair and rubbed his forehead. "I've publicly called upon Solomon to run for president many times. He refuses to and says our elections won't be legitimate until we've restored technology to every outpost in America. My people on the ground are trying, but rebuilding a country is no small feat. We'll eventually accomplish the task, but it will take several more years. I just hope he doesn't try to seize power by force. That's not going to end well for him."

"I couldn't agree more. And to confirm your question, all of the super-soldier serum in Solomon's possession has been destroyed. I was on site and am confident it's eradicated."

Arthur smiled at his assurance. He was a valuable member of his team and loyal to a fault.

"Thank you, Zayne. That gives me great relief."

"Of course. Will there be anything else? I promised Gabriella I wouldn't be home past midnight," he said, referencing the woman he'd started dating several months ago. "Unless you need me..."

Glancing at his watch, Arthur realized it was almost eleven o'clock. "No, you can go. Thank you for coming in at this late hour. I'll make sure you get a Friday off soon so you and Gabriella can take a long weekend vacation. Lord knows you've earned it."

"Sir, it's an honor to serve you. It's because of you that Gabriella and I have a future." Rising, he saluted, and Arthur saluted back before he pivoted and strode from the room, closing the door behind him.

Unrest and foreboding pulsed in Arthur's body, and he reached over to tug open the top drawer of his desk. After emptying the contents, he removed the slab of wood, revealing the false bottom that hid several vials.

Lifting one of the vials, he studied it against the ceiling lights of the Oval Office. If anyone discovered the stash, he would be removed from office immediately. After all, he was the one who'd written the decree that every last vial of Luthor's super-soldier serum must be destroyed.

To his knowledge, all vials on the planet had now been eradicated except the ones that remained in his desk.

The ones he hoped to never use against anyone, but increasingly feared he might have to use against Solomon...or someone else who tried to assume power but didn't earn it...or wasn't worthy.

Only a just and fair leader could rebuild their world. One who understood the people, who the people *chose*, and one who was capable of guiding them into their prosperous future.

Decrying the heavy thoughts, he slipped the vial back into the drawer and replaced the wooden panel before closing it tight.

Rising, he released a slow breath and trailed from the office, determined to protect the new world he'd created...

Never realizing how closely his inner thoughts mimicked those of the last leader who'd ruled over society before ultimately ending it.

Before You Go

W ell, dear readers, they did it! Our amazing team of dystopian survivors saved the world. As always, I HAD to leave the door open just a little bit. Will Arthur continue to be the leader the world needs, or will he devolve into someone evil like Luthor? My hope is that he remains true, but with anything in these perilous times, one never knows!

Thank you from the bottom of my heart for reading this steamy dystopian trilogy. I absolutely loved writing it and have been heartened by your lovely messages and feedback that you enjoyed it too. The six main characters of this series were some of my favorite I've ever written, and I appreciate you joining me on the journey.

Please make sure to check out all of my books and other bookish goodies at **RebeccaHefnerBooks.com** and thank you for supporting indie authors! Until next time, happy reading! –Rebecca

ALSO BY REBECCA HEFNER

The Sendaxa Chronicles
Book 1: Repressed Echoes
Book 2: Scorched Redemption
Book 3: Fated Salvation

Etherya's Earth Series
Prequel: The Dawn of Peace
Book 1: The End of Hatred
Book 2: The Elusive Sun
Book 3: The Darkness Within
Book 4: The Reluctant Savior
Book 4.5: Immortal Beginnings
Book 5: The Impassioned Choice
Book 5.5: Two Souls United
Book 6: The Cryptic Prophecy
Book 6.5: Garridan's Mate
Book 7: The Diplomatic Heir
Book 7.5: Sebastian's Fate
Book 8: The Solitary Protector

Prevent the Past Trilogy
Book 1: A Paradox of Fates
Book 2: A Destiny Reborn
Book 3: A Timeline Restored

About the Author

USA Today bestselling author Rebecca Hefner grew up in Western North Carolina and now calls the Hudson River of NYC home. In her youth, she would sneak into her mother's bedroom and read the romance novels stashed on the bookshelf, cementing her love of HEAs. A huge Buffy and Star Wars fan, she loves an epic fantasy and a surprise twist (Luke, he IS your father).

Before becoming an author, Rebecca had a successful twelve-year medical device sales career. After launching her own indie publishing company, she is now a full-time author who loves writing strong, complex characters who find their HEAs. Rebecca can usually be found making dorky and/or embarrassing posts on TikTok and Instagram. Please join her so you can laugh along with her!